IS THIS ALL THERE IS?

A bit of a giggle novel

Copyright © 2002 R. Driver

All Rights Reserved

ISBN 1-59113-093-X

Published 2002

Booklocker.com, Inc.
2002

IS THIS ALL THERE IS?

A bit of a giggle novel

R. Driver

IS THIS ALL THERE IS?

Author's Words

I am a grandparent. There is no gratuitous sex or violence in Is This All There Is? If you want more than moderate character assassination then please look elsewhere; I offer only rib-tickling titillation.

I have sailed around the world twice; flown around it twice; lived and worked in England, New Zealand, Australia and Canada.

Work always involved writing, plotting and conniving, therefore I was rather good at selling advertising space for newspapers; writing television scripts; producing a single-frame photography puppet television show, and in my spare time, writing novels.

Now I am retired I shall pursue my love of novel writing with a determination borne of a desire to succeed.

Introduction

<u>Is This All There Is?</u> involves two characters in a near mid-life crises.   No matter from which perspective they are viewed empathy will abound: that could be me or someone I know.

What does a person do when they have been kicked in the teeth by events? Roll over and die? Get up and fight back? Reinvent themselves?

Jessica takes the latter course.

How does a stodgy scientist catch the bus before it is too late? Jack hitches a ride and suffers the consequences.

Have a giggle at their antics; be sad at their failures and frailties, but delight in their romantic romp.

APRIL 2000

Chapter One

Jessica's statement almost unseated her parents at their dinner table in Victoria. "Ronnie's gone to live with his girl friend." She helped herself to a tablespoon of mashed potatoes from the tureen before she passed it to her open mouthed father.

"Well I never." Mrs Mayhew paused with a serving spoon of roasted parsnip and potato for her plate, and turned to her husband. "You heard that Father, Ronnie's -"

"I'm not deaf." He glared at his wife then swung brown eyes back to his daughter. "The bugger's gone to live with his fancy woman," and dug savagely into the potato tureen. "So where does that leave us?"

"I don't know about you, Dad, but I'll be leaving Vancouver after the house is sold." Jessica helped herself to Yorkshire pudding from the dish and wondered once more why hers never turned out as nice, melted in the mouth like candy floss. She made them just the same as her mother, hot fat, hot oven, but hers were always flatter and stiffer. It didn't seem fair somehow. "The divorce won't take long since there's no contest."

"He was the reason we emigrated to Canada." Mr Mayhew brandished his knife. "He was the one retrenched in Bradford, not you. "Why the hell didn't the inconsiderate devil desert you before we left England, if he was fed up with you?"

Jessica took a serving from the center dish of peas and sweet corn. "He hadn't met his bit of fluff, then, Dad."

"Aye," Mrs Mayhew helped herself to mashed potatoes. "If it hadn't been for Ronnie we'd never have left home to follow you."

"I'm sorry, Mum, Dad." Jessica poured gravy on her plate avoiding the Yorkshire Pudding, which she didn't like soggy. "If only I'd realized what was going to happen within a year, I'd never have left. But you know he was determined; emigrate and seek fresh opportunities in a young country."

"And he made sure of his opportunities, getting a leg over a young, fresh filly." Mr Mayhew reached over and patted her shoulder. "Nay, no one's blaming you, love. It's the fault of that bloody Ronnie and his hot little hands, isn't it Mother?"

"Don't be so descriptive, and stop that swearing." Mrs Mayhew shook her head at her husband, who suddenly concentrated on his plate.

"Makes me feel like a broody, old mare put out to grass." Jessica could have cried at the humiliation but under her parents' gaze she had to smile, bravely. "I suppose it's character strengthening, something like this."

"You're not thinking of going back home, are you, Jessica love?" Her mother stretched a gentle hand across the table which Jessica clutched for strength. "Because if you are we'll go back with you."

"You won't, you know, Mother." Mr Mayhew glared at his wife. "I've started a nice job going in self employment. I'm not chucking it in to go gallivanting across an ocean every time our Jessica's got a problem."

"That's you, selfish to the core!" She quickly released her daughter's hand and concentrated on pouring water into her tumbler.

"Don't argue, you two." Jessica jumped in quickly before they really got stuck into one another. "And there's not much point going back, is there, with retrenchment still going on?" She knifed peas onto the back of her fork. "Mind you, I might be all right, I wasn't the one who was retrenched. But I'm so annoyed. I've made friends at the office and the rowing club. I don't fancy putting down fresh roots at forty years of age." She mouthed the peas thoughtfully. "At thirty eight going on for thirty nine it didn't seem so bad. But knocking on forty? How's that going to look on a Résumé?"

"We put down fresh roots." Mrs Mayhew concentrated on serving peas for herself from the dish to avoid looking at her daughter. "We made the change. At sixty five!" She turned to her husband, extended the full spoon of peas. "Have some peas, Father?"

Her husband nodded acquiescence. "By gum, he's a rum'un that Ronnie. A fresh start in a young country, he said." His slammed hand on the table caused the extended spoonful of peas to scatter across the tablecloth. "By God, he's got it with a bit of How's Your Father, half his age."

"Watch your manners Father!" Mrs Mayhew scooped up peas, deposited them on her husband's plate until he pushed away her hand. "All right, no need to get shirty!"

"I'm sorry, I know how distressing..." Jessica turned from one to the other. "I'd sooner it hadn't happened... If only..."

"If only you'd used your loaf our Jessica would never have married him." Mrs Mayhew glared at her husband. "Typical!"

"Eh?" Her husband looked flabbergasted.

"You're a man! You should have known what he'd be like! He never gave us any grandchildren, did he?" She turned to Jessica. "That hurt, not having any little ones to come, after us. Your dad always has plenty to say afterwards though, you notice?"

"Providing I get the chance," careful to aim his low voice towards the dinner plate.

"Why should you have to leave lovely Vancouver because of that idiot, Jessica?" Mrs Mayhew cut into her sliced roast beef viciously. "I've a good mind to give him a clout across the ear behaving in such a disgusting manner. And I will if I catch up to him."

"You'll have to stand in line, Mother." Mr Mayhew commenced to smash peas onto his fork with his knife. "If I catch a look at him it'll be more than a smack on the head. I'll clobber him, good and proper."

"Bit late in the day for being masterful, isn't it?" Her mother stretched to run a loving touch over Jessica's hand. "Don't throw away friends and family because of that rotter, love. Don't run away again."

"I didn't run away last time, Mum. We emigrated! You knew Ronnie couldn't get another job in England at his age."

"I call it running." Mrs Mayhew chewed on her tender beef. "You left and we followed, like little sheep."

"Aye, your mum's right, love. Let that silly bugger leave, not you."

"But I'm the one making waves, Dad, not Ronnie or his girlfriend. I'm the one expendable at the office. Anyway, this'll give me an opportunity to make a clean break from the past; try to make a new life for myself somewhere as far away from him as possible."

"But to leave BC. altogether, Jessica love." Mrs Mayhew's eyes brimmed with unshed tears. "I might never see you again if you run to Montreal or Toronto. You'll be gobbled up in a big city on the other side of the country."

"Okay Mum, I'll not go far. But I've got to put as much distance as possible between Ronnie and me." She moved the Yorkshire Pudding from spreading gravy. "I couldn't stand being in the same city as him and his girlfriend."

"Where will you abscond to this time? Timbuctoo?" Mr Mayhew glared at peas piled high on his fork before mouthing them. "I can't get over us following you across an ocean like flaming mother hens," inadvertently spattered peas across the table towards his wife who glowered at him.

"Alberta!" Jessica sounded as if she had just thought of the idea, but she hadn't, she'd given the matter of her removal from Vancouver a great deal of thought. "It's the next province. Their economy's on an upward curve, and I've got a lot to offer Edmonton Social Services. They'll jump at my experience."

"Ooh! We'll be able to pop over and visit you often, then love." Mrs Mayhew turned to her husband. "That isn't so far away just next door, Father, is it?"

Jessica didn't correct her. That night after their daughter departed to sleep in a house that was up for sale, Mr Mayhew opened his road map and spread it across the table.

"Bloody hellfire!" His shout reached his wife in the kitchen washing up the dishes. "We'll have to cross the Canadian Rockies to get there!"

"Well, it mightn't be so bad, Father. We used to have lovely walks on the Pennine Chain; picnic on Saltaire Glen and Ilkley Moor." Mrs Mayhew turned with the scrubber in her hand, and smiled fondly. "Remember the purple heather, how springy it was to walk on?"

"These aren't hilly moorlands, Mother. They're bloody big mountains!"

"Ah, I was looking forward to a picnic. It'll not be level ground for sitting down." She resumed washing up thinking back to Yorkshire Dales; gently sloping hills covered with purple heather, and the, to be avoided, rolled up turds from moor sheep.

Mr Mayhew rolled his eyes up to heaven.

JACK HAVERSKY SAT at the breakfast table and watched Brian, his condo mate, pack for a trip to Toronto. Brian would charge to his bedroom and return with more items to squeeze into a bulging bag. Between visits Jack cast glances out of the window of the condominium; the river valley sprawled from east to west of the high rise, various shades of green trees and bushes flanked the track alongside the twinkling waters of the North Saskatchewan River.

"I should've gone for a walk instead of watching you pack all that gear." He reluctantly dragged his eyes from the inviting outdoor scene. "Exercised outside, filling my lungs full of fresh air."

"Yep, exercise'll sure do a lot for ridding yourself of that paunch, Jack." Brian paused from pushing rolled up underpants into shoes. "You'd better think seriously about that spread in the middle."

"I'll see to it after you've gone." Jack patted his girth. "I've consumed more than my usual since you moved into the condo," eyed his plate. He'd have to consider seriously leaving more than a few crumbs; learn to push away the plate.

"You don't have my energetic lifestyle jumping out of planes, that's why I eat well." Brian maneuvered the shoes into the side of the case. "I need food for energy."

"I don't pack that amount on a field assignment. Why so much?"

"You don't go in for entertainment after work. I do."

"In the bush there's no need for party clothes." Jack indicated the dress shirt hanging over a chair waiting to be packed. "No one to impress accept drillers and jackrabbits."

"You don't go partying when you're in town." Brian pushed everything flat in the case then went for the shirt. "When was the last time you dated a girl at a party?"

"I'm long past partying, thanks. I prefer the long haul sort of friendship; sort of introduction you get through an acquaintance."

"You ought to try the Introductory Service, like I did." Brian carefully folded the shirt to lie on top. His blue eyes twinkled looking over at Jack. "I've great replies from girls wanting to meet an all right guy. Help yourself to them while I'm away, if you like." He snapped shut the case.

"How much are they charging you?" Jack's grin was intended to be mischievous, but failed miserably: he was envious of the younger man.

"There's an Yvonne, a Myra and a Jean. No mention of charging, or I'd be away."

"You must be joking, joining a love sick service. That's for pitiful guys who can't express themselves face on. A skydiver should have sufficient stamina for facing up to a girl at a disco or a dinner party."

"Yes, old guy." Brian laughed out loud, tied the drawstring on his duffle bag. "You do your thing at your dinner parties and I'll do mine where I get results."

"Okay, so I'm old fashioned." Jack assumed an unusual belligerence. "You imagine it's entertainment taking a girl to watch you perform at hockey or skydiving. To me that smacks of the worst kind of egotism."

"What's your problem?" He crossed over to Jack. "It turns them on."

"It'd turn me off."

"But you're not a female, are you?" He leaned into Jack's face. "Your advice sucks! You'll soon be too late to do anything, Jack. Look at your gut spilling over."

Jack surreptitiously pulled in his stomach.

"Go on, get in!" Brian prodded with a finger. "It can't, can it, little porky pig?"

Jack's effort turned his face a different hue.

"See! You're galloping into middle age, Jack. Get a life before it's too late!"

Jack took a swing at the teasing face, but missed. Agile Brian leapt backwards and went for his luggage. Jack stood up and smiled, implying he wasn't hurt by his friend's remark. The smile was still there when Brian carried his suitcase and two bags to the door.

"I'm out of your hair, what's left of it, for four weeks or more, Jack. Make the most of it. Don't go dragging your oars with that midlife stomach bulge, you hear?"

"That's a promise. I don't hanker after you pushing my buttons when you return." Jack opened the door. "Many soft landings, Brian. Make sure you walk in the door, not carried back on a stretcher, you hear? Have a nice day!"

14

He closed the door after the young man; relaxed his features and stomach with a sigh of relief; eyed the wall clock and hurried into his bedroom, he'd have time to do something before going into the office. He stripped down to under-shorts, pulled them down to the hairline under his bulging stomach and winced at the dressing table reflection.

"Sure thing, it's obscene. A strict diet and exercise routine, that's my intention from hereon. I've four weeks to get in shape before Brian returns. I'll show ..."

He turned sideways, pulled in the hanging bulge with a tightening of muscles, and viewed with difficulty the balding patch on his crown.

"Give me a break! How do I produce hair growth in four weeks? No wonder I don't attract ladies. I'm a wreck!"

He dropped to the floor, rolled over onto his back and started to peddle vigorously an invisible bicycle.

JESSICA PERSUADED her parents to fly to Edmonton for a weekend rather then drive from British Columbia, a few days after settling into her new environment. She collected them from the International Airport where her mother beat her father getting into the offside front seat of the Cavalier.

"Have you met any Christian men, love?" Mrs Mayhew asked once she was settled in the car.

"My new boss Dick Chalmers could be considered manly, but definitely not Christian." Jessica started up the car. "Buckle up, Mum."

"I meant, at the 'Y'." Mrs Mayhew strapped herself in. "Should be plenty of Christians there at the YWCA."

"I'm not in the market for men of any description, Mum, whether they're Christians or Muslims. Jessica eyed her father through the rear vision mirror struggling with his belt. "You okay back there, Dad?"

"Some nana threw up on me on the plane."

"You should have let him pass, like he wanted." Mrs Mayhew shot venom over her shoulder, then eyed Jessica. "Pigheaded at times, your dad."

"He'd already been to the loo twice. I told him to put a knot in it." He stroked his trouser legs as if vomit still adhered. "Bet he did it on purpose!"

"We'll drive next time, Father." Mrs Mayhew twisted round to peer at him. "You won't get anyone throwing up on you when we're crossing those mountains accept me. And I'll be considerate. Use the window." She cast sad eyes at Jessica. "I never liked switch-backs at the fairgrounds. That slow climb up and the whoosh back down fair gives me the willies."

"There's a roadway through the mountain range, Mum." Jessica concentrated on leaving the car park. "And it's practically level, you won't even realize you're climbing uphill to three thousand feet above sea level."

"Haaa! That makes sense. Hey, Father!" Mrs Mayhew struggled to eye her husband examining his fly front. "That three thousand feet we've to climb. There's a roadway through the mountains, not over!"

"He could have held onto it, the spiteful devil!"

"Oh, give it a rest, Father." Mrs Mayhew looked at Jessica. "He never lets up once he's got his teeth into something."

JESSICA TOOK her parents along to view her purchase in up-market Bonnie Doon. The sight of the house beneath builders' papers and the unkempt front garden when they exited her car, had them pause.

"You'll be needing more than a few nails in this lot, luvvy." Mr Mayhew stood on the front garden path, viewed the missing tiles on the roof and the broken down pipe; went and knocked on wood and listened for scampering wood lice; lifted a corner of the window paper to view the interior. "You'll be needing a bloody miracle."

"The previous tenant couldn't be evicted the Realtor said, but I can see possibilities, Dad, can't you?"

He snorted in disgust and strode along the side path to the back of the house.

"It doesn't seem worth the airfare money to come and see it, Jessica." Mrs Mayhew eyed the neighbors' houses with pristine lawns and flowerbeds. "I'm glad we did a bit of sightseeing first, otherwise I'd have been disappointed."

"It's still early days, Mum, give it a chance.

"It loses out on comparison with West Edmonton Mall."

"Their budget was over fifty million, Mum, and that was when the dollar went a lot further. I'm only playing with thousands, here."

"Still, I'm glad we're staying with you at the 'Y'."

"Of course, it isn't ready yet, Mum. But you just wait and see, in a couple of weeks' time once the builder and landscape gardener get through with it -" The bellow from the backyard interrupted her.

"What flaming idiot allowed a house to fall into this state?"

Jessica spun around, biting hard on a sharp rejoinder. Her neighbor across the road emerged through his front gate. She grinned, and not saying a word indicated him to her mother.

Mrs Mayhew's face dropped when she observed a man with an invisible dog on an invisible lead stand by the curb and encourage his dog to pass water.

"Nay, lass." She shook her head from side to side. "It takes all sorts." Then caught Jessica returning his friendly wave. "Hope your dad doesn't see him. He's got enough problems on his plate with your divorce and dilapidated house. He couldn't take on a pixielated chap, as well."

Her parents returned to Victoria, saddened at leaving her to face the repairs all alone, especially her carpenter father. But 'She had made her bed and she could lie on it': a Yorkshire expression they thought suited the occasion.

SHE OFTEN VISITED her house to check progress, was pleasantly surprised at the speed of the workmen and on each visit the thought occurred: This was her home, hers alone; a new start, bought outright after the sale of the joint home in Vancouver, thinking she would have no financial worries.

Chapter Two

Jessica opened the envelope fearing the worst. The mail had been delivered to her dream house that morning, and this was the first occasion she'd had to enjoy the luxury of opening her own mail, delivered to her own address in a home that was completely hers.

"Been waiting for you to come," the mailman had said. "You've a backlog of mail and advertising. Hope you'll get yourself a mailbox."

"Thanks very much. I'll get one as soon as I've moved in properly."

She had promptly piled the mail and flyers onto the foyer shelf and continued with sweeping, following the departure of furniture men who had considerately put on overshoes to prevent spoiling her new carpets. She would just sweep the wooden foyer floor then dash back to work.

And now, having arrived home again via the back door, she had sped through the hall to the foyer and picked up the mail. The advertising could wait, she wouldn't waste her time, she'd done enough spending for a while; since changing provinces her hand had been forever in her pocket, or other people's hands. She was constantly handing out gratuities. What was it this time?

She immediately felt guilt when she read the invitation to a forthcoming festival. The YWCA was demonstrating activities. 'Would you care to volunteer in the tent?'

"Not content with my money they now want my body!"

Yet she was quite chuffed at anyone wanting her services, free or not. It was good for her ego, especially when thoughts turned to a traitorous husband who had cast her aside for a bit of hanky panky with a tart. She placed her handbag and Safeways shopping bag full of groceries on the kitchen counter.

"Stop regurgitating old news! I'm in a new city. I'll soon make friends. I won't look back. I'll look forward! Someone's out there for me. I'll draw on courage and hold on!"

She looked out of the kitchen window at the garden where she alone had chosen   flowers and plants, that is, if she didn't count the expertise of the landscape gardener.

The second letter was addressed to a Jean Morningbird. What a nice name. Must be for the previous, tenant. No return address. Curiosity won. Jessica ran a finger nail along the gum line, but it didn't give.

"Someone's used a lot of spit."

Fear of contracting AIDS had her drop the envelope on the counter and put on the electric jug to steam it open. By the time water came to the boil, clothes were hung, groceries tidied into the fridge, pantry and the Lazy Susan in the lower cupboard.

How sadly empty her cupboards looked. Since leaving two homes, the one in Bradford since their marriage, and the Vancouver home shared with a worthless being for nearly a year, she had lost most of her crockery. But she didn't mind, she'd no wish to be reminded of the wasted years with a stupid man who didn't realize, or appreciate, the treasure he was losing for a, bit of the other, with a nymphet. She'd fill the cupboards with dishes and foods of her own choice; not have to consider the feelings of a nerd. Alone, she...

The bubbling jug brought her back to the task in hand, stifling forlorn thoughts. She held the envelope over the steaming spout; gradually, the flap loosened. She threw the too hot to handle envelope on the counter to cool off, poured boiling water over a Chamomile teabag in a mug, and hoped it would settle her stomach after the burger and fries with Dorinda at the hurried office lunch.

It was a matter of moments before the letter was retrieved from the soggy envelope.

> Dear Jean,
>
> Great to hear from you via the Introductory Service. You sound kind of busy with kennel activities and the Reserve. Guess you like animals, eh? You say you're into canoeing. Me too, only I don't have opportunity because of skydiving. I'm into white water rafting, though, are you? You'll have me beat with your ballroom dancing technique. You can teach me, I'm a willing learner.

Jessica poured two cups of boiled water into a pan, added a packet of chicken noodle soup before she continued her read.

I'm writing before I leave for an air show with Airborne Brothers, City Airport. Hope I return in one piece and meet up with you. Ha-ha!

You sound interesting. A photograph would be great.

Guess now you'd like to know what I look like. Well, I have all my own teeth, great vision and hair. And what wasn't included in my ad: I don't have any bad habits. The guys at work say I'm an okay guy.

Hope to hear from you soon. Regards.

Brian Swartzkoff.

Jessica felt a tingle imagining she was the intended Jean. Umh, nice! He must be under forty to be a skydiver. She made soup and toast and pondered over the letter propped up on the servery.

Morningbird... Morganburg becoming Anglicized to Morningbird? She'd accompanied Sylvia Stevens in Bradford to the Synagogue more than once; her family name had been changed from Stein to Stevens, and she knew lots of Jews in Bradford and Leeds in the clothing trade changed their names.

Brian Swartzkoff probably wrote the Introductory Service for partnering with another Jew. He'll be disappointed when his letter's returned saying messy Jean has skipped leaving no forwarding address.

A smile started, an idea taking root. Why disappoint the man, she was as lonely as this Jean replying to an ad. in an Introductory Service? She could pretend to be her. Then reality struck. That'd be stupid! If she met him she'd be stuck with being this Jean. She picked up the letter; another thought intruded. She could say Jean's gone but she was available.

"On your bike!"

She threw the letter onto the counter. She didn't want to sound desperate, even if she was. She raised her eyes to the ceiling.

"Oh, you rotten sod, Ronnie Walters! You've made me feel worthless, unwanted and unlovable."

With the light meal on a tray, seated on the couch in front of television watching Hercule Poirot solve yet another case, Jessica came to an important decision.   Henceforth, Jessica would be Jean.   No more the loneliness of separation. She would sally forth and live again. Brian deserved her!

IT TOOK NO TIME for Jessica to reinvent herself writing to Brian. On her way to work the next morning she dropped her reply into the mailbox at Bonnie Doon Centre and bought writing paper and envelopes: she was going to need them.

Arrived back at her parked car she discovered a deep scar where a careless shopper with a buggy cart had crashed into her rear mudguard. Jessica looked around for the miscreant, but naturally, no one was waiting to own up.

She drove downtown musing on the reason behind the accident to her car. Was it fate?   Was she being punished for lying about herself to Brian, misleading him?

ONE WEEK OF exercise later Jack was relieved to find the pain became more tolerable with each period. He advanced from exercising in his condo, then the gym, to a jog around the River Valley track, conveniently close for running off the pounds.

He stepped on the bathroom weighing scales after jogging four miles, two there and two back. He had gained weight! At six two he should be under two hundred pounds. The muscle of course! Fat converting to muscle weighs heavier. He stepped off the scales and saw himself in the full length mirror.

"Don't expect miracles. You're targeting."

He dropped to the floor and commenced a vigorous exercise of pushups. Soon, he rolled onto his back and rode his invisible bicycle: it was kinder to his body.

JESSICA HAD MORE reason for self doubt over her actions when she arrived at the Claims Department of Social Services in Jasper Avenue, where she was supervisor.

"You're presence is required in the director's office," Dorinda informed her.

"I wonder what the lecher wants now?" Jessica hung her coat on the wooden tree stand. "He's singled me out for attention ever since my arrival. It's getting up my nose, I'm telling you for a fact."

"You're still new, he's trying you out for size."

"I only made matters worse when I asked to leave early yesterday for moving into my new home." She giggled. "Still, I suppose after morning break time is half a day off, not a few hours. Maybe that's what he's wanting to see me for."

"You never know what the reason is unless you find out, my David says."

Jessica gave a half smile. She hadn't been there long enough to ascertain just how credible was Dorinda's husband, with his peculiar sayings.

"He won't take 'No' for an answer. He tries breathing down my neck when I tell him to get on his bike!"

"Good luck." Dorinda went in the other direction when they left the partition opening and tried not to giggle at the newcomer's problem.

Jessica determined on appropriate action going along the corridor to Dick Chalmer's office, she wouldn't give him chance to insinuate or leer. She knocked and entered.

He was seated at his desk wearing a smart business suit topped with a wide grin; large white teeth glistened and resembled a wolf eyeing a choice morsel.

"Come in, don't be shy, Jessica. Come and stand by me," patted his thigh in encouragement. "I want to show you how things are done in Alberta. You had a different method in BC. I'd like you brought up to speed."

Jessica stood in front of the desk out of arm's reach. "I can hear quite well from here Dick, and there's nothing wrong with my eyesight." She leaned forward, peered at the marked paper in front of him. "I even possess the ability to read upside down."

"Intriguing! No doubt you're familiar with the hundred different positions of the Kama Sutra. We shall have to evolve a plan and discuss the merits of -"

"You want to discuss a different format for filling out Claim Forms, it looks like." She'd given him an edge, curse it, and waited, holding her breath, eyes boring in on his. She wouldn't give him the satisfaction of knowing he'd struck pay dirt with her nervous system: stomach tightened, vomit rose in her throat, head felt light, but she smiled.

"We prefer inserting brackets round the reason for non-payment of claims."

"Is that all?"

"That's enough for now." He held a magnifying glass up to his face with a 'come on' grin. "I'm maintaining a close watch on you, Jessica. I don't want you misled using different methods. You're destined for managerial promotions, next March. I wouldn't want anything preventing your rise up the advancement ladder," his eyes monstrous under magnification. "I'll even hold it for you. From below, naturally, and I hope you wear a skirt."

"And nothing will prevent my promotion... providing..." It was pointless finishing the sentence.

"Providing we understand one another. A sensible woman won't have that problem." The message was clear. He lowered the glass, looked her up and down undressing her with his eyes.

She turned on her heels, crossed quickly to the door, annoyed she was unable to make a smart retort. Saliva filled her mouth as she scurried along the partitioned corridor and into the washroom. She bent over the handbasin and dry heaved, but a strong stomach held onto breakfast. A toilet flushed and Dorinda emerged from a cubicle exhibiting concern.

When Jessica first encountered Dick Chalmers intentions she had mentioned the matter over a cafeteria lunch.

"Is it just me he makes amorous advances to, Dorinda?"

"No way!" Dorinda had beckoned work colleagues from the serving line to join them. "Dick's trying out with Jessica."

"Welcome to the club," was the general consensus.

"If he's a lush with everyone, why don't you complain to -" Jessica eyed in turn, girls from nineteen to twenty-five.

"Complain about a director?" Veronica's eyes were raised to her eyebrows. "Which planet are you from?"

"We've got equal rights in the work force, haven't we?" Jessica said. "Why doesn't someone make an issue of it?"

"She's got to be kidding," a tall thin girl said.

"Yes, equal rights." Veronica answered for them all. "We've the right to work alongside men and not complain when they grope."

"Certainly, complain." Jessica was envious of the girl's wrinkle free brow. "The union should - "

"It's male oriented," they all chorused. "Go figure!" The gaggle of females had laughed and returned to the counter line-up.

Dorinda washed her hands in the next basin. "Did he get to you again?"

Jessica's nodded, a hand over her mouth. "Yep!"

"Pity he can't be castrated like a bitch of a dog, my David says."

Jessica imagined a strapped down Dick on the operating table. "And without the benefit of an anesthetic."

They left the washroom arm in arm, giggling. The sight of Dick Chalmers leaving his office at the far end of the corridor had them scuttle through the partition opening of 'Claims'. They immediately started looking busy at their desks; the staff got the message from Dorinda's eye signals and hand waving in the direction of the director's office, and they too lowered their heads.

However, Dick walked past the opening and onto the elevator landing and everyone breathed a sigh of relief.

"I feel like a silly schoolgirl hiding from a headmaster." Jessica's words were agreed upon by all within earshot.

"Yes, and even a school principal," topped Dorinda.

JACK DRIED HIMSELF after the shower; ambled back to the foyer to pick up the mail he'd collected from the letterbox in the entry after his early morning run; two bills and a typewritten envelope for Brian. He noted the return address: Jean Morningbird who lived at Bonnie Doon.

Brian had mentioned an Yvonne, Myra and a Jean. This must be an answer to Brian's advertisement.

He pondered on what action to take and tapped the missive against his teeth. He could inform the girl of Brian's absence for four weeks. Brian had suggested

24

he should help himself to one of his penfriends. He set the envelope on the telephone stand to contemplate.

He couldn't 'Return to Sender', that'd be cruel. And if she didn't hear she'd imagine her letter hadn't touched the heart of the young Lothario. He could send it to Brian in Toronto, but quickly brushed aside the idea: Brian would have plenty of action on the tour. Go for it! He grinned. Okay!

Dear Brian;

It was nice to hear from you. I hope I'm in time to reach you before you go on your skydiving tour. What an interesting occupation that sounds, but short-lived, one presumes. Ha-ha! I don't really mean that in a horrible way, it just seemed appropriate, but now I realize it's probably in bad taste. I meant, you couldn't hold down that job into your sixties, could you? And there I go again. Sorry!

Jack towel dried his head; scrutinized the bald patch in the bedroom mirror then continued to read with a feeling he was touching the heart and mind of this person.

I work amongst dogs and cats at SPCA downtown; the kennel-maid, feeding, giving haircuts, injections and pills. I particularly enjoy walking dogs in parks and reserves. I can't get enough skiing during the year. I was at Banff this last season where this photograph was taken.

A heavily clad skier against a mountain background.

I know you enjoy canoeing. I love the thrill of pitting myself against the river, but I don't go in for white water rafting. Perhaps we could go on the river together sometime. Hint, hint!

Your new friend,

Jean Morningbird.

Jack was entranced. She's honest and sincere, pleasant, not pushy. Looks a happy soul; about thirty, but it's difficult to tell buried beneath skiing gear.

"In fact, Jean sounds the sort of companion I'd like to meet." He hurried to the telephone, checked the number on the letter, and paused. Yes, the telephone

25

was quicker than a letter, and anyway, his writing, especially his signature, was different to Brian's.

"Pinch his girlfriend, yes, but forgery? No way!" He drew a deep breath and punched telephone buttons. After several rings he realized Jean must have gone to work. Should he be presumptive and telephone the SPCA? But then, she would be at work, surrounded by co-workers, and maybe not appreciate a call.

Feeling despondent for some inexplicable reason, Jack continued dressing for work; he'd been on cloud nine at the thought of speaking to Jean, and now was undergoing pangs of letdown. Then he remembered Brian had already received replies to his advertisement from the Introductory Service.

He raced out of his bedroom and into Brian's, and without compunction looked through the stack of correspondence by the computer, and found the girls' letters. He picked out Jean's handwritten answer, sat in the chair, and drew a deep breath.

> Dear Advertiser,
>
> I'm interested in your request to meet a companion of the opposite sex. I'm Métis, mid-twenties and good-looking, and work as a kennel-maid.
>
> I used to visit my grandparents on the Reservation. My grandmother showed me how to bead belts. Grandfather showed me how to catch fish through ice holes. It's great you requesting a canoeist companion. My father and grandfather taught me and I've never forgotten.
>
> I've won medals at ballroom dancing. I look forward to hearing from you.
>
> Yours truly,
>
> Jean Morningbird.

A smile creased Jack's face. He felt years younger; imagined he was touching this person. She must have been a happy child visiting her grandparents on the reservation. Which one did she go to? He was familiar with Ontario bands having learnt of them in school. He must look up Alberta reservations.

His breakfast consisted of cornflakes and 2% milk with tinned peach halves in their own juice; to follow, black coffee without sugar or cream: he was learning! It was strange how the prospect looked brighter since Brian's departure after castigating him for sloth. He'd have something to exhibit when he returned; a girlfriend on his arm. He'd show him not to sling-off at his elders ...

Whoops! He had to get out of that mind set. He was an eligible bachelor!

JESSICA CAST A glance towards the director's office at the far end of the corridor. If she were quick, she'd make good her escape before Dick sussed out the rest of the staff had departed and she was alone. She turned around the partition at the elevator landing, looked back and saw Dick Chalmers emerge from his office. She sped into the ladies washroom and thankfully leant back on the door. Foiled him, goodie!

After wasting time fixing her hair and shining her nails for four minutes she judged it safe to emerge. Mistake! Dick was at the elevator doors and smiled graciously.

"I couldn't leave without you, Jessica," his welcoming arm resembled a vulture wanting to encircle her with its wing. "I've rung for the elevator."

Get in a lift with him? There'd be no escape! He'd have his hands all over her. Not if she could help it!

"I'll see you tomorrow, Dick," hurried to the Emergency Exit door and stone steps.

"But the elevator is coming, Jessica, dear."

"And I'm a-going, Dick." She dashed through the door, ran down the first flight of steps before she realized he'd beat her to the underground car park; be waiting! She slowed panic-dash to a lingering, easy stroll down seven further flights of stairs. "Let the stupid bugger wait."

However, when Jessica finally arrived in the basement car park, there was no sign of Dick or his Daimler. She'd bested him!

WORK DRAGGED for Jack at the office despite the interest of geological data gained from his last trip; never in his life had he been a clock watcher, but today was different. Today was the first day of the rest of his life. He aimed to reach

27

out for opportunity with both hands; get off his butt, find and marry a girl and start a family.

He traveled home from Shellack Oil Exploration in Kingsway, to the corner of Victoria Park Road and 116 Street in a high state of expectation. He'd better slow down or he'd be toast on the road. Anyway, why hurry? She might have had answers from other guys as well as Brian. A near miss of a pedestrian who chose to chance it dashing across the road without benefit of the traffic lights, brought a heavy foot on the brake.

Right on, an accident on the way to future happiness with a lovely girl.

Why hadn't he taken this opportunity to contact a girl through an introductory service before?

"Because you're chicken; you didn't want to be demoralized by rejection."

Everyone made mistakes.

"Your problem was thinking you weren't growing older."

He parked his car in the basement beneath the condominiums, warm in winter and cool in summer, raced to the elevator and punched the button for the twentieth floor. By the time the elevator shushed to a halt the door key was ready for inserting into the lock; inside the apartment he hurried to the telephone and came to a stop.

Slow down and think!

"For what? A reason for not doing anything?"

He placed his briefcase and computer Notepad on the telephone chair, removed his jacket and eyed the telephone; counted up to ten slowly, took a deep breath and punched out the numbers imbedded on his retinue. The ringing out tone sounded and once more, there was no reply. He felt like yelling in frustration; all day he had been anticipating hearing her voice and she wasn't available, yet again.

Maybe she did shopping on her way home from work.

Yes, that would be it. He replaced the receiver, glanced at the wall clock above the entrance to the open kitchen; just before five o'clock, he would try again after he'd sweated ounces jogging along the river.

On the way to change into running gear he ran a speculative finger and thumb around his waistband. It was certainly slimmer than when Brian had prodded it, and firmer. Soon it'd disappear entirely.

Sure thing, he'd impress Brian and also Jean, when he finally met her. There'd be no more sitting on the sidelines watching life go by, girth spreading, hair thinning; there was a train at the station and he intended catching it.

He couldn't do much about his bald patch, could he?

He puzzled on the matter, then when lacing up his runners caught a glance of his head in the dressing-table mirror, and a light bulb went on.

JESSICA PLACED DIRTY dishes in a sink full of soapy water and mused on the amount of waste for only one plate, knife, fork, fruit spoon, teaspoon and mug. It was really uneconomical living alone; two or three settings could have been washed in the amount of hot water and dishwashing liquid she'd used; but then, if she hadn't bought a small tub of yogurt she would have dirtied a fruit dish.

The telephone rang. Maybe it was the 'YWCA' asking about her answer to volunteering. She wiped her hands on the hand towel and picked up the wall-phone.

"Yes?"

"Is that Jean Morningbird?" The question, in a deep masculine voice, had Jessica imagining a Goliath of a man.

"Yes." The answer to her letter. She mouthed her knuckles like a schoolgirl.

"Hi, this is Brian Swartzkoff."

"Oh, hello Brian. I'm so pleased you called."

"I tried phoning you this morning but I guess you'd already left for work."

"Um, probably. I leave around seven-forty for an eight am start."

"You must fly, to reach SPCA in twenty minutes in Coliseum rush-hour traffic."

Wow! She'd been caught out in her first lie. Naturally, she'd been thinking of Social Services on Jasper Avenue, just across the river from Bonnie Doon.

She giggled. "Er... I may be bragging a little." His return laugh made her heart skip a beat. What a lovely deep voice. "I'm not a roadhog, I assure you."

"That's sure a quaint accent, Jean. Not your average native Canadian."

"What do I sound like, Brian?" She swallowed hard.

"Well, at a guess, I'd put my money on north of England. Am I right?"

"Brilliant deduction, sire. Ha-Ha-Ha!" The laugh to gain time. "Er... I've had long spells with Youth Services Abroad." She crossed soapy fingers. "And I was billeted with a Bradford family for two years. I picked up their accent, I think."

"You've got to be kidding! You sound as if you've recently arrived by plane."

"Er... Maybe it's because I spent time with my mother in Halifax when I was ten." How easily the lies spewed forth; it was just as well she wasn't eyeballing him, she could never have kept up the pretense.

"Nova Scotia? With an accent like that?"

"Halifax, Yorkshire!" Flipping heck! What persuaded her traveling the road of deception would be easy?

"That would do it. We assimilate accents early in life and retain that certain inflection, that special way of saying things. Like a Newfoundlander for instance; extremely difficult to follow if you're a westerner."

"And numbering. Here, it's four, four, four. In the UK on the telephone it's double four-four or treble four."

"Our way's on account of street numbering, I guess. One hundred and forty four on forty-fourth Street."

"Your accent's Canadian, isn't it, Brian? Swartzkoff sounds as if you're of German descent. Am I right?"

"I'm a third generation Canadian, from Austria."

"Isn't this a nice way of introducing ourselves?"

"Sure is. How about we meet tomorrow? I'm looking forward to seeing you in person, nice as the photograph was. Say, about halfway between us."

Now she was for it, hoist by her own petard; he wanted to meet the girl of the first letter, not a discarded wife.

"That would be lovely!" Now, what part of her said that? "I'd like to meet you too before you go on your skydiving tour." There was a silence on the line. She bit her lip, had she said something wrong?

"I was thinking, Jean. How about Sir Winston Churchill Square for a quick lunch. There's a Works Festival. We meet in a sociable atmosphere without the trappings..."

What a sensitive man, considerate of her feelings. "Lunch would be fine with me, Brian. I can change my lunch-hour if twelve to one o'clock isn't suitable."

"That's okay by me. How shall I recognize you? Don't suppose you'll be muffled up in a ski suit, like in the photograph? Ha-Ha-Ha!"

He has a sense of humor! Jessica hugged herself. And he didn't think her too old, or he wouldn't have phoned.

"Er, let me see. I'll wear a dark blue dress with a white bib front and carry a ..." What sort of identification should she carry, a carnation or rose?

"Purse," and he laughed.

"Yes, an imitation alligator purse." Good thing she hadn't mentioned handbag, a dead give away. "But what do you look like, I don't think you mentioned how tall you are?" Dear God, make him over five-ten, please?

As a five-foot-eight-inch girl she had been mocked in her youth for choosing partners smaller than herself. Her ex. had been over six feet, which had immediately endeared him to her: however, his negative points far outweighed the positives.

"I'm six-two and well built."

She spun around, held the receiver to her cheek. He's tall! He's tall! And a bonus: well built, not scrawny.

"Naturally, an athlete needs to be fit." Another silence followed her remark. What had she said wrong again?

"Precisely, a sore point, Jean. I guess I missed this skydiving tour because I'm overweight. They prefer us guys landing lightly on our feet. Ha-ha!"

"Oh, lucky for us, meeting before you're off on another tour."

"Right on. I'll see you around twelve noon at the statue in Sir Winston Churchill Square, eh?"

"Rightio, Brian. Bye then."

"Bye, Jean."

Jessica held the receiver to her hot flushed face for a moment, then feeling silly replaced it on the wall cradle.

"I have a date! A date with a mature male with a voice that'd cream butter!"

What footwear to match the outfit? She hurried into her bedroom, glanced down the rack of footwear in clear plastic containers: obviously, cuban-heeled alligator sandals.

Decision made, there remained nothing else to contemplate in the wardrobe. Jean returned to the sink, finished washing dishes, her mind not on the task. She was in seventh heaven, had a date! A haunting thought struck her. How could she make herself appear younger? She hurried into her bedroom, posed several different ways in front of the dressing-table, hands on hips; stuffed nylon stockings down her bra, pinched the ends to make pert, pulled in the waist-belt an extra notch.

"I'll have to watch my food intake or I'll strangle myself." She placed a hand behind her head nonchalantly, lifted her hair to one side and laughed gaily at her reflection.

Did her teeth have a yellow tinge? Were those lines around her mouth? She practically shoved her face onto the mirror to observe this intrusion on beauty, but after several movements in and out with her lips, gritting teeth and grunting like a chimpanzee she concluded they were laughter lines, and laughed with relief and at her stupidity.

This was exciting, she had something to look forward to. She was no longer alone, she had a date! Maybe this man would obliterate the memory of betrayal.

"No!" She slapped the back of her hand. "Don't look back, Jessica. Look ahead! Be joyful! You can still attract a man... even if it is someone else's."

Realization struck.

"Hecky thump! I'm no better than that floozie in Vancouver going after Ronnie."

She eyed her reflection. A floozie? More like a tired businesswoman. But she was good, honest and decent; she'd hold onto that thought. She smiled, and performed an exaggerated sashay from the bedroom with her head held high.

"I'll show the world you can't toss aside a woman like me and have her roll over and die. Up and at 'em, Jessica!"

Chapter Three

Sir Winston Churchill, the solid bronze statue in the square named after the hero of the Second World War, witnessed many people meandering around. Their interests were not on him but in the many booths and activities vying for attention at the Works & Entertainment Festival.

On the circumference of the square, down the east side, booths served Indian, Chinese, Vietnamese, Italian, French, Ukrainian and Canadian food. Several long picnic tables occupied a dining area in front of the large stage which promoted a continuous supply of entertainers; other tables, conveniently placed under the spreading branches of trees on the perimeter, catered for patrons who valued their hearing. Eight side fountains sprayed steady streams of water into the pool at the foot of City Hall; the carillon chimed twelve noon, went into ecstasies of bell-ringing which rivaled the output of a hootenanny singer with back-up guitars.

Jessica shook her head to clear her ears when she neared the statue. One thing at a time please, she didn't want to overload her circuits! But everything was gorgeous; a noisy crowd, lovely day and meeting a man.

She'd managed to escape early for lunch, scrounged a few minutes from Dorinda, who, like Veronica, was interested in Jessica's blind date.

"Stay longer if you find him difficult to leave, Jessica. I'll fill in for you so Dick doesn't catch onto the fact you're missing." Dorinda stood off to examine Jessica's dress length with a keen eye. "A rare find is hard to find, my David says."

Which statement left Jessica slightly perplexed, so she merely smiled her appreciation.

"Say again how you know about him, Jessica?" Veronica touched up the sleeves of the dress to sit straight on Jessica's arms. "It sounded romantic the first time."

"A friend in Vancouver gave me his phone number and said to phone him once I was settled in my own home." Jessica repeated her spiel. "So I did. A bit clinical really, Veronica, not romantic." She patted side curls over one ear. Think they're a bit much?"

34

"And he said?" Veronica insisted, and attempted to span Jessica's waist with her two hands. "You've a small waist Jessica, I wonder why you don't show it off more."

"No, he didn't say that, silly." Jessica kept her face straight. "He said he'd like to meet me, that's all."

All three had a quiet giggle. Jessica looked to see if typist-clerks at their desks had heard, but they discreetly carried on working.

"You should wear tightfitting dresses often, Jessica." Dorinda turned her gently from side to side. "This way your waist shows off your bust."

"Yes, I thought so too." Jessica patted ear curls to deflect their attention from her boosted bosom. "Think I'm overdoing it with the curls, umh?"

"You're a free woman, and if you have it, flaunt it." Veronica touched the curls. "And I like the hairstyle."

"Think it makes me floozie-like with curls, shampoo highlight and pins?"

"No way!" Veronica ran a finger under the forehead kiss curls. "Reminds me of those black and white reruns on TV, Dorinda. What do you reckon, eh?"

"Gosh! Thanks a heap, Veronica!" Jessica pushed off feeling hands. "I needed that."

"She means, you look romantic, Jessica," Dorinda hastened to add. "Just right for a first meeting."

"Yeah, Jessica." Veronica patted her. "You'll turn on his lights, for sure."

Jessica left in the knowledge she wasn't making a fool of herself tarting up; and to save time trying to park downtown she'd hopped on a bus.

She looked at the clock from the shadow of the statue; she wouldn't be missed here, she couldn't be closer otherwise she'd be standing in 'Winnie's' flowerbed.

Why hadn't Brian given her a more comprehensive description of himself? Fat, glasses, hearing-aid, tanned? Six feet two inches said very little about a person. He could have mentioned his hair color and type of jacket and trousers he was wearing.

35

IS THIS ALL THERE IS?

JACK WALKED UP THE STEPS from the underground parking by the library, pulled in his gut beneath the sweater for practice; he hadn't entirely lost his spare tire, but was getting there. At street level a cacophony of noise assailed him. Why on earth had he suggested the Square with a Works & Entertainment Festival, hardly conducive to entertaining a lady?

Trees gave shade to tents which covered the outer area; owners submitted their wares, expertise, Frankfurters, ice-creams and cold drinks.

Jack crossed the road, strode through the happy throng who walked aimlessly from booth to booth exhibiting no concern for using walkway matting. He was tall so could see over bobbing heads, the slim, dark haired lady in a dark blue dress with white bib front, beneath the statue.

His heart began to pound. Was he going to have a heart attack? He slowed his pace but his heart continued to race. The lady looked in his direction and he could see she was lovely, and happy to see him.

His heart 'boinged', resembled a jackhammer ripping up concrete. His own face gave a return smile; blood pumped through vessels at a rate usually reserved for jogging the last yards of a marathon.

Oh, lovely, he's tall, well-built and handsome with a head of hair thick and wavy, and of a luxurious brown she bet he didn't get with Harmony High Lights, like her.

Jack drew level, stretched out a hand in greeting.

"Hi, Jean! Or should I say: Hello Jean, I'm Brian Swartzkoff," and felt a colossal fraud and wished he hadn't started the charade. This was no lady to fool around with; he wanted to be honest, be himself not a substitute.

"Hello, Brian." Jean liked the firm hand grip, he wasn't a wimp with a damp clasp; she could trust this man with clear, dark blue eyes and strong white teeth, like he'd indicated in his letter: obviously an honest man. "Hi Jean's, all right if you don't mind being reminded of sanitary pans." Why did she say that? She would put him off! Quickly, say something! "You managed to get off early?"

"No problem for me, I'm my own boss more or less," his heart returned to a normal beat, eyes imprinted her features for all time in his memory bank.

"I suppose the pilot calls the tune though when you're parachuting?" He appeared stunned. What had she said wrong? What could she say to sound clever? "I came by bus." Wow, that was clever!

R. DRIVER

"Did you?" Jack touched her arm, indicated the food stalls and tables across the square and down from the bandstand. "How come? Don't you have a car?

"I didn't want to buck the noon traffic; then there's the parking -"

"I'll take you back, then cut along 118 Avenue to Kingsway." He halted when Jean froze in her tracks.

Hecky thump! She'd forgotten she was supposed to be working at SPCA on 122 and 67 Street. But wait a second, the Coliseum was near. Brian mentioned it last night.

"It's all right, thank you, Brian. Er ... I've planned returning to work by LRT, getting off at the Coliseum."

"Nonsense," took hold of her arm, headed for the tables. "It's no problem for me."

"Er... I've arranged to meet a co-worker in Churchill Square Station at 12.45. She's parked her car at the Coliseum and is driving me back to work."

"That's disappointing. I'd have liked more of your company. This three-quarter hour isn't long enough for us to get to know one another, that's for sure."

She wished she had never started the seemingly innocent escapade. Why, oh why had she pretended to be someone else?

"Which is it to be?" Jack indicated the stalls when they neared. "Chinese, French, Canadian or what-have-you?"

"I don't mind, but I do enjoy Chinese for a change."

"Chinese it is, then." They threaded their way past tables. Jack courteously took hold of her elbow and only released it when they stood in line at the stall.

She liked the proprietary hold and missed it when it was gone. "Smells nice. It's making me hungry, Brian." They watched assistants ladle food onto plates from several piping-hot containers for customers ahead of them.

"I suppose with your service abroad you've built up a comprehensive range of different foods." The fringe on the canopy caught against his head when he entered the serving area so he missed Jessica's sudden start of surprise. His mind in turmoil at the thought of discovery, he put up both hands and caught onto the hairpiece studiously stuck onto his head prior to leaving the office washroom.

37

"Did you catch your head?" The last thing she wanted was to lose him before they'd become acquainted.

"No sweat." His toupee was still attached and firm as per the instructions. "I have a hard head. Got to in my job. I'm often banging up against overhead rocks."

"That isn't fair! Your life shouldn't be on the line every time you jump."

Wahoo! He'd forgotten he was Brian, the skydiver. Fortunately, the Chinese cook indicated they were next in line, so he concentrated on choosing from the wall menu.

"I figure Chow Mien and pork balls Jessica, eh?"

"Good choice," thankful he wasn't a Muslim, she liked pork.

The plates were piled high and handed over. "There you go." Jack paid the man in correct change.

"Thank you Brian." She smiled, and they left carrying their plates.

"You're welcome."

"I'll pay next time."

He was delighted. That meant she wanted to see him again, expected to, liked him enough to. They wended their way towards a dining table farthest from the bandstand. He'd nearly blown it with his hairpiece almost detaching, and the slip about banging up against overhead rocks. At geological digs they often worked under rock overhangs, all part of the job. He'd have to exercise care if he wanted to retain his hidden identity.

"The trees aren't shading the tables too much." She put down her plate and seated herself. "And we can both see and hear the fountains, here."

"And, what's more important, it's away from the stage. We'll be able to hear ourselves speak."

DURING LUNCH they conversed a little, both carefully skirted around the edges in their search for a safe topic.

"I enjoy canoeing, Brian. How much have you done?"

"Enough. But what I want to know more is about your canoeing. What rivers have you been on?"

"I've paddled in Quebec, Toronto, Saskatchewan and Alberta and," a quick afterthought, "BC." He was waiting for her to continue, smiled sweetly at her. "At The Peace River convention we camped at Notikemin Provincial Park."

"Did you manage to canoe on the Muskeg River at Grande Cache? That's a marvelous area for trekking over Willmore Wilderness Park."

"No, missed that one, but we competed on the South Thompson River at Kamloops."

"Ah, yes, west of the Monashee Mountains. Been there on a rekky. Anomalies of efflorescence proved interesting. Osmium cobalt hydroxide, which was unearthed - "

"Get away!" Brown, wide eyes, stared in amazement.

Immediately all his senses were on the alert. "You don't want hearing me report on this dry material. Tell me about yourself, apart from the canoeing."

"For jumps, in Monashee Mountains? That'd be dangerous with turbulence coming up the mountains, wouldn't it?" She didn't want to talk about herself, it was dangerous ground; best to invite him to open up about himself. He was interesting, sounded intelligent, even if she had no idea what he was talking about.

Jack smiled, his stomach in knots at his slip-up. "I'm impressed with your knowledge of airflow." He indicated the plate. "This is real good."

"You're not kidding."

"But there's a lot of it." He gamely continued to eat, enjoying her company, the ambiance surrounding them as if arranged especially for their benefit; but a tightening of the waistband was a warning; gradually stomach muscles went into spasm and he broke out in a sweat.

Jessica was unaware of her partner's difficulty in his mid-section, but she could see him shifting on the wooden bench. Has he caught a flea, or maybe a mosquito got into his trousers. He looked very uncomfortable, charming, but ill-at-ease. Jack caught her look of inquiry, and smiled.

"A splinter." He looked down at the wooden bench, ran a hand over the smooth, freshly repainted planks.

"Flipping heck! Shall we go and sit over by those trees?" Jessica set down her utensils, picked up her alligator purse. "I don't mind, I've had more than enough to eat. Chinese meals are so filling. I won't be able to work this afternoon." Her purse caught a pork ball smothered in sauce which landed with a splat on her sandal. She tutted, bent down to wipe away the disgusting residue with a paper napkin.

"You okay, Jean?"

"Yes, but I'll have a few animals sniffing curiously at my feet for the rest of the day."

"Fortunately, your dog-walking will get rid of unwanted calories." He took the opportunity to stand and ease the waistband through the sweater and draw breath; blood circulated once more in released flesh.

Oh, certainly, walk a dog? She'd be running from one.

They deposited their plastic utensils and paper plates in a container on the periphery of the dining area.

"Good, they have plenty of garbage bins around." Jack used the napkin on his hands before tossing it away.

"Um, keeps the place tidy. I love walking in towns without untidy litter around the trees."

"Yes, dogs would be attracted to it."

"What, to the trees? Cock a leg, you mean?"

Jack laughed loudly. How honest and refreshing she was. "I guess that's what I meant to say."

"Er... In England there were large signs everywhere: 'Keep England Green' and there was no spitting in the streets either, like here."

"Yes, I saw those signs when I was over on a business trip. 'Don't Expectorate'. I wondered at the time if the landed immigrant understood what 'expectorate' meant."

"They soon did, once the police warned them they'd be fined if they spat again."

"I don't go a bundle on spitting." He took hold of her arm to head for one of the benches beneath the hanging branches of a giant spruce. "In hockey it's common practice to spit on the ice. I suppose it's a hangover from youthful days: it's a guy thing to do, sort of."

"I hate seeing them spit on the Wimbledon Tennis Courts when I'm watching television. I've got to turn my head away." She hurried her pace and glanced at her watch. "Hope we get a seat before they're all taken." Time was flying and she hadn't got to know how he ticked, as yet.

"I envy you, Jean, having the trust and companionship of man's best friend."

She'd be in front of a computer terminal processing claims, not on her knees clipping man's best friend. Her spirits sank. How she wished she hadn't lied from the outset, it was depressing having to watch every word she uttered. If she were smart she'd let him know the truth. She looked up at him striding alongside her, smiling at a dog frolicking with children at a picnic. But she would lose him, he was obviously a man of integrity; he wouldn't want an association with a liar and a cheat.

Jack dusted the bench with a tissue from his pocket. "Don't want you should get dirty."

"Thanks a lot Brian, that's very considerate of you." She sat and smiled up at him.

"You're welcome." She's wearing a nice perfume, and has a lovely wide smile with teeth that almost outshine her bright brown eyes; when sunshine catches strands of her hair it resembles burnt chestnuts. She sure has a lovely nature; was greatly concerned for him in the skydiving act. Gawd! If only she knew the truth about him.

Then he remembered his hairpiece and the trouble he'd gone to; the salesman assured him during the fitting it would not come off even when swimming. Oh yeah! It darn near ended up a disaster under the awning!

"There's a big crowd here, Brian. You wouldn't think a Works & Entertainment Festival would attract many visitors, would you?"

"It's the entertainment factor. Entertainers come from Europe and the States. It's a big item on their agenda, and a great draw for the public." He looked at her fully. "Don't you come to many festivals?"

Whoops! "Sometimes." She quickly searched her mind for something else to contribute. "Aren't there a lot of booths, all flogging their own speciality? It looks like a Middle East bazaar."

"It pays to have a booth at festivals. They sure make a bundle." He nodded in the direction of the fountains. "Ever skated here when the pool's frozen over, Jean?"

Oh, geez, what should she tell him? She hadn't been through a whole winter yet, especially an Alberta winter; it had rained in British Columbia, Vancouver Island in particular, and she couldn't recall seeing an outside skating rink. In fact she hadn't ice-skated at all. Roller-skated, yes, when she was twelve. Anyway, did Jean say she ice-skated in her letter? So she changed the subject.

"Oh, look at that dog with the children."

They both watched the cavorting dog fascinated by a strip of paper attached to a string which was pulled back and forth by his small owners.

"You speaking of a Middle East bazaar poses a question, Jean. Where did you travel on your Service Abroad? Ever get to Israel?"

Of course, he's Jewish, that's why he's interested in Israel. She noticed dried gravy on her handbag; commenced flicking it off with a fingernail in order to gain time to assimilate her thoughts.

"Er ... Yes. I had two months in a kibbutz. What a workload it was too." She had been the recipient of woes upon the return of friends in Bradford conned into working holidays, who arrived home worse for wear. "We arose early in the mornings, worked to breakfast-time, worked to lunch, worked to dinner time."

"From dawn 'till dusk." Jack handed her a clean tissue from his pocket. "I'm aware of the work output."

"Of course, you would be. The rest of the time was our own." She spat on the tissue and wiped clean the handbag. "We were too tired to go out and enjoy ourselves, though. It was a relief to get home where work output, earned money."

"I've been through Israel," screwed his eyes trying to remember. "Now, when was that?"

"Naturally, you would. Which kibbutz was it?"

"Not on a kibbutz. It was Saudi Arabia and the Lebanon, we..." He couldn't state they were sounding out the viability of Middle East oil wells. "We'd an air-show."

"Over Muslim areas. Really? The desert Arabs must have been impressed by your aeroplanes after seeing nothing faster than a camel."

"Oh, don't you believe it. Arabs know about airplanes and fast travel. You ought to see Rolls Royces vying for space in the narrow confines of alleys packed with street vendors balancing wares on their heads. It's a work of art. These large vehicles manage to avoid bicycles, and stall contents overflowing onto the streets. Arabs are extremely knowledgeable about computers and television, and up to the standard of Israelis."

"Oh, did you witness a camel race? I saw one on a television program about racing camels spurred on by nomads."

"Witness one?" He laughed loudly. "I even rode one. Do they ever bounce up and down! It's impossible to remain upright, you're swaying from side to side."

The dog came over to sniff Jessica's foot. "Go away little doggie, I'm not on your menu." She waved it away before breaking into a sneezing fit, her allergic reaction to long-haired dogs well known by friends.

"There's a good dog, go back to your master." Jack patted the animal who decided he preferred that to a wave-off, and lingered by Jack's legs. "I envy you having dogs and cats around you all day, Jean."

Oh goodie, back at the kennels again! "Have you got dogs or cats at home, Brian?"

"I'm in a condo and it's against the rules."

"Oh, of course, what a shame." Inwardly she was delighted. There was nothing to prevent her visiting him since he didn't have animals.

"But, I've a guy who shares and keeps me entertained as much as any frisky dog."

"Hecky thump! A dog or a bitch?" She laughed, lifted her face to the sun that flitted through branches and remembered the Kennel Club Show Ring where she had been showing their dachshund bitch when she was seventeen.

A boisterous dog stood next in line to be judged, took little heed of his owner's instructions to stand straight, he was more interested in sniffing her little bitch's bottom. The young man's apology lost something in the translation; Jessica was fascinated to observe the frustrated dog cock its leg and wee-wee on the leg of its owner.

What a lovely person she is, so natural. "I hope it isn't indelicate of me, Jean." He smiled into her eyes. "I can't get past the English expressions. Would you mind telling me which tribe you belong to?"

Jessica was open-mouthed, literally. Sylvia Stevens in Bradford hadn't mentioned they belonged to tribes. She remembered from Bible study endured for half-an-hour every school morning that there were tribes of Israel. Was it seven? No, that was seven plagues of Egypt. Which tribe was hers? She decided to follow her chess strategy: when in doubt, attack!

"Which tribe do you belong to, cheeky blighter?"

"Sorry, Jean," his face a picture of contrition. "Pretend I didn't say that."

"How do you expect me to forget you wanting to know which tribe I belong to? That's an impertinence."

"I was wondering which Reserve you came from, that's all. If it was a Cree band in Alberta or what? But, forget I mentioned it, will you?"

"Forget it? You've just said it again!" Her mind whipped along at a fine rate assimilating this new thought. The Reserve mentioned in the letter was not the parkland she'd assumed.

"I'm sorry, Jean. I'm a clumsy asshole. Please try to ignore it. I'll never ask you again. I can see it's distasteful... distressing for -"

"All right, then." She would be only too happy to ignore it; she hadn't the faintest idea she was Indian.

Her education had been sadly neglected apparently since arriving in Canada. Previously, the only North American Indians she was familiar with were the television reruns in Bradford: Indians surrounding Custer's last stand at Little Big Horn; John Wayne fighting gloriously; Errol Flynn dying with his boots on, and the Classic 'Last of the Mohicans'. Indian and Pakistani pupils she had gone to school with in Bradford, didn't qualify. Wrong continent!

She should have realized Morningbird was indigenous. There were many unusual names which gave room for thought in the register at both Vancouver and Edmonton Social Services. Henry One Tooth, Yes! Wind In Belly, Yes! Sam One Toe, Yes! Jim First Born, Yes! But never a Morningbird!

The latest addition to her knowledge of names was the reported New Brunswick Lobster pot confrontation between Mic-Mac Chief Knock Down of Burnt Church Band, and the Ministry of Fisheries. The band wanted to harvest

44

five hundred pots, not just forty two pots, enough to feed their own people. The Ministry was averse to allowing them leeway when the rest of Canada had to stop catching lobster altogether, at least until the breeding season showed there was sufficient in number to allow lobster to once more go on the nation's dinner menu. Cree Chief Matthew Coon Come went on Television and Radio to make the point, but failed to dissuade the Ministry of Fisheries.

The names of the chiefs were nothing like Morningbird.

"I'll delve into my ancestry when I know you better Brian. That all right with you?"

"Gee, thanks a lot, Jean, that's sure a relief. I should never have asked. You must think I'm..." He couldn't say a racist, that'd suggest he was!

"Maybe I should be the one to say: forget it, Brian," holding out a conciliatory hand.

"Forget what?" He took hold with both hands. It appeared Jean had hopes of meeting him again.

"Tell me about your skydiving, Brian. How long have you been jumping?"

"Quite a whiles." Jack released her hand, looked around the square for inspiration; drew on memory of Brian's life before he entered a career in skydiving. "I was in the Air Force and developed a taste for flying."

"As a pilot?"

"No, as a bombardier." Brian said they sat in the little turret like squirrels guarding nuts: flak, a bombardier's nightmare. Thank the Lord he hadn't been one; his preference was terra firma, the reason behind Territorial weekend soldiering.

"What decided you to take up skydiving then?"

"I suppose it was seeing the guys floating down on their parachutes." Jack strained for total recall. "I had a bird's eye view of them in my camera following them in free-fall, 'till their chutes opened, and saw them swinging backwards and forward like a symphony of motion," emulated Brian's enthusiasm. "Gave me a kick! That's what I'm gonna do in civvy street."

"Bombardiers have guns not cameras, don't they?"

"You're half right. In peacetime they use cameras; in wartime they film before and after bombing and use their guns when under attack from enemy aircraft."

"I've never wanted to parachute." Jessica didn't know how to ask the next question with any degree of delicacy, but she had to know. "I... I suppose there's an age limit for skydiving. I mean, I suppose you can get too old for it. I mean, aren't you too mature to be skydiving?"

Jack laughed out loud, placed a hand across his midriff to hide the bulge. "Nice one, Jean."

"Oh, I'm sorry I was so indelicate, Brian. It's nothing to do with me how over..." His look stopped her. "I've done it again, haven't I? He nodded, tried not to smile at her obvious discomfort.

"But you did say you were left out of this tour because of being overweight. And I can see the tightness..." She pointed at the roll under his sweater. "You're definitely too heavy for performing aerial calisthenics."

"It's okay, Jean," patted her hand. "You're only stating the obvious. I'm overweight. I'm fast approaching the stage where younger performers will, or should replace me." What a great cop out to exit skydiving completely!

"That makes sense."

"I've been considering leaving the skies for awhile. I guess that's why I've gained weight. I'm leaving the game to younger, more pliable bodies than mine. Let them take the falls."

"Good for you, Brian. It's an occupation more suited to a younger person. Why, you could easily snap an ankle on landing, carrying all that weight. Whoops!" Her face screwed up at the lack of tact. "Sorry!"

"Talk me out of skydiving, Jean," patted the hand now on her knee. He couldn't keep his hands off her, what was wrong with him? "You'll be doing me a favor."

Jessica wished he could talk her out of being an aborigine. She glanced at the clock tower, the carillon started to chime the three-quarter past the hour. She checked with her own watch and stood with a smile of reluctance.

"That's me for meeting my friend at the LRT."

"I'd like to see you again soon, Jean." Jack stood up quickly. "That okay?"

"That'd be very nice, Brian," smiled sweetly. "Let's shake on it."

"This is great." He retained hold of her hand whilst they walked towards the edge of the entertainment area of the square. "Better than expected when I phoned you."

"You're right there. Been perfect from when we first met. Where are you parked?"

"In the parkade under the library. I can go with you down the stairs to the subway."

"Together a bit longer, then." Flipping heck! She hoped he wouldn't insist on accompanying her onto the platform; he'd begin to suspect something if he saw her board a train going in the opposite direction to the Coliseum.

"Where would you like to go next time, Jean? The movies, dinner or...?"

The playful dog caught onto Jessica's pork ball scent and sniffed around her ankles.

"Somewhere away from dog activity, Brian. I get enough of it during the day."

"I get the message. No animals on our date."

The children called it back but the dog had a mind of its own; pestered them almost to the LRT glassed shelter.

"Go back to your master, little doggy." Jessica released Jack's hand, waved the dog away. Hey, dog, you'll get a foot in the face if you don't cease and desist!

"Gee, dogs sure like you, Jean."

"No doubt he likes pork balls better! Ha-Ha-Ha!"

The small owner whistled and the dog mercifully left to rejoin loved ones.

"No, you're wrong. Dogs always sense a trustworthy person."

"Postmen might differ with that assessment; dogs are their worst enemies on postal deliveries."

"That's for sure," Jack nodded his head thoughtfully. "The mailman's got it tough in the canine department."

Mailman not postman, idiot, she was supposed to be Canadian. She smiled wryly going down the subway stairs; how much more could she take of this incessant hammering at her brain to do and say the right thing, the correct thing in accordance with Jean Morningbird, native to this country? Change the subject for heaven's sake!

"I don't think I'd enjoy free-falling from ten thousand feet, Brian. What's it feel like?"

"Great, couldn't be better."

It had been his intention to accompany her along the platform, see her onto the train, but discretion was called for. The subway branched right for trains and left for the parkade. "I'll telephone tonight and arrange something," holding out his hand.

"Thanks for the lunch." She clasped hold of warmth.

"You're welcome."

"I'll hear from you tonight, then. Ta-ta!"

"Have a nice day! Or should I say, Ta-ta?"

Their hands parted reluctantly, neither wanting the break; each went a separate direction relieved beyond measure they had not divulged a guilty secret.

Gawd, if only he hadn't been a smart-ass adopting Brian's mantle. Jack scowled when he passed through the doors to the parkade.

Jessica descended the escalator, saw the Coliseum train departing, and made certain Brian wasn't watching from above. On the platform she hid behind an advertising display and train timetable stand; took occasional squints at the escalator to see if Brian was observing.

When the University train pulled into the station she scampered across the intervening space, entered an almost empty carriage then squatted on the edge of the seat until the train started to move, before she felt able to relax.

"You fooled him, but good, Jessica. Proud of yourself, you accomplished liar?" She quickly looked around to ascertain she was not within earshot of fellow passengers.

Chapter Four

Jessica alighted at the LRT station, walked a block to Social Services, elated, thinking of her newfound man-friend. Dorinda on the landing pounced on her immediately she left the elevator.

"How'd it go, Jessica, and what's he like?"

"He's tall, handsome and with lovely hair." Jessica took her arm to walk to their section. "About my age, and he's so charming. And get this Dorinda, he's a skydiver!" Not a word about the lie in which she had buried herself; ashamed to divulge the depths to which she had sunk: reading someone else's mail and pretending to be the pen pal.

"A skydiver." Dorinda gave Jessica's shoulder a gentle punch when they rounded the partition to enter the Claims office. "You didn't say he was a skydiver before."

"Well, I didn't want to brag, it mightn't have come to anything. And I honestly thought he meant he parachuted out of planes when it was necessary. I didn't realize he did it for a living." She placed her handbag in the desk drawer. "But he's so nice, Dorinda. Really easy to talk to."

"Does he have a friend who'd like to meet a co-worker?"

"Ha-Ha-Ha!" She couldn't introduce anyone from Social Services to Brian. "I think your David would have something to say about you making up a blind date."

"Hey, how about that? We could have a foursome, some time. David and me, and you and Brian."

"Um, should be nice."

Inwardly Jessica quaked. She switched on her computer terminal, the signal for Dorinda to leave and start up her own computer; but Jessica's thoughts refused to leave the image of the four of them at a restaurant table, laughing. At what? Her stupidity pretending to be someone she wasn't, of course.

Work occupied her mind until almost home time at four o'clock, before she remembered her 'Tribe'. She tapped into Edmonton Library through Edmonton Community Network, and looked up books on the subject of native culture in

Alberta. She would go to the library and bury herself in homework; she didn't intend being sideswiped by questions on her Indian background again.

What had been said in Jean's first letter to Brian? Obviously, she was part Indian, for Brian to ask which tribe she was from. No one in their right mind would assume Jessica was full-blooded. Jean must be a quarter or sixth part Indian. She knew from her Vancouver period there were Métis, Innu and Aborigine. Which was her group?

Jessica's family on both sides were Yorkshire borne and bred. Her mother, fair-haired with blue eyes, followed the Anglo Saxon coloring; her father, however, had a complexion which easily tanned, brown hair and eyes, obviously of Norman ancestry following the conquest of Britain in 1066. She knew he was of Norman descent; her uncle Albert, on her father's side, had traced their lineage to the twelve hundreds and discovered one of their ancestors had been hung for sheep-stealing, adequate reason for the name change. Uncle Albert had declined further research into personal history, much to the relief of living relatives: apparently, a bad lot, those Normans.

Um, she had taken after her father, that's why she resembled First Nation People. It had been easy fooling an unsuspecting man, and didn't she make him feel bad when she'd verbally attacked him? Her skin crawled with self-disgust.

At home time Jessica was the last to leave the office. She put on her coat, felt a hand reach from behind to assist, and swung around. The hand fell to her hip to settle, fondly: leering Dick.

"Haven't you got something better to do with your hands?" Instantly realized she had left an opener; his hand slid down to her upper thigh.

"If you like, it can be in my office or in a motel."

"In your dreams!" She raised her arm threateningly.

He removed his hand. "I'm disappointed but not deterred." He moved to stand between Dorinda's vacant desk and the bookshelves. "You'll come to appreciate my attentions soon enough, Jessica, I've no doubt at all."

"I'll look forward to it like a dose of the clap, umh?"

"Ooe, naughty but nice thoughts, Jessica. In the nether regions. That shows where your mind is, my dear."

Jessica removed her handbag from the drawer, checked her keys were inside. Out of the corner of her eye she noticed him lean back on the desk and push forward his hips so she would brush against him when leaving.

"You believe in living dangerously." She swung the shoulder strap in a semi-circle. The leather handbag at the end of its pendulum swing connected with his crutch. He doubled over in slow motion and held himself like a goalie on the receiving end of a kicked football.

"My regards to your wife." She pushed him to lean over Dorinda's desk. "And if she wants to know about your alligator bite, tell her to phone me." She was still smiling when she caught up to Dorinda waiting at the Emergency Exit door.

"What was that about?" her whisper for Jessica only. "Did he have his evil way and manage to touch you?"

"I touched him, but good, Dorinda."

"What? Where did you touch him?" She held open the door. "I knew something was happening." They started to descend the stairs.

"He tried it on after you'd all left the office. So I landed him with my alligator where it hurts."

"You kicked him with your alligator shoes?"

"No, my handbag. I let fly with it. And you ought to have heard the clunk when it connected, in the, You Know Where!"

"Wow, way to go, Jessica!" At the turn in the stairs she looked over her shoulder. "He waits to catch you on your own, the ratbag."

"Why doesn't Dick-head chase after you, Dorinda? You're younger and more attractive?" Then quickly, when she caught up to her. "I wish I hadn't said that, it's demoralizing."

"He caught sight of David when I first started work, and he's left me alone ever since. He pursues you because he knows your ex. is in Vancouver."

"Stupid git of a man!"

"Who? Your ex-husband?"

"Well, no, I was thinking of Dick-head. But 'Stupid git' applies to Ronnie, as well. More so, the Dilettante of the Department of Devious Behavior."

Dorinda burst into an explosive laugh which immediately encouraged Jessica to see the lighter side of the situation. They descended the remaining flights nudging one another and laughing. At basement level Dorinda pushed open the door into the garage and they headed for their cars parked side by side.

"Even if your parents visited you at work he'd keep his distance, Jessica."

"That's hardly likely. Dad's business is taking off in Vancouver. They won't take time out to be visiting me for a long while."

"They could live here. Your Dad could apply for a Start Up business loan in Alberta." Dorinda opened her car door.

"I don't think he'd be pleased if I asked him to pull up stakes and follow me again. I had an incentive to move from Vancouver, getting away from an ex-husband and his bit of extracurricular activity on the fanny front, but they haven't."

"I love how you express yourself, Jessica." She giggled, held onto the car for support. Get on your bike! Shove off! Thickhead! Hecky-thump! And, Flaming-hell!"

"Pleased I amuse. I wonder if that's why my putdowns aren't having the desired effect on Dirty Dick? I'm turning him on, not off."

"There you go again!" Dorinda stifled a snort with a hastily clapped hand to her mouth. "You make it sound so funny!"

"I've noticed since I arrived in Canada I've become more polite. I should resort to good old Yorkshire put-offs. Like," spoke loudly over her shoulder. "Sod Off, You Dirty Bugger!"

Dorinda almost fell into her driving seat with the shock. "That'll do it!"

"So I see. But I don't want to lower my standards just because someone else is in the gutter." She opened the door of her Cavalier. "I wish the silly sod would leave off, though, he fair gets on my wick!"

"That's why it's a good idea to have a man friend like Brian come and collect you." Dorinda leaned out of her car. "Dirty Dick will see him, and leave you alone."

"Good idea! Umh!" She waved good-bye to Dorinda.

However, several things were wrong with that proposal; she was supposed to be at an animal shelter, not a government office for distressed unemployed;

meant to be a Jean, not a Jessica; pretended to be somewhat younger to acquire someone else's man-friend.

Jessica Walters was a devious person indeed. That's another thing! When did she revert to her maiden name of Mayhew and drop the nerd's where it belonged:

In The Depths of Hell!

ALL THE WAY TO the library she was thinking of Brian; the epitome of everything a woman could possibly want. He wasn't a romantic Lothario. He was settled, extremely intelligent, a little heavy, but obviously, out of training. Anyway, she liked cuddly, love handles to hang onto; being overweight was something that could be adjusted, unlike her lying to him out of her skull. And now, she was obliged to look up her ancestors and invent an identity to go along with her lies.

"I'm researching Indian tribes for a novel I'm writing," Jessica informed the librarian. "Can you point me in the right direction?"

It took only a short while before Jessica discovered what she needed to know. The Eskimos, known through school years as people who lived in igloos in the northern hemisphere, were grouped, Innu.

Nice, she knew she wasn't Innuit.

Indians were Natives, First Nation and Aborigine. She wasn't one of them, they were too pure bred.

That eliminated Indians.

Métis were the result of native and landed white immigrant coupling in early days.

Oh, yes, Métis sounded like her.

She studied where they lived. In cities; with full-blooded Indians on reservations; particular trades followed, depending on the reservation being near a town or river. She chose the reserve close by Calgary, a distance away but in the same province.

"Find everything about indigenous peoples?" The librarian asked at the turnstile.

"Yes, thank you very much."

Jessica left the library, a happy little camper, prepared to offset any question put to her about her tribe.

JACK TELEPHONED whilst she was dining on a sardine sandwich.

"I'd like to invite you to a dinner-dance tomorrow night, Jean. Does that sound attractive?"

"A dinner-dance sounds lovely, Brian. We'll be able to exercise on the dance floor between courses, won't we?"

"Yes, not overload ourselves with Chinese food."

"You're right there. My tea tonight is a sardine sandwich. It's all I felt like after that huge lunch."

"You couldn't face supper, eh?"

"Er... No, nor dinner." She screwed up her face at the obvious mistake. "I'm back in Yorkshire, I suppose, thinking of tea after four-thirty and lunch or dinner at midday. Supper there is a late-night snack around nine pm." Enough of the explanation! "I'm looking forward to tomorrow's outing."

"Okay!"

"What time shall we meet?"

"I'll call for you about seven. Bye! Or, Ta-ta!"

"Bye! And Ta-ta!" She waltzed around the living room, hugged herself and sang disjointedly. "He likes me! He does like me!" She bit off the hanging sardine tail, and danced towards the large picture window.

The neighbor across the way walking his invisible dog on the footpath, waved. Jessica returned his wave before she commenced a sedate walk into the kitchen.

JACK HUNG UP the receiver thoughtfully. Jean was such a sweet person, bore him no ill will for putting his foot in his mouth enquiring about her tribe. He wouldn't broach the subject again; accept her as she was, a delightful person who had no false inhibitions. She called a spade a spade, which he thought... nice.

The toupee in his hand resembled a rat, a wet one, after cleaning it in the bathroom before telephoning Jessica. He gave it a savage shake and remembered humiliation.

In the Library Parkade he'd removed the toupee and used spit and tissues to clear gum residue from his hairline; craned his neck to view in the driving mirror the unsatisfactory operation. Still polishing his cranium he walked into the geological department at Shellack Oil Exploration, went to the washroom and washed the back of his neck, forehead and around his ears; he wasn't going to be the butt of jokes.

Jeffrey Olivera walked in, saw Jack drying his head on paper towels.

"Give me a break, Jack. No towels at home, eh? You've gotta sneak in and shampoo your bit of thatch at the office?"

"A bird decided to make a deposit." Jack smiled through the long mirror over the washbasins. "Pity you weren't around, Jeffrey. Your big head would've presented a better target."

Jeffrey eyed his larger than usual head in the mirror. "Okay!" Yeah, he had more brains than Jack.

Jack hid his smile. What a nerd the guy was.

JESSICA TWIRLED IN front of bedroom triple mirrors, admired every angle of the long sleeved satin blouse and calf length knife pleated muslin skirt. It had been a long time since she had gussed up for a dance. A dinner dance indeed! How lovely! She twirled more. The dangling necklace swung dangerously close to her mouth.

"Watch it, Jessica, you might do yourself an injury," which brought her up short. "Oh, dammit, I'm Jean! Jean, the Métis girl who loves animals!"

Oh, why, oh why...?

JACK RANG JESSICA'S front door bell at six forty-five the following evening, groomed for an evening of dining and dancing. The dress shirt with front panel pleats would be appropriate if it became too warm on the dance floor and he removed the jacket.

He was looking forward to this evening. Brian had been right-on about his leading a sedentary life. In previous years he used to dash to a site and still feel refreshed when he returned. But now, travel had become a drag. He missed putting up his feet, having a beer, watching televised hockey matches, and, if energetic enough, going curling: however, the sweeping required more energy than he was prepared to give, of late.

There was excitement in the exploration of a new oil patch; titillation pitting his wits on the outcome in boardrooms. But conditions in the field were rough. Battery power was insufficient to operate electrical equipment on a site, he was obliged to sit in a hastily constructed shed on cane furniture; use packing crates as a specimen table, and if lucky, listen to a battery operated radio, and use the battery Notepad for Internet connection, that was, until oil was a certainty and an electric generator assembled.

He waited for the opening of the door. Would this relationship be established before his next trip in three weeks' time? He pondered on the merits of continuing his successful climb to the top, or stepping off the escalator and living life at a more leisurely pace as a consultant, with a wife and family at home.

The door opened. Jessica's face with bright brown eyes and generous smile showed he was welcome.

"Hello Jean." He forgot about trips of discovery; he had made one right here and wasn't about to lose it.

"Hello, Brian," reminded she was Jean ensured she was extra careful. "You found me easily enough, then?"

"Sure did," smiling a glow of guilt. It had slipped his mind he was an impostor; been Jack for forty two years. "It couldn't have been easier."

"Come and have a look at my home," beckoned him in.

The neighbor walked his invisible dog through his front gate. Jessica waved at him. Jack was intrigued to observe the man's arm extended as if with a dog on a leash. The neighbor grinned and returned Jean's wave.

"That's the neighborhood eccentric," Jessica said.

Jack stepped across the threshold, his arm brushed against hers and drove thoughts of the man out of his mind.

"I haven't been here long and the place isn't up to much just yet, but I'm getting there." She felt a thrill of excitement at the close contact, before she closed the door. "You'll have noticed the absence of the mail box and realize I'm not quite settled in."

"I didn't give it a thought." Jack eyed the sparsely furnished living room from the entry foyer. "It looks comfortable." He followed Jessica to the picture window overlooking the street.

"I've got a lovely outlook onto the park down that street opposite. And there's a school further down but you can't see it behind the houses."

"Nice neighborhood." His Cadillac was parked at the curb directly at the foot of her garden path; the neighbor, pretending not to be looking into Jean's window, tugged on the invisible leash.

"Interesting guy, your eccentric, Jean. Is he a problem for you?"

"Naw, he's harmless. And his dog doesn't bark at night." She giggled and touched his arm. "Here's the dining-room and kitchen," a handwave encompassed the whole, and French windows opening onto a verandah.

"Everything looks bright and new, Jean."

"It's been completely refurbished, and of course the furniture's brand new." Jessica ran a hand over the island servery which separated the kitchen from the dining-room. "I enjoyed choosing different items."

"I like that." Jack indicated the bubble-glassed chandelier hanging over the large oval table. "What a massive table for one person." Has she been married? But she says it's all brand new.

"The dining-room called for a full-size table, I thought. Do you think it's out of place, Brian?"

"Not at all, it's a large area. Red Cedar calls for a large piece of furniture and you were fortunate, this wood's considered a rarity." He ran his hand over the smooth tabletop bare of decoration. How tidy she is. He hated untidiness, followed by an afterthought: almost as much as lying.

"I like what I've accomplished so far?" Her taste, encouraged by the salesman at Sears Furniture Department in Bonnie Doon, was simple, leading to the austere, she didn't care for flamboyancy in furnishings. "I'm taking my time looking for paintings and drawings. That's why my walls are bare."

"Good idea. A painting lasts forever, and if you chose unwisely it'll be disappointing in the long term." He walked into the kitchen, looked into the back garden through the kitchen window. "You're fortunate having a backyard. That's what I miss in my condo. I see by your yard you haven't been here long."

"Not long enough for my garden to get established. The landscape gardener said my trees were too old and the bushes too young, but he liked the other things I had growing. In fact, he was highly amused. I don't know why." She opened the verandah windows, beckoned him outside with another giggle. "Want a tour of the estate?"

"I guess we've time before the dinner-dance." Jack checked his watch and followed her onto the verandah. "I understand you're more than above average in ballroom dancing. I hope you don't put the rest of the diners to shame with your expertise."

"Ha-ha!" Her laugh to gain time. "Methinks you exaggerate a little, sire. I'm nothing spectacular on the dance floor."

"Not according to your letter. You've won ballroom dancing medals."

"I'm no professional Brian, just an ordinary dancer." What on earth did Jean say in her introductory letter? "And anyway, I won the medals in my teens. I won't embarrass you by tripping the light fantastic, I assure you."

"I like the picturesque terminology, tripping the light fantastic. It conjures up visions of Peter Pan flying around Captain Hook and the crocodile."

"And Wendy and the boys chasing in and out of trees, swarming up and down the ship's side."

He joined in her laughter, eyed the pine trees at the bottom of the garden casting shadows across the back lane and creeping towards the house. He'd visualize her in this setting when alone at night, twenty floors up in the air, lonely and fed-up with himself.

Jessica led the way down the verandah side steps, passed the back door to tour the side garden with its rockery and raspberry vines.

"I enjoy fresh raspberries with cream and ice-cream." Jack touched the leaves of a vine gently. "When I was young I'd accompany my mother to Pick Your Own."

"And help eat as many as you could whilst you were picking. I know, Brian, I've done that." She trailed her hand along a stem. "I'm looking forward to eating these when they're ripe. Maybe raspberries will be on tonight's menu." We're a match, he likes raspberries and canoeing.

"They'll need to be imported ones from the States, Mexico or Brazil." He attached a vine to the string. "Canadian raspberries won't be ready for a few weeks, yet."

"Of course." She turned, realized she should have been aware raspberries were not in season. "You've seen the front, so we'll peruse the rest of the estate."

They walked past shrubs lining the side fence, ferns and bushes set amongst rocks. The overhanging mountain ash tree cast its shadow over more ferns, the delicate variety, a huge patch of frilly fronds that waved in the breeze.

"That your choice of weed, Jean?"

"They're pretty, aren't they?" She veered towards them. "I left the selection to the landscape gardener. Some things were here when I moved in, but others he planted."

"What did he say about the weed?"

"It's funny you should ask, Brian." She leaned over, ran her fingers along a frilly leaf. "He wanted these uplifted, but I thought they were so pretty I said they should stay." She looked up at Jack. "He laughed out loud and said: 'On your own head, be it, lady'. I don't know why he was amused. They probably spread like a weed, but don't smell unpleasant. You sniff it."

"It's cannabis, Jean." He pushed her hand away from the plant. "An attractive hemp, certainly. The stem makes the hallucinogen and is favored for its medicinal value. But, if the police enter your back yard and see this they'll have you arrested, and your house and all your properties seized.

Jessica's eyes were wide. "I've only just bought the house." She looked at her lovely new home sparkling in the evening light. "And the car's only one year old," cast him a look. "How could they do that?"

"I'm sure sorry, Jean. The authorities will consider you bought them with money gained from drug trafficking."

"I don't even imbibe, let alone smoke pot!" That Jean, she's a... a...

59

"The police don't take that into consideration. They're after traffickers who make money out of misery. You, unfortunately, would be swept up with the rest of the garbage."

"Thank you." Boy, what a charmer!

"You're welcome. Glad to be of service," assuming she was grateful informing her she was operating outside the law. He pulled out a fern, roots and all. "See how the fronds separate and point at the tips? That's how you recognize this fern is one of the milder, but addictive drugs."

"Who'd have thought?" Jessica rubbed a finger and thumb on a leaf then put them to her nose. "You can't smell anything different, but then I'm ignorant about pot."

"No, you only get high when lit-up," tried to keep his face straight.

"That stupid gardener not telling me it was an abusive substance. Really, the amount of money that man was paid, he should have warned me. He just laughed at my ignorance, the stupid git." She looked around, afraid more disclosures would jump up and bite her. "Is there any heroin, cocaine or opium thingies around?" She pointed further along to a spread of brightly colored buds emerging on long stalks. "I have Iceland Poppies down there."

Jack walked towards the other side fence. "Not the variety of poppy that makes opium, Jean," cast an inquisitive eye over plants that surrounded the lawn.

"I thought it was too good to be true. Just when everything's going right, something comes along and bites you in the bum when you least expect it."

"Relax, you're free apart from that clump," looked away and tried hard not to smile at her choice of words. When he looked back, Jessica was pulling out the insidious weed. He glanced at his watch and rejoined her.

"They were so pretty and now I hate them! Hate them!"

"I can come out tomorrow and finish pulling up the rest." Why was he presumptive, implying they were going steady? "Where did you live before, Jean?"

Where oh where, her mind in turmoil. Should she say the 'Y' or Vancouver? She reverted to the Yorkshire axiom: 'If in doubt, say nowt', but in this case she'd avoid it.

60

"I'm so annoyed, they looked decorative and frilly. I was looking forward to having them in a vase." She eyed the plants lying on the ground, no longer the innocent decoration for a vase on the dining-room table, and used her foot to stomp the life out of them. "I'm annoyed with myself for being so gullible and idiotic, Brian."

And so was he! He wasn't Brian, he was Jack. A jack-ass! He touched her arm gently. "You go inside and wash up. I'll garbage these you've pulled out in case anyone decides to investigate."

"Thank you."

"My pleasure."

She walked into the house feeling sorry for herself. The gardener had tried to warn her but she hadn't listened. She needed a keeper; hadn't much luck with her choice of husbands and paid the price for stupidity. Now, she couldn't buy a house without endangering herself. What other actions had Jean taken to place the next occupant in jeopardy? She'd already altered her race and made a career change.

Was Jean's guardian angel punishing her for pretending to be her? Was God getting even with her? Were the fates against her? She'd already lost a husband; got Dirty Dick and a scratched car. She might lose her new home and her belongings. She'd certainly lose Brian after he discovered her duplicity when she was up before the beak in court; she couldn't hide behind Jean's identity there.

It isn't fair, you hear, up there! It isn't fair!

Chapter Five

Edmonton Queen was a glorious, unexpected romantic sight when Jessica and Jack stepped on the short gangplank that lead to the deck at Rafter's Landing. Fairy lights hung from the radio mast to the cabin, along the top of the rail to extend all around the upper deck.

Jessica had been delighted when Jack parked the car and they'd sighted the paddle wheeler, with its backdrop of Edmonton skyline, waiting for guests.

"Oh, Brian," her eyes bright, rivaled the lights from the ferry reflected in the water. "What a wonderful, beautiful venue you've chosen."

"Thought you'd like it." He helped her out of the car and hoped she'd continue calling him Brian, or he'd forget. "How are you on the high seas? Do you suffer from seasickness?"

"Naw, waves don't bother me. I've been across to Ireland on a very choppy ocean and wasn't affected." Take care, she'd mentioned Ireland; maybe Jean hasn't been there. Oh, what she wouldn't give to read Jean's first letter to Brian.

"The North Saskatchewan River suffers in comparison to the Irish Sea."

"How so, it's wet?"

"You'll see."

The moon outdid the luminescence of the fairy lights; a huge orb in the late evening sky looked down on the river which lapped at the sides of the river-boat and enveloped everything it touched with a silvery, magical sheen.

Their coats taken care of by an attendant, Jessica and Jack strolled to their place names at the set dinner-tables. The Dixieland jazz band played familiar melodies, some dancing rhythms, others for easy-listening, whilst dining.

Jessica was pleased she had opted for wearing the long flowing skirt, it would flare out when she twisted and twirled on the dance-floor. The gold and black metal earrings matched the necklace and brooch enhancing the lustrous satin of the blouse. She felt elated every time she caught Jack's admiring glance over a glass of red wine.

"It's tasty and fruity, Brian. You are driving, aren't you?"

"Yes, I'll only drink during the meal, no problem."

"I was just thinking. I'll be able to become slightly pixielated seeing I'm not behind a wheel."

"Go for it, but don't get drunk. I hate drunken women."

"I'll remember." She raised her glass. They both drank looking into one another's eyes. "When the waiter suggested House Wine I wondered if it was brewed on the boat," giggled at the thought.

"Shouldn't think so. But when the average householder brews up from a domestic blend, anything is possible."

"I have a large cellar. I could brew up wine, couldn't I? Her thoughts turned to insidious cannabis plants sprouting, oh so innocently, in her garden. "That is, if it isn't against the law?"

"Why haven't I met anyone as compatible as you previously, Jean?" He leaned on his hand, elbow on the table and gazed into her eyes. "Where have you been hiding yourself?"

"What a lovely way of saying you like me, Brian." She forgot all about the garden and swam deeply in blue eyes that reminded her of the Opal pool at the Open Air Swimming Baths in Bradford.

He loved the way she smiled, became more radiant looking. Previously he'd gone for glamour and youth; what a mistake, maturity was better. How old was she? She didn't look Brian's age, more like his own? But then, it had never been his prowess to determine a lady's age, and he wasn't crass enough to ask. He'd made one error regarding her tribe, that was sufficient.

The band struck up an old-fashioned waltz tune and drew their attention.

"You don't object to dancing with someone not a professional, do you, Jean?"

"Like I said, it was ages ago I took ballroom dancing. Now, I dance just for enjoyment." She hoped that would suffice, she was getting fed up with Jean's attributes on the dance floor.

They rose, Jack held out his hand and she went into the enveloping circle of his arm with a feeling of homecoming; placed her left hand on his shoulder and without hesitation, his hand in the small of her back, moved into the slow waltz.

IS THIS ALL THERE IS?

"You're as light as a feather. Make me feel like an expert, Jean. Let's dance like this all night and forget about the dinner, eh?"

"I'm having similar feelings. Let's play it by ear." Wow! It was a long time since she had felt a man's body next to hers. She couldn't count Dirty Dick, he hadn't got lucky enough. Or her ex-husband. It had been ages since they'd danced, and never an old-fashioned waltz: Ronnie had two left feet.

Jessica had attended ballroom dance classes in Bradford from the age of eleven; danced with other beginners like herself, eyes fixed on her partner's tie, not daring to raise her eyes beyond a chin beginning to sprout whiskers. Each young couple on the dance floor moved stiffly to the sound of big bands coming from the huge speakers. The dance instructor walked up and down and whacked a large cane in time to the music, exhorting them to 'feel the rhythm, move your feet not your body'.

Whatever the tune, fast, slow or medium, it had always been the same with Ronnie. One-two-three, one-two-three. How boring and she hadn't realized just how much until now.

"This is so wonderful, Brian. You're a lovely lead."

"I aim to please." Jack swirled her around the dance floor of the deck cleared for action, pleased he'd learnt old fashioned ballroom dancing.

In his youth he kept quiet about dancing lessons, having no wish to be thought a sissy by his peer group of hockey and football players at junior high. His mother had accompanied him at first to dance lessons ensuring he didn't goof off. Later, when he appreciated that girls had to dance with him, he told his mother she needn't escort him any longer, it wasn't a chore. At his first school dance Jack had appreciated the lessons; asked girls to accompany him on the dance-floor, watched and envied by fellow sports players standing around the doorway shuffling their feet and trying to appear, gung-ho.

The music on the soft night air encouraged other couples to accompany them on the road back to a bygone age when dancing was akin to loving in public. Jack's hand stretched wide in the small of her back felt the heat of her. He would need to wipe his hand after the dance, he didn't want to sweat-mark the lovely material. No wonder gentlemen wore white cotton gloves in the old days when couples galloped around the ballroom in fine style.

The whistle blew; the anchor rising dragged metal against metal; the ferry started away from its moorings in the direction of Dawson Bridge. Jack and Jessica stopped dancing, hurried to the bridge rail and leaned over.

"Look at the luminescence falling off the paddle." Jack pointed to the rear. Water lifted on the wheel, balanced at the top of its arc then cascaded down to splash into the ship's wake where it spread twinkling, clean and bubbly on the river surface.

"That's so lovely. But doesn't the boat move slowly?" She felt disappointed the boat wasn't flying along; the ferries in Victoria cut through water. "Maybe it'll pick up speed as we go?"

"I doubt it. We've to waste time on the river. We're supposed to take two hours to 115th Street and back aways to 90th Street, the length of time for dinner and dancing. So it won't be going much quicker, I'm afraid."

"From 90th Street to 115th? Is that all the distance we're going?"

"The North Saskatchewan River isn't deep enough further on; we might end up on a sand bank." He grinned at her. "We don't want the skipper ordering us to: 'Apply shoulders to the hull and manoeuvre this ferry back mid-stream'," delighted his imitation made her laugh.

"All the same, only a few blocks either way." If only he could read her mind. She visualized pushing a ferry off the sandbanks of the Pacific Ocean; they'd have needed diving suits. Not quite the same thing, a low water river in prairie country. "I see what you mean now about there's no comparison with the Irish Sea."

Jack laughed, put his arm around her, it seemed the right thing to do; he was happy and apparently Jean also, albeit she was disappointed at the slow pace pf the vessel.

"You should have been on the ferries I've ridden," he said. "The hydrofoil to Devonport or Waiheke Island in the Hauraki Gulf, whip along at a mighty rate." He smiled at wide open eyes, so bright and brown in the moonlight. "Ferries in New Zealand are a convenient mode of transport for the workers."

"Oh, doesn't that sound a lot nicer than bucking traffic downtown?" It was, she'd done that in Vancouver.

"It sure is. You relax on ferries after work. You don't experience the hassle of congested roads and traffic hazards."

65

"New Zealand? How long were you there, Brian?"

If she hadn't used the name he would have blurted out the reason; negotiating with bankers on behalf of Shellack Oil Exploration, drilling offshore, Poverty Bay.

"We had an air show in Auckland. Afterwards we went to Wellington and then crossed to Christchurch, South Island."

"Did you see Ruapehu, the volcano that erupted this week?" She was pleased to remember the name reported on television news, just two days previously.

"Yes, but it wasn't erupting then. This is a phenomena, it shouldn't have erupted. There's three mountains in that area: Ruapehu, Ngaruahoe and Tongariro. It's Mt Ngaruahoe that's supposed to be active, not Ruapehu."

They both moved closer when another couple leaned over the rail next to them and Jack continued in a quieter voice.

"Then there's White Island, just off Auckland; the safety valve for earthquake activity. It's difficult to understand why Ruapehu's erupted. It's been dormant for years."

"Why do you know so much about volcanic eruptions? Are they a concern for skydivers, apart from being in the near vicinity, that is?"

"Er… volcanic eruptions emit powerful disturbances in the atmosphere. Anything airborne's a hazard to skydivers."

She was hanging onto his every word. He turned, leaned back with his elbows on the rail and continued remembering a pleasant interlude in New Zealand.

"I've stayed at The Chateau, a Tourist Hotel on Mt Tongariro. We skied on great slopes. A neat break from doing acrobatics in the skies to skiing down soft, snow covered mountains." He inhaled deeply. Well, that part of the lie was true, he had skied during the talks in Auckland; he and his counterparts from NZ Petroleum and the merchant bankers took three days vacation to enjoy the majesty of the mountains.

"You've traveled a lot more than me, Brian. Even with service abroad trips, my experience is nothing compared to the wonderful sights you've seen." She definitely wouldn't brag about Blackpool lights at Christmas time.

66

"Yes, I've traveled, but it's great to be home and dancing with you."

He edged her back onto the dance floor before she could ask any follow up questions that would really put him in the mire.

Jessica didn't mind the interruption to what sounded so fascinating; she loved dancing with him, his arms around her. It felt comfortable, suggested she'd returned from a long, hazardous journey; safety, security.

Most of the other couples returned to the dance floor with similar thoughts. To watch water cascade from paddles and form a luminescent wake was pretty and interesting for a while; scenery slipping past inch by excruciating inch though could be likened to watching paint dry on a deck: to dance and dine had more pull.

JESSICA KNEW SHE was falling in love with this wonderful man who knew what to say, was so interesting and thoughtful, and smelled nice, manly. She wished she could be herself, not a cheat; she'd enlighten him of life prior to arriving in Canada.

How she'd gone through the English school system, elementary and college; early work years prior to marriage; love to inform him of her parents living in Vancouver. A tear came unbidden; she was denying their very existence taking on this foreign personality. If she could turn back the clock she wouldn't pretend to be someone else, especially not a native Canadian. Why, oh why had she acted so stupidly? No amount of feeling unwanted, unloved, was worth this agony?

She couldn't be herself, so settled for the dance, the moment of being in his arms.

The music finished, they reseated themselves. The paddle wheeler commenced to pass beneath Dawson Bridge. Both eyed their watches, then laughed out loud; seemingly other passengers were comparing their timepieces and laughed at the absurdity of the ferry's pace.

"Way to go, Jean. Nice and leisurely, eh?"

"The pace certainly won't give us a heart attack."

It was a marvelous meal in wonderful company for Jessica, and she hoped he was enjoying it too. He'd made an excuse of touching her hand when he passed the salt. Over dessert of peaches and ice cream set in a meringue bombe, they eyed the dancers on the floor, the band, passing scenery, and a comfortable silence fell between them, friendly and assured.

Jessica's heart started to pound. She mustn't give herself away behaving like a silly schoolgirl, even though that was how she felt; young, alive, attracted to this lovely man.

"They didn't have raspberries on the menu, Brian. Were you disappointed? I wasn't, not really. I enjoyed the peaches. I wonder if they were from BC?"

"Probably. Do you like kids, Jean?"

"Yes, I love them." She assumed he didn't mean baby goats. She had to be careful though, kids were close relatives of dogs and cats.

"That's what I figured. Kids and animals need similar loving." He took another sip of wine; there'd be no hindrance to his plan for having a family. But hold on a tad, maybe her biological clock was advanced to the stage where a healthy baby was not the norm? Maybe... He smiled at her. Why did he have to think of abnormality when she was so obviously intelligent?

Oh dear, don't let him ask why she hadn't had any children, please? She sipped at her wine although she could easily have gulped it down. In one respect it was a relief she didn't have to consider children when Ronnie left her for his treacle tart. But then, she would have loved to have had a warm body to kiss and cuddle, hold close, not to be alone, surplus to requirement.

"We could head north and have a picnic lunch on Saturday, if you're not doing anything, Jean." Jack put to rest all negative thoughts. "Should be nice weather."

"I enjoy picnics." Jessica's face lit up at the change of subject. "Since I was little. Dad would fish and mum and I would..." Wow, what would Jean and her mum do?

"I can imagine you as a child running along collecting shells."

"Mum and I collected seashells." Whoops! They were in prairie country. "Sorry, shells, not seashells. And we'd sometimes make sand castles and forts."

"Was that before your mother went to England? Was that when your grandmother on the reservation showed you how to bead belts?" He could see bright brown eyes cloud over. "Each tribe has a different design. What was yours?" Why didn't he leave it alone, she wasn't impressed by his mentioning her tribe?

"You know what little girls are like. They enjoy doing beadwork, embroidery, flower arranging and things." What on earth did Jean tell Brian in her letter?

"Did you go to a native school?" He could have kicked himself when her face went blank. "We heard natives objected to western style education. They were ordered not to speak their own tongue, and abused in many ways."

"No, I went to an ordinary public school, then a composite high, and of course, with the break in English schools." She daren't say college. How many Métis went through to higher education? She quickly revved her brain. "Have you been skydiving by Fort McMurray, Brian? They have air shows up there, don't they?"

His brow furrowed trying to remember Brian's itinerary around Alberta.

"Yes," a logical decision, he knew the area, been on an exploratory site north of Fort McMurray. "Putting down a bore in the peace and tranquility of the country was great. Unlike the city noise which..." Wahoo, what was he saying?

"What did you put down a boar for? Did it squeal too loudly in the peace and tranquility of the countryside?"

"Er ... a water borehole for a farming friend. After the air show it was time for relaxing in the country." He indicated the dance floor. "Like to trip the light fantastic again, eh?"

Neither realized the amount of relief the other felt when they escaped to the dance floor. Bodies clung, felt every nuance of movement; electrical particles bombarded sexual organs with an old age message: enjoy and procreate. An effective diversion which ensured loose tongues did not divulge secrets.

JACK TOOK JESSICA home, bid her goodnight at her front door and shook hands. He was unable to resist the impulse to pull her close, look into her eyes and kiss her forehead. She lifted her face, eyed his lips: a clear invitation.

The kiss was tender and friendly. He admired her too much to push for anything more; not at this stage, maybe later. His needs and desires would for now go on the back burner. Jean's feelings were paramount, not his. And he was also scared; in unchartered waters.

Jessica went indoors on cloud nine.

Jack walked down the path and licked lips that had caressed a newfound love. The neighbor in his garden across the road walking his invisible dog received a friendly wave from a man obviously pleased with himself and the world when he climbed into his car.

Jessica kicked off her shoes in the foyer, danced through the living room into the kitchen in a dream state, the music of the night still ringing in her ears. She switched on the electric jug for a cup of chamomile tea; danced into the hall and into her bedroom switching on lights; removed her sponges and tossed them onto the bed gaily like a striptease artist, before she had a good scratch.

Still scratching and dancing to inner music she returned to the kitchen, then suddenly ceased her gyrations. Not only the living room lights were on but also the kitchen and foyer lights; she'd be observed by the whole street, the curtains weren't drawn. She hurried to the living room window; fingers spread wide covering un-sponged breasts and peered out.

"Brian's Cadillac's gone, thank goodness, he didn't see me dancing like an idiot."

But the neighbor with his invisible dog on the footpath in front of his house, waved. Had he witnessed her dancing in gay abandon? She returned the salutation.

"I wonder just how daft he is?"

JACK PARKED HIS CADILLAC on Waterdale Drive, looked at the river valley below with a feeling of contentment.

"What are you doing right now, my Jean? What is it about you I admire the most? Your eyes, your mouth, your face, your figure?" That's dangerous ground, think of her face again.

"Her shell like earlobes which looked even smaller with those heavy looking earrings."

He could imagine a few precious stones gathered during the course of his career polishing up into earrings. He had a few stones displayed on shelves and even more boxed away in the walk in wardrobe. His happy thoughts hit a low.

Geez, if Jean ever visits he'd have to hide them; Brian wouldn't have geological specimens showcased round the condo. His thoughts turned to the prospective trip to the North West Territories. Conditions were excellent for a field opening up north of Yellowknife, northeast of a recently discovered diamond vein. Maybe he'd pick up a diamond or two and give them to Jean for earring settings.

He hit the steering wheel a resounding blow with his fist.

"Geez, why did you start this charade, you smart-ass, you can't be yourself now?" He pulled off the toupee; knew pain would follow his own hairs removal from comfortable follicles.

Chapter Six

During her lunch break Jessica went to Edmonton Centre to select a mailbox. She loved the convenience of shopping at Eaton Centre, Edmonton Centre and The Bay, joined by basement and first floor walkways. Overhead Pedways stretched across downtown streets from one building to another, and inside the undercover complex, a miniature city. Shops, Railway Transit, walkways to the Citadel Theatre, City Hall, Centennial Library, Sir Winston Churchill Square, and Canada Place where immigrants and the unemployed registered, and other points of interest.

She was in pig's heaven! No traffic. Only fellow shoppers like her. And wasn't it nice to have an artist playing his violin at the bottom of the shrub-lined slope leading to the transit system. Like many others she dropped money into his open violin case: a small price for his easing the spirit.

There were several varieties of mail boxes on the shelves in the home style shop; metal, wood and metal or just plain wood. She opted for plain wood with a gold paint trim; afterwards sauntered around furniture displays comparing what she had purchased from Sears at Bonnie Doon. She hadn't done too badly with her choice of furnishings: downtown was more expensive.

She sat in an easy leather chair with an adjustable foot cushion; just the thing after a day at the office to sit and relax with a cup of coffee in front of television.

She shot out of the chair quickly, an image of Brian standing by her coffee table in front of the television set at home bringing her to her senses. She was supposed to be in her twenties, not sixties! Just went to show how tired her body was. It was the difference in lifestyle she'd undergone in the last few weeks, obviously.

First, to discover she was not the meat in her husband's sandwich; second, left Vancouver and settled into a new position in Edmonton and desperately tried to evade the grasp of a randy chap; third, found the perfect house for herself alone, not to share with an ungrateful spouse whose aim in life was to satisfy the flesh, regardless with whom; fourth, a second life according to cannabis Jean Morningbird, the Métis, not someone of the Jewish faith with which she was familiar.

She should never have pretended to be years younger, five maybe. It was difficult trying to remember all about druggie Jean? She must be brain tired as well.

Jessica went around the chinaware displays, was unable to resist the eggcups, four of them with matching saucers and side plates. She didn't require four of anything, maybe two, but never four. What the hell! She gladly had the assistant wrap them and placed them safely inside the mailbox. When her parents visited, they'd use them.

After leaving the store she speculated on the whereabouts of Jean Morningbird. The Realtors neglected to inform her why the previous tenant left, or where she had gone. At the time it seemed obvious why someone would want to leave the house and garden which had been allowed to fall into such disrepair. What idiot would have stayed there? And what sort of an idiot could see the potential for improvement?

Only an idiot struggling for self worth after a failed marriage. Maybe, if she'd done more with her looks; been less wifely, more glamorous, then Ronnie's eyes might not have strayed.

"Like hell they wouldn't!" She flung open the car door, and buckled up the mailbox in the offside seat. "He was hot to trot!" Then a possibility struck why Ronnie was made redundant in England.

"Oh, dear Lord, was he given the push because he was playing the field?"

She drove back to the office, her mind eliminating one young girl after another at her husband's former office in Bradford. By the time she parked the car, she decided it didn't matter one jot: it was all in the past.

"To hell with Ronnie, the bastard: he's history. I'm here in the present, and with a future to look forward to."

DICK CHALMERS WAS not around when Jessica arrived back at Social Services. She stood at her desk and demonstrated to Dorinda how the doors opened on the mailbox for mail and another door for flyers and unwanted junk.

"The postman will be pleased I've finally plunged, buying a box. He's been holding onto stuff he can't deliver behind my screen door, he says."

"I doubt it, Jessica." Dorinda shook her head from side to side. "Mailmen dump it at your front door if there isn't a mailbox."

"Oh, and there I was thinking he was being nice."

"He wants something, that's for sure, Jessica. Like my David says: Watch out for what you can't see."

"Um, yes, neat trick."

Dorinda picked up the egg plate. "It's easy to see why you bought this egg set, the blue flowers seem to leap off the porcelain."

"Yes, I like the yellow background, reminds me of morning sunshine, and..."

"Easy on the eye, like other things I could mention." Dick Chalmers stood close. "You've been busy during your lunch hour, Jessica." His hands covered Jessica's on the box and she quickly withdrew hers to leave him holding the box on his own.

"I'll continue with that work you gave me, Jessica." Dorinda hastily left them.

"I can have your house number stenciled on it, if you like." Dick peered into Jessica's face. "Ninety-two fifty-four, isn't it?"

"You don't need to bother, Dick," she backed away. "There's a large number on the house itself." Annoyed at giving in, she stepped forward and tried to reclaim the mailbox but he pulled it teasingly out of reach.

"I'm sure I could add to its attractions with a little touchup of mine," eyes wandered over her breasts. Had she started to wear an uplift in order to impress him? If she had, she'd succeeded, the points stuck out provocatively? "And I'll stay for an egg breakfast with no encouragement at all."

"I'm not issuing any invitations, Dick."

"Her boyfriend's installing it." Dorinda added her contribution from over by her desk. "Good thing he's handy with carpentry isn't it, Dick?"

Dick handed over the mailbox without further demur, turned on his heel abruptly and spoke over his shoulder: "Jessica, your section is falling behind in its output of unresolved claims. Rectify that situation, immediately."

"Will do, Dick." Jessica watched his departure. She had to be careful of this man, complaints about him landed on his desk, a no win situation; the victim had a choice, put up and shut up, or leave!

"I told you." When he was out of sight Dorinda gave a delighted chuckle. "Once he knows you've a man, he'll leave you alone."

"I wish." Jessica placed the mailbox under her desk. "The alligator bite didn't seem to deter him. In fact, it's made him more aggressive."

"I've told you. Have Brian come to the office and show him around. Dick'll get the message, for sure."

"He asked me if I liked children, Dorinda. What do you think he meant, that he wants to have kiddies? I hope so."

"I reckon," Dorinda ambled back, leaned over seated Jessica. "Why didn't you have children during your fifteen years of marriage? You'd have made a good mum."

"I married a man whose sperm were poor swimmers."

"I'm sorry for laughing... sorry." Dorinda clapped a hand to her mouth to muffle exploded laughter. "You are funny, Jessica."

"Flaming hilarious," determined not to be hurt. "Do you think I should ask Brian if his sperm comes equipped with fins?"

Dorinda leaned over the desk and they both laughed hilariously.

In his office Dick telephoned Vancouver Social Services and asked the switchboard for Mr Ronnie Walters.

AT HOME TIME in the car park Dick Chalmers struck again; waylaid Jessica. He crept up from behind when she stretched to secure the mailbox on the offside seat.

"For a sweet lady whose smile I treasure while lying on my bed of thorns."

"What?" The proffered bunch of flowers perfuming her rear had Jessica exit the car smartly. "Get off, you moran!" She ducked to evade his nearness.

"Your husband suggested I woo you with flowers." Dick thrust the daffodils, pansies and assorted ferns onto the driving seat before Jessica could seat herself. "Don't say he gave me a bum steer?"

"Have you been speaking to my ex-husband in Vancouver?" Jessica paused, one foot inside the car. "You've been stirring it up with Ronnie Walters?"

"Just ascertaining the lie of the land, Jessica," hands held in mock capitulation. "Nothing nasty, I assure you. I just want to know you better."

"Very nice, Dick." Jessica picked up the flowers, thrust them at his chest and released her hold so abruptly he was obliged to grab them. "I suggest you bugger off and take them home to your wife. I'm not interested in either you or your flowers." Was this how her husband behaved with the full bosomed dolly bird in Vancouver?

"I could make you more than interested if you'd give me a chance, Jessica. You're a healthy woman with a woman's physical needs. I want to be the one to satisfy your… your sexual drive."

"Not on your Nellie!" She smiled sweetly, closed the door. "Bye for now, Dick. Go home to your wife, and I'll see you in the morning!"

She started up the engine, was disappointed when she observed him jump away from the car and a possible crushed foot. Still, she couldn't have everything; she'd bested him in the matter of the mailbox, or at least, Dorinda had, saying her boyfriend would fix it for her.

Jessica revved through gears going up the slope to ground level. Should she ask Brian to fix the mailbox, pretend to be helpless?

"When you learnt carpentry at your father's knee? No thanks, you're not pretending to be something you're not." The contradiction struck her immediately.

"Well, not more then I am right now being Jean Morningbird."

JACK LEFT HIS Cadillac, walked briskly up the path and rang the doorbell early Saturday morning. He turned, waved at the neighbor across the road walking inside his garden. The dog wasn't visible, naturally, but the guy handled himself as if he had a dog on a leash. He waved back across the hedge then quickly ran forward, head back, arm extended: the dog obviously getting away from him.

Jack felt fitter than anything he'd experienced in a long time. His early morning runs were hardening muscles; calves and feet not inclined to go into cramp at night. That had been pure murder. He'd crawled out of bed, staggered to the tiled floor of the shower until the spasm ceased. But now, he was okay.

If he drew in stomach muscles the trousers no longer nipped his spare tire, that was, until he had to breathe. He'd maintain the exercises until there was no necessity for punishing himself so hard. But for now, he would continue losing the fat and sloth of years: had to, in order to impress lovely, shapely Jean.

His hair, he couldn't do much about. Each time before setting out on a date with Jean he applied gum around the hairline and carefully attached the toupee. What a shame his own hair had never looked as thick and lustrous as the hairpiece; and thank God it wouldn't become detached at the slightest puff of wind, the salesman asserted.

He touched it now to make certain it was in place, then noted the slightly askew mailbox and smiled. Well, she was a lady after all; no one expected a female to do carpentry. The door opened and a bright smile greeted him through wire mesh.

"Hello Brian. So pleased you came early, we can get off to a good start."

"Hello, Jean." Jack gritted his teeth. Blast that Brian! "Hand me a screwdriver I'll straighten your mailbox while you collect your things."

"What's wrong with it?" Jessica pushed wide the screen door, stood next to him on the door mat. "It looks all right to me?" She nudged him. "But then, I'm not a perfectionist like you, apparently."

"Nothing wrong, just needs a shove up a tad this side." He opened the box, wiggled it. "There's plenty of play with the screws, it'll be no problem." She bent down with him for a look inside the box, and he could smell the essence of her. "See, there's another ratchet hole to move this side and level the box. I'll sort it in a tad."

"Whatever turns you on."

She went indoors thinking her father should be here to see how his daughter screwed up; carried along the hall, down the back steps to the foyer and basement stairs. The basement was huge, ran the length of the house and at present bereft of furniture; the floor smooth enough for roller-skating, which she didn't, not nowadays.

She went into the furnace room and searched out pliers, screwdriver and a spanner from the toolbox next to the gas burning monster that would prove to be a lifesaver in winter, she had been informed by the installation engineer. She returned shortly to the screen door to hand out implements to the man of her dreams gazing into space.

"These are what I use. Are they all right?"

"What's the spanner for?"

"To hit the screw if it doesn't go in place properly," and called back through the closed screen door. "I haven't got a hammer."

His raised-voiced admonition: "Remind me not to have you undertake repairs on my Caddy!" made her jump.

"I promise," she grinned back at him. "I don't do any repairs on my Cavalier. I don't like dirty fingers," which produced a picture of Dick Chalmers at his desk ogling her through pyramided fingers. She started across the living room.

"How's the uprooting going?" The voice snaked in through the open door.

What? Jessica paused and looked through the window. What did he say? She sidled back to the door.

Jack smiled apologetically through the screen and unscrewed a plug. "I didn't come and pull out weeds like I promised. Will you pass inspection by a visiting RCMP officer?"

"Oh, yes." She breathed a sigh of relief. Really, she was in Dick's sewer mind too much. "I thought I told you. I pulled out every little blessed plant and put them in the dustbin, out back."

"Good. Just so you're okay. I don't want to lose you to the law."

"Me neither," she giggled and left him.

It only took a few minutes for Jessica to pack sandwiches, fruit pies and biscuits into a picnic hamper; thermos flask of instant coffee with 2% milk and water; small cartons of fruit juice packed around the flask to hold it upright, and she was ready for departure. She'd have one last look at herself, there was time according to the sounds of activity on the mailbox.

In the long mirror of the bathroom just off the kitchen Jessica tweaked out hair to surround her face. She still wore her new style but it showed more face than previously. It seemed the older she got the longer her ears grew, or was it the weight of earrings pulling them down? She leaned over the vanity unit for closer inspection. She mustn't show too much flesh, her neck wasn't the skin of a woman in her twenties.

"Hah! No pimples." The young had problems.

She stood side on, eyed her bosom, then from the front on position. It looked lopsided. She plunged a hand up her slim fitting machine knitted jumper, pushed up the sponges in the brassier and checked the cello tape was attached to the flesh; stepped back, turned this way and that admiring her outline.

"Madonna? Who's she? Now, who looks as if she's knocking on forty years of age? Not this gal!"

In the kitchen Jessica picked up the picnic hamper, checked electric switches were off, and the back door locked, before she returned to him.

"It's squared off now." Jack placed the tools on the shelf beneath the foyer mirror. "No discerning mailman will denounce you for using a lopsided box."

"He's a very nice mailman, Brian. I've no complaints about him. He's put up with having to deliver my mail behind the screen door." She lined up the tools tidily. "But I wish he'd forgotten to deliver those blessed advertising sheets, they're a bore. And I dare say I'll have no complaints about you once I've examined your handiwork."

"Go have a look." He relieved her of the hamper, took it down the path with a backward glance at Jessica locking the door.

The mailbox certainly looked better it wasn't at an angle. Wow! Handy with tools. Nice!

They got into the Cadillac, the neighbor across the road waved from his footpath then patted the invisible dog's head to say 'Good-bye' too.

"Bye!" Jessica smiled hugely in return.

"Nice guy," Jack waved at him, and out of the corner of his mouth: "Hope you realize I'm waving to him, not his dog."

IN THE CADILLAC Jessica stretched her legs, there was more legroom than in her Cavalier. She had been so absorbed sitting alongside him on the dinner dance date, she hadn't thought of anything beyond how nice he looked, and his manly smell. Now she peered at his feet on the pedals; plenty of room for him to stretch out his legs too. Maybe that's why he'd got the Cadillac. Roomy!

"Where are we picnicking, Brian?"

"A place for relaxing and contemplating nature." He took his eyes off the road momentarily. "I won't divulge the destination. See if you can guess on the way."

She looked so right sitting next to him, her head halfway up to his neck; a snug fit. At last, he had found the perfect companion. He lowered his window and inhaled fresh air, road traffic having lessened in volume, looked at her and smiled. She answered with a smile that stopped a heartbeat.

Had she packed enough to eat? She could've made steak and kidney pies. They were nice cold at a picnic, or pork pies, they'd have been better still. Why didn't they make Stand Pies in Canada? They went down a treat in England, especially in Yorkshire where Stand Pies at Christmas were considered a necessity. Father Christmas always had a slice of Stand Pie and a choice of Christmas Cake or Mince Tart at each home visit with a glass of Sherry or Port Wine. Glutton and drunkard, never crossed the mind of a child on Christmas morning upon examining the bottles and plates.

Canadians weren't interested in tripe and onions either. She inwardly giggled. Then there was Haggis, another food they didn't go in for. What else? Oh yes! Brains and Sweetbreads. But then, not many English people fancied eating items from the top and bottom of the animal. She could remember the repulsion as a little girl, her mother explaining how her mother-in-law used the whole rabbit in the rabbit stew.

"The head too, Mummy?"

"Aye, love. And with the eyes still in."

THEY WENT ALONG Stony Plain Highway heading for Highvale in a state of euphoria, neither daring to speak in case they said the wrong thing; didn't want to break the spell of togetherness, it was too precious a moment. A word out of context would disturb the ambiance, the serenity of a delightful occasion.

A sign informed they were approaching Hasse Lake Provincial Park. Jessica eyed Jack in happy anticipation, this was all new country to her.

"Does it look familiar?" Jack asked quietly.

Jessica's stomach did a flip-flop. She looked around the countryside; hills, mounds and trees. Nope, should it? Nothing familiar about this place for her, but, what about Jean? She smiled briefly at him, then caught sight of a hoarding on the other side of the road which announced a Native Reserve ahead where trinkets could be purchased.

Still she didn't answer. The sign flashed by. She would have to say something about her ancestry, he'd be thinking she was ashamed if she didn't mention where she was from. She inhaled deeply and spoke in a voice higher than usual.

"Er... My people are from the Bearspaw Band."

"That's interesting. I've heard of the Bearspaw Band."

"Er... Stoney Indians. My great grandparents came from the Kootenay Plains and settled in Rocky Mountain House Reserve. Chief David Bearspaw was a great chief."

"Yes, so I heard. Did a lot for his people."

"He died in 1956." She hoped she'd remembered it correctly, there'd been so much historical detail in the library she'd been hard pressed to decide to which tribe and band she belonged.

"Ah yes, the Sarcee tribe were devastated by his demise," nodded his head as if recalling accurate details. "Pretty heroic bunch, the Sarcee."

Sarcee? She smiled, nodded her own head too, but in disbelief, too paralyzed to say anything. She quickly searched in her handbag for the packet of sweets; unwrapped a barley sugar and belatedly offered him one. He declined with a smile.

A stag ambled onto the road ahead, obviously thought he was king of the highway.

"Oh look at that animal, it's going to get hurt ignoring the traffic signs," and felt a complete idiot mouthing such an inanity.

"Yes, all members of the deer family should be taught to read at birth." After he stopped grinning, he continued. "The Déné Indians were decimated by smallpox, we learnt at school." He slowed down to avoid the animal now grazing in the middle of the highway off droppings from motorists' discarded half eaten sandwiches and chocolate wrappers.

"They didn't have the immunity," she stated simply.

"After General Wolfe scaled the walls of the Quebec Fort, the French surrendered."

81

She'd also taken history at school. "Yes, I know. The battle of Quebec."

"But you weren't told what the British did afterwards, I guess." He looked sideways at her face in repose and continued. "To punish the Indians who'd fought alongside the French, the British presented them with blankets impregnated with smallpox. The disease had been rampant in immigrant settlements, so this gift to Indian villages was in the hope they'd decimate the Indians. They succeeded. Tribes broke up and scattered."

Wow, what a history lesson. Her English school had kept quiet about that bit of skulduggery. "Very nice, I don't think."

"I didn't think you'd be aware. In the east we were also ignorant until recent facts surfaced about the first use of biological warfare." There was no reply from her. "The Sarcee finally settled in the Bow Valley on the Morley Reserve between Banff and Calgary."

Jessica swallowed hard, he knew more about her ancestry than did she. Naturally, he'd learnt it throughout his formative years. She'd been adult arriving in Canada, had to learn as she went along. She knew more about Indians, Pakistanis, Jamaicans and Ugandans but not native Canadians. She felt such a dope.

"I like venison." She swung her head, gazed after the stag then turned back to him. "Is it a traffic offense hitting an animal out of the hunting season?" That should change his concentration.

"If we down one, we'll store it in the trunk then hand it over to RCMP for distribution on the Reserve. I don't want a fine for eating road kill." She'd deliberately changed the subject about her tribal background; been forthcoming and then stopped for some reason. Don't broach the subject again, leave it for her.

What a clot she was! An aborigine would have been aware it was an offense for motorists to benefit by road kill.

Gradually, came the realization she was being let off the hook, he wasn't nattering on about natives and reserves. He was driving, his eyes fixed on the road ahead. She relaxed, started to hum to herself watching scenery slide by.

"I'm hungry, but I ate a good breakfast, did you?"

82

"For sure. But I'll enjoy whatever you've packed. We'll soon be at Edmonton Beach picnic grounds." He smiled at her. "I'm looking forward to relaxing stretched out on the beach, and then," paused enticingly.

"And then..?" What happens then? No more about reservations, please?

"We'll hire a canoe and I'll see how good a canoeist you are. It's okay to say you're an expert but I have to be convinced," twinkling eyes opposite to accusative.

"I am a good canoeist, Brian." She didn't have to lie. Her heart lifted; eyes widened in joy. "I've even done some kayaking, but I'm not keen on it. I'm afraid of overbalancing, and I dislike having to scrunch up my legs."

"Me too, I don't kayak for that very reason. It's paralyzing on long legs."

"We're alike in so many ways, Brian, it's incredible." A flood of relief swept through her whole system, she could have soared up to the sky.

Chapter Seven

After picnicking at one of the tables under the trees that surrounded the lake, they packed their gear and took it back to the car. Then, hand in hand, ran down to the lake where canoes were for hire.

At the landing stage, Jack held steady the canoe whilst Jessica seated herself. Likewise, Jessica maintained a steady craft until Jack settled on the seat in front. Both picked up a paddle to manipulate the canoe away from the staging and head for deep water.

They stroked in perfect harmony, each pleased with the prowess of the other. We're a pair, a canoeing couple, a perfect match! Hearts sang in rhythm with dipping paddles until they reached the other side of the lake, took a right turn to continue along the bank.

"How long have we got, Brian, I don't want this interlude to end."

"As long as we like." His arms rotated stroking expertly to avoid a free floating branch. "There wasn't a lineup for canoes, so this can be 'till nightfall."

"I'd like to stay until the moon comes out. See with every lift of a paddle water break up into shining waves like it did on the ferry."

"Sounds nice," glanced over his shoulder. "I'll try to arrange it."

Unseen by either, driftwood below the surface came into their path. The prow of the canoe pushed it to one side but Jessica's paddle connected with a clunk and catapulted her overboard, headfirst, with Jack a close second.

The canoe tipped over and hit Jack on the shoulder. He went under.

Jessica, dogpaddling, saw the incident. She ducked beneath the surface and grabbed hold of Jack's head and shoulder to resurface with him, his eyes wide and startled. No more surprised than Jessica, a hair flap in her hand and a bald patch beneath. She quickly replaced the toupee and pressed it down firmly. With her other hand under his chin for leverage, commenced a dogpaddle towards the upturned craft.

"I'm okay, Jean," through a clenched mouth, her grasp was so firm. "Sure enough, you can let go now."

"I don't want to lose you." Jessica did not release her hold until certain his hairpiece was firmly attached. She had a fleeting vision of saturated breast sponges enclosed in machine knitting float almost at neck level before she pushed them below the waterline.

"Let's get to the shoreline quick," his thoughts not for himself but how to save the situation. He grabbed the canoe with one hand, the other held his shoulder. "It's okay up on the right. Head that way."

"I'm with you."

They dogpaddled and pushed until their feet struck bottom, then up-righted the canoe. Jack immediately left her, struggled unsteadily through tree roots in a search for a place to sit.

"Hang on, Brian, I'll be with you." She tied the mooring rope to an exposed tree root and splashed after him; arrived, placed a hand under his elbow. "There's a comfy patch of grass under that tree," and led him up the slight bank and assisted him to sit.

"I'm okay," and tried not to appear the embarrassed fool.

"Let's take a look at your shoulder, Brian." She proceeded to examine his injuries; worked fingers and thumbs along his shoulder and upper arm.

"I should be looking after you," his eyes downcast.

"If I whack myself you can feel for breaks and tears, I promise." What an opening! Good thing Dirty Dick couldn't hear. "You are brave, Brian. I suppose you're used to injuries as a skydiver, but I'd hate it."

So did he, hated being a fraud, not the man of her dreams. He was no skydiving hero; a mere mortal, and Jessica's prodding at a shoulder muscle made him wince: vulnerable too!

"There's no major damage, just this bruising apparently where the muscle's thin on your shoulder joint." Jessica sat back on her haunches and cast an inquisitive eye over him. He was looking decidedly sorry for himself because he wasn't in charge. Like her mother said: A man likes to be in control of the situation. Don't take over from a man or you'll lose him. Her mum made sense at times!

She stood up. "Ouch!"

"What is it?"

"Oh, it's nothing," with a sudden grasp at her waist.

"Yes, there is." He lurched to his feet. "You're hurt, aren't you?" He made a moved towards her with his left arm. The muscles in his shoulder protested but he ignored them, reached out to touch her waist.

"I'm not injured, not really." She should win an Academy Award.

. "Did you bang into the log or the canoe?" He reached an arm around her drawing her to him. "I don't figure on you being hurt, Jean." He pulled her to him; their bodies melted into one. He kissed the upraised face gently, each eyelid received a blessing. "You mean so -"

A sudden douche of hot water cascaded down his chest.

Some kiss!

Jessica pulled away from the perfect man in surprise. The sponges were spilling out lake water! No wonder it was warm, she'd been cooking it on her breasts.

"I'll go to that tree," Jessica indicated a large spruce nearby. "Wring out my jumper, er... sweater." She escaped his touch, walked sideways like a crab, not wanting to spoil the precious moments of togetherness yet realizing the necessity for repairing her attire.

"Tell me if you find bruising, Jean." He released the lingering hold of her hand, finally let go of her fingers. "I'll kiss it better."

She smiled, clearly not wanting to leave, her face streaming wet and glowing. "I'll let you kiss it better, even if I'm not hurt."

"It feels mighty good to be wet through and glowing inside like a glowworm," his smile spreading. "That's how I feel, like a glowworm. I've seen them at Waitomo Caves, Jean. Glowworms suspended from the ceilings emitted lights like distant stars on a clear, black night."

"That sounds pretty. Like a prairie sky at night."

"Unfortunately, someone's hungry stomach growling in our boat produced a ripple of laughter which caused the glowworms to switch off."

"Isn't that typical? Good thing your stomach grumbles can't put out starlight."

"I remember the quietness of the trip along the waterway. The guide pulled the boat along by the rope attached to the sides of the passages like balustrades, and then we emerged in the huge cavern." His good arm described an arc in the sky and dripped water. "There we sat in the boat and craned our necks to peer at the majesty of the high ceilings with its splendid glowworms."

He smiled at droplets of water on her ears as she backed away clearly hanging onto his every word. "I'd love to take you to New Zealand Jean, and show you the sights I've seen."

"I'd like to go too. I love to travel and soak up knowledge like a sponge." Good thing she was an easy learner with all the tribal history she had to learn.

When she was hidden from inquisitive eyes Jessica pulled up the jumper, wrung out one breast sponge at a time, thankful they'd retained their shape. But to make sure she pulled and pushed at the sponge to make the nipple points. Then she wrung out the jumper, first at the front, then the back and both sides. Her bosom looked okay too.

A Madonna figure again!

She sneaked a look around the tree trunk, observed Jack with his shirt off rubbing and flexing shoulder muscles. Hmm! Fine figure of a man, Brian. His rotating arm caught his head and he quickly put up both hands, pulled down the thatch then cast a hurried look in her direction.

Jessica quickly withdrew from sight. Hey, what about that hairpiece? She giggled, then stopped abruptly.

Now don't laugh at the poor man's misfortune having a bald spot; maybe it was a family trait, in the genes. Her father had a full head of hair, a bit thinner, but it still covered his head. Did Brian cover up to make himself appear younger? Realization struck quickly. A fine one she was to castigate Brian; she was wearing a padded bra and extra -

Oh Lord! She'd been smart-alecking about Brian's bald patch. All her makeup must have washed off! And he must have speculated, when he met chest on, her leaking bra!

Jessica came out of the trees reluctantly, barefaced in front of him; wanted to impress him, not turn him off.

Jack watched her approach and love smote him in the pit of the stomach. She looked vulnerable without the facade of makeup; obviously didn't realize she had lost an earring. With her hair flat to her head and ringing wet, not a curl in sight, she resembled a lovable puppy caught in a sudden downpour.

"You remind me of our drenched dog after a storm."

"Thank you very much! I needed that!" About turned and stalked off in the direction of the canoe. So much for a man she assumed worth loving. He had the sensitivity of a gnu.

"Sorry, Jean!" Jack hurried after her, tried not to laugh. "Hang on, don't go off in a tantrum!" His pace increased to match hers.

Jessica's feet shot out and water sprayed as she neared the mooring rope. She'd teach him, the monster, likening her to a dog. Thank goodness, he hadn't said, bitch!

Jack closed in on her, flung himself forward noting her intent, to unloosen the knot, and brought her down on the beach in a football tackle. They rolled over and over until they came up short against tree roots. He held down flaying arms determined to have a piece of him.

"Get off me!"

"I meant you looked like a lovable puppy we used to have at home, Jean. I adore you. I think I love you."

Her struggles ceased, glaring eyes turned to love orbs. "You could express yourself better than that, lad."

"Teach me, my dear."

"There's only one way to teach you, my lad." She freed her hands, held onto his head and pulled his face onto hers. They kissed gently then more urgently, familiarity coming with practice. They came up for air and smiled at one another.

"I sort of go for the lad, bit. Makes me feel young."

"What sort of dog did you have, Brian?"

Oh God, he wasn't free to make love to her; he was a usurper, a no-good man hiding behind another man's name. He smiled wryly, rolled off her and sat up.

"A Heinz 57 variety. What's your favorite dog, Jean, you're the animal expert?"

Jessica groaned inwardly. She'd blown it. She'd noticed the change in him instantly before he rolled off her. Had she presented herself too quickly? Was he disgusted with her sexual drive? She made to sit-up and was surprised when he assisted her upright with a hand under an elbow. She wasn't untouchable, then.

Jack stood, helped Jessica to rise. "Careful where you place your feet."

"Thanks, tree roots don't make the best footing."

"Not when you have a small foot like yours."

Jessica looked down at her feet. Yes, they were smaller than Brian's by a few inches, and narrower. She smirked inwardly; she had neat feet, even when the shoes were soaked.

They returned at a leisurely pace to release the canoe. Neither spoke, there seemed little to say. They pushed out the canoe and Jessica climbed aboard.

"It's not the first time I've hand paddled, Brian," indicating. "I can see oars over there by that log."

"It isn't the first time for me either." He pushed the canoe to deeper water, then climbed into the front seat. "I lost paddles on a fast flowing river. They weren't as easy to reach as these."

They commenced paddling with their hands. "How's the shoulder bearing up?"

"Okay." Jack reached for the paddles. "A bit closer."

Jessica leaned over the other side of the canoe, her hands paddling gently. Jack stretched to his utmost and managed to float a paddle towards him. The thatch left its back mooring and flopped over his face. Jessica instantly averted her gaze in case he caught her looking.

"Got it!"

She cast a hesitant glance. He held a retrieved paddle aloft and at the same time pulled the partially attached thatch off his head.

"Oh, don't Brian, it'll hurt!" She caught hold of his arm, the hairpiece lank, no longer thick brown waves.

"I'm thankful to be rid of this piece of vanity." He hurled the toupee far into the lake; turned, saw consternation in her eyes, not blame. "Don't worry, Jean, it didn't hurt, it was only attached by a few front hairs. The gum must have come unstuck with the swim." He struck the canoe with his good hand. "That's great! They assured me it wouldn't come off in water."

"Oh, that's so funny!" Jessica couldn't control a loud bray before she clapped a hand over her mouth. She eyed the other paddle waiting to be rescued and commenced a desperate hand paddle towards it.

"You think having a toupee's funny?"

"No, not really." Her mouth wouldn't stay straight, and stretched in a grin. "If I was balding I'd wear a wig."

He eyed her askance over his shoulder. "Wait 'till I get you ashore, laughing at baldness." Then he too joined in the amusement.

"No, it wasn't the lack of hair, honestly. It was the funniness of everything. The canoe tipping. Your hair. My, my, oh my..." She simply couldn't mention her saturated sponges.

At the landing, picnickers glanced across the lake, intrigued to hear chortling laughter.

THE NATIVE STALL at the side of the road contained a great many artifacts, and the owners resplendent in traditional Cree clothing. Visitors searched for that special gift to take home to relatives and decided to ignore, the damp, bedraggled pair examining wooden totem poles, duck eggs and Canada Geese.

"Look familiar to you, Jean?" Jack picked up one of several strands of wooden beads. Her wan smile made him realize he shouldn't have insisted on dropping in at the stall on the way home. She obviously felt uncomfortable; maybe had unhappy memories of reservation days.

"Not really, Brian. I don't recall that beading."

"I'll hang them on the kitchen overhang to remind me of this memorable day when we went for a canoe ride and ended up swimming."

"Hope you don't put your head into it or you'll hang yourself," her smile wide. "I think on the side of the overhang would be a better place." She ran a hand over the hand carved bird. "I'll get this Canada Goose for the foyer."

"Should look neat reflected in the mirror. Make it look like the bird's in water."

"Yes, you're right. What an imagination you have, Brian." She deposited the bird and beads on the counter.

Jack opened his wallet for the cashier in full chief headdress. "Do those head feathers take much cleaning?"

"Only need a soaking in soapsuds and a rinse off." His eyes followed dripping water escaping from the wallet in the search for dry notes. "In clean water like that on my floor."

"Oh, sorry about that, Sir."

"My credit card's all right, Brian, it was in the car." Jessica opened her handbag and removed her wallet before she realized she'd have to sign her own name.

"I don't mind who pays." The cashier held out a hand.

"All the same, you shouldn't be paying." Jack closed his wallet; felt obliged to justify himself to the big chief. "We fell into the lake."

"That'd do it every time, eh?" He took Jessica's card.

"What do you think of those designs, Brian?" She indicated beaded purses at the far end of the counter. "Recognize any tribe?" The ploy worked. Jack obliged and left her to examine purses. Jessica signed her own name on the account slip.

"Hold onto that bill, Jean, I'll reimburse you," Jack called.

The chief checked out her signed name, and Jessica smiled at the man disarmingly when he handed back her credit card with the purchases. Why had she worried, it was J for Jessica and Jean, and Brian hadn't used, 'Morningbird'. But, he hadn't better get a look at the docket with the name of Walters on it, had he?

"Hand it over, I'll pay for these items." Jack held out his hand when she joined him.

"No, you paid for the boat ride, Brian. I'm paying for the bird and beads."

What a nice, thoughtful person she is. Her heart equals the generosity of her smile. Jack tucked her hand through his crooked arm and they left the store.

91

Chapter Eight

On Monday Afternoon Jessica arrived home from work; parked her Cavalier in the garage off the back alley and admired her back garden from the short path to the back door. Pity she hadn't accepted the bouquet Dirty Dick offered last week, her flowers weren't up to their full potential yet. Still, she wouldn't have cared for what accompanied the offer.

She replaced the back door key in her handbag ready for the morning's departure, propped open the door for fresh air and walked down the corridor past the open doors of two bedrooms; hers at the front of the house, the other, going to be a study once she'd acquired a desk for the computer currently sitting on the wooden crate it had traveled in from Vancouver. It hadn't been cause for dissent between the divorcing couple: Ronnie had his Apple, she, an IBM.

She opened the front door to create a draft, noted the police presence in the form of a cruiser parked directly out front. The two officers seated inside observed her in the doorway and emerged from their vehicle to walk up the footpath towards her.

Many feelings of guilt crossed Jessica's mind she was unable to prioritize. She had refrained from felling her husband a lethal blow before leaving Vancouver; paid her electricity and telephone accounts promptly; smacked Dick's hand off her hipbone that afternoon. No one called in the police for a silly thing like a reprimand. What on earth had she done wrong?

"Jean Morningbird?" Big feet paused on the landing.

Whoops, it wasn't Brian asking, but police. "No, she was the previous occupant. Can I help you?"

"Mind if we come inside?" The look of skepticism spread over unsmiling faces.

"Certainly, I've nothing to hide." Jessica stepped aside and ushered them indoors. She was innocent, an honest person. Well, almost!

They stood in the foyer, eyed the interior of the living room. Jessica indicated the recent purchase sitting on the mahogany shelf reflected in the mirror as if floating in a lake.

"I bought the Canada Goose at a road stall, if that's what you're after."

"It isn't."

One of the officers stepped into the corridor, saw open bedroom doors and decided to investigate.

"I've been in Alberta about three months. My name's Jessica Walters. I came from Vancouver and work at Edmonton Social Services." She indicated the officer looking into the bedrooms. "What's he up to?"

"It's all right, no need to worry."

Jessica peered down the corridor at the man now looking into the bathroom. "He's a nosy sod, isn't he?"

"Just doing his job, lady." He went into her living room and tried not to smile whilst he assessed the contents.

Jessica followed the first officer leaving the bathroom and about to descend the stairs to the basement. "Where do you think you're going, you cheeky beggar?"

"Just downstairs, madam, no need to worry."

"It'd be a nicety if you asked instead of just moving in as if you owned the place."

"Won't take long, madam," and turned to descend the basement steps."

"No, you won't, because there isn't much down there to look at." She walked to the dining table and saw the other officer examining her wall unit."

"The television set's paid for, I've got the receipt."

"You're in Social Services, eh? I didn't think you looked like your average hooker."

"What?"

"You don't look like Jean Morningbird, hooker."

"She's a kennel maid at SPCA. What do you mean, hooker?"

"Oh, yeah, a kennel maid? Since when?"

"You've got to be kidding! She's a prostitute?"

"I kid you not, lady."

"The basement's clean," the returning officer said when he entered the kitchen.

"Of course it is, you cheeky sod! Everything's brand new and I'm a tidy person." They were getting more and more up her nose. But she'd better be careful; they were after all, policemen.

They both peered out at the back garden hiding smiles.

"Got anything of interest in your backyard?"

Instantly, Jessica was on the alert recalling her and Brian's weeding; the only thing was to be upright about it. "I pulled out some ferns a friend of mine said were cannabis from the hemp plant, or something like that."

They looked long and hard at someone from a strange planet. No one could be so dumb. No one would volunteer such damaging information. One of them fiddled with the latches on the French window and managed to open it, then the two of them stepped onto the deck.

"Where were they?" The second one paused for Jessica to catch up with them at the front of the verandah.

"Over there in front of the Mountain Ash tree." Jessica waved a nonchalant hand and remained on the deck to watch the officers stride purposely up the garden. And each pulled up a plant! Curses, she'd not thought to see if they'd re-sprouted!

The search for more plants was thorough, even covered the periphery of the garden. Both entered the garage and she could hear oilcans and the lawn mower being moved. They were hoping she'd provide them with more stupid plants? Or maybe a Still for making gin?

She waited in trepidation in case they found something to further implicate her in wrongdoing. They emerged from the garage, closed the door and headed towards her with fronds that waved in the breeze.

"They're so silky and frilly, and don't they grow quick?" Her attempt at levity eased off when she saw their stern faces. "I thought I'd got them all."

"Don't grow quick enough for pushers."

"It's such a shame they're for smoking, I enjoyed just having them." Jessica leaned over, gently touched one of the ferns. "I haven't an established garden yet, but the landscape gardener's made a good show of it. The poppies aren't the heroin or cocaine thingies, so I can leave them in."

They nodded, eyed her, the garden and the weed.

"And of course, the rocks help. Later on, when I'm more settled in, I'm going to paint some rocks." She knew she was rambling but couldn't stop herself. "You know the sort, like little foxes and dogs and cats. It's easy with acrylic paint, I've heard. And they do look nice, either in the garden on a footpath or inside on a window - "

"You say your landscape gardener knew of these?" One of them waved a fern when they mounted the verandah steps.

Oh dear, she was putting in the boot to the gardener. "He wanted me to discard them but I persuaded him to leave them in." She gave a nervous titter. "He was a very nice person, but said: 'On your own head, be it, lady.'"

They eyed one another, then her, speculatively.

Were they thinking of charging her for illegal possession like Brian indicated? Was she going to lose everything she'd worked to acquire?

"It was a friend of mine told me they were hemp cannabis thingy, and helped me pull them out." She trailed frilly fronds through her fingers. "It's such a shame they're used for smoking, they're so attractive. They'd make a nice show in a vase with tall flowers."

"We'd like you to accompany us downtown to make a statement." One of the officers touched her arm.

"Why? I can make a statement here," removed her arm. "Don't be familiar, you cheeky sod. I don't like to be touched."

"It's more convenient, downtown." Each took hold of an elbow, lifted her, feet cycling, through the French windows.

"I don't think this is very nice police procedure!"

They set her down and relocked the French windows. "Don't make difficulty for us. You're wanted downtown."

"Difficulty-fifficulty. I couldn't care less about you and your problems. I've been working and want my dinner."

She went to the fridge, removed a Pyrex dish of cooked sausages. But before she could take out mashed potatoes from last night, one officer gently pulled the dish out of her hand and replaced it in the fridge.

"You'll be fed if we find it necessary to detain you."

The other officer went to the back door and she could hear it being locked. He returned, picked up her handbag. "Your house keys in your purse?" At Jessica's nod feeling utter inadequacy, he held it out for her. "We'll leave now. The sooner we're gone, the quicker you're back."

"Oh, I'm coming back? You're not going to imprison me?"

"Think you deserve jail time?"

She shook her head, not answering; she was only putting her foot in her mouth.

"Come along, then, madam."

She cast sad looks around her friendly living room and foyer before the door closed after them; felt such a fool being escorted down the path to the cruiser, imagining neighbors across the street and the ones on either side getting an eyeful of her being taking in by the police. They'd think her a criminal. She felt like shouting: I'm an innocent victim of circumstance!

It wasn't until she was in the back seat of the cruiser she realized her nosy neighbor with the invisible dog wasn't in evidence.

Ha! He wasn't so stupid after all. He hadn't got a dog license.

IN THE POLICE STATION Jessica saw the workings of a stretched police force. She waited by the sergeant's desk whilst he absented himself twice to answer calls at the front desk to settle a dispute from a drunk, then a prostitute who insisted she had been framed by an officer pretending to be a client.

"Entrapment!" she screamed, her mouth red and wide.

Jessica could not help but admire her knowledge of the law. But the police weren't impressed, it made them surly and disagreeable. The sergeant still smarted when he returned to continue the interrogation.

"You say you and a friend pulled out the marihuana plants?" He waited, pen poised over the statement form.

"Yes."

"The friend's name, please?"

"Why do you want to know that?" She couldn't give Brian's name. They'd ask him questions and he'd say she was Jean Morningbird. Wow! Hoist by her own petard!

"Just give me the name."

Instead, Jessica looked across the busy operations room and thought of the Edmonton Queen; dancing and dining and being in Brian's arms; another flash of them paddling in rhythm across a placid lake; rolling on the beach in a death struggle until finally kissing to make-up.

"Why don't you divulge the name? Is it because this person is nonexistent?" He noted the shrug. "Did you uproot the marihuana by yourself?"

"Probably."

"Who told you they were from the hemp plant?"

"The landscape gardener suggested they weren't a good thing to have in my garden."

"But you asked him to leave them in. We've contacted him, and he's having to come up with a reason why he didn't notify us. Don't be silly, we know you didn't realize they were an illegal plant. So, who told you they were?"

"Why don't you ask Jean Morningbird these questions? Why ask me anything? I'm an unfortunate victim of circumstance." Well, at least she'd managed to get it into the conversation, it was too good a line to pass up on.

"I'm asking you."

"I repeat. Speak to the previous occupant."

"That'd be a neat trick. She works the streets as a hooker and pusher. And when not, she's on a reservation where she can't be reached. You're our best chance for a conviction."

"I don't think that's fair."

"Drug pushing isn't fair. We need verification of what action you and your friend took on learning you were growing marihuana, and what you did with the plants."

"I put them in the rubbish.

"Where?"

"In my rubbish bins.

"And the garbage was conveniently collected. When?"

"The next day, I believe. I haven't been there long enough to know when the rubb... garbage men come."

"Who helped you garbage them?"

She shrugged. So what can they do, throw me in jail? Stupid gits! She wished her father was there to deal with them. He'd soon put them in their place, he would.

The solution was swift: confined to a cell for the night to think it over.

THE CELL WAS not too unpleasant, but the cot blanket looked suspect. Who had occupied the cell previously? A drunk, a derelict, a prostitute, or maybe an addict with AIDS? Eeek!

The small aperture in the door opened, a face appeared, eyes searched the cell and landed on her standing in the center.

"What do you think I'm up to, cheeky?"

"Just checking."

"Could I have a clean blanket, please?"

"That's a clean blanket."

"It doesn't look it."

"You're not at the Hotel Hilton."

"I want to go home."

"Retain that thought, and in the morning you'll get your wish, providing..."

Oh cripes, if she wasn't released early enough she'd never arrive at work on time. Just the sort of excuse Dirty Dick needed for having her on the carpet: literally!

The slot closed bringing loneliness nearer; isolated from humankind. A feeling akin to the emptiness when she realized her husband had cast her aside like so much undesirable refuse. But she was also closed in here, an unnatural environment. She couldn't see anyone, talk to anyone.

Hey! She looked around the high walls and ceiling. Where's the television they say they spoil prisoners with? A lot they know, there's nothing here but a cot, washbasin, and a toilet with a lid, for which she was truly thankful.

She went to the door and banged. The small aperture opened, eyes peered in.

"Where's my television set?"

"You should be so lucky." The slot closed smartly.

JESSICA WAS RELEASED the following morning immediately after a tasty breakfast of croissants and coffee. Don't they eat well in a lockup?

It was a good thing her mother wasn't around to see her dip the croissant in coffee, she'd have gone spare. Her dad would have appreciated the dunking, though, he dunked when his wife wasn't looking.

Last night's meal had been exceptionally good. Chilli stuffed in a baked potato and mixed vegetables with a buttered bun; dessert of plums on custard squares and coffee to follow. The only things they'd missed out on, were biscuits, cheese and wine.

The sergeant was not present at the desk when the constable returned her handbag.

"Do you have anything to add to your statement?"

"No, nothing further, you've had it all."

"Sign here, please."

The form was handed over. Jessica read she had pulled out marihuana plants and garbaged them. No mention of anyone assisting her. She smiled and signed her name. She was safe from discovery by Brian, he wouldn't find out she was a liar; even been incarcerated so she wouldn't divulge her guilty secret.

Jessica went down the steps of the Downtown Police Station and wished she could undo her actions. She pretended to be someone else in order to fill the aching void of losing a marriage partner, and had demeaned herself. Clot!

JACK TELEPHONED Jean the next morning before seven o'clock, concerned she hadn't answered her phone the previous evening, even after several attempts. When again there -was no reply he decided upon action. He had to see Jean and explain his deception, pretending to be Brian. She was already aware of his vanity with the hairpiece, maybe she'd extend her humor to accepting his purloining Brian's name.

"Oh yeah, don't forget the glamorous job. Sky diver! I wish!"

There was no way he was continuing the charade; he had to be his own master. If Jean didn't like him after his confession, then he'd walk, learn to live with it. But the sinking feeling in the pit of his stomach indicated he wasn't going to like it. He slipped into his Cadillac, eyed his bald spot in the driving mirror, drew a deep breath and set out to vindicate himself to the love of his life.

JESSICA ARRIVED at the office. Buses were plentiful for morning rush-hour, consequently she arrived before seven forty-five; the guard on duty at the main desk on the ground floor, the only witness to her arrival.

It was empty on the eighth floor when she switched on her terminal, sat down and sought out Jean Morningbird through the welfare files. Bingo! Jean Morningbird was listed, not as Morningbird but Morning Bird.

"No wonder I didn't connect with an Indian, she joined up her name. And they should bring their files up to date having a hooker and drug pusher at my address!"

She discovered there was quite a long list of Jean, the cannabis grower. She had been on welfare for years on and off, between the times she had spent in a woman's prison, in fact for street prostitution. No mention of being a kennel maid. That was too respectable an occupation for a hooker and drug pusher. The liar!

Jessica placed her arms on the desk and bowed her head in them. What had she got herself mixed up with? She hadn't chosen an ordinary person to impersonate but one with a criminal, unsavory record? She sat up and sought out further information, going back into Jean's history.

She was descended from Shuswap Cree of the Blackfoot Nation, who lived on the Athabasca headwaters. The footnote stated: Iroquois, Sekani and Salish affiliations.

"That's why the police couldn't get to her on the reservations; she's got too many bolt holes." She'd been nowhere near Jean's ancestry when spouting off to Brian!

There was a rattle indicating the elevator had arrived at her floor. Jessica quickly came out of the welfare files and closed down the terminal. Footsteps approached along the corridor and sounded like Dirty Dick's. She opened her handbag to appear busy; inside was the toothbrush and small tube of toothpaste given her for, The Use Of, by a police guard.

Opportunity presented to brush away sins and reflect on her actions.

JACK ARRIVED AT Jean's door and felt the nakedness of bare truth about his head when he rang the bell. He waited, courage slipping away like quicksilver, and there was no answer. He could see the next-door neighbor attending to the hedge which separated the two properties, the while maintaining an alert watch on the stranger standing on the doormat, no doubt already formulating in his mind a report to the police on burglar activity.

Jack nodded agreeably to the man, walked down the side of the house through the gate and up the garden path to the verandah; jumped up and crossed to the French windows. He looked inside under a sheltering hand to eliminate reflection, and noticed nothing out of the ordinary. Jean wasn't lying on the floor of the dining room or living room; the kitchen floor however, was hidden by the island servery.

If she wasn't at home, where was she? Had she been and gone between his telephone calls? There was plenty about Jean he didn't know. Maybe she led a secret life; there was obviously something in her background that made her shy off.

The slight breeze rustled through the branches of pine trees, bushes emitted a sweet scent; everywhere his eyes landed in the yard he visualized Jean. He swallowed hard, maybe he'd better leave and allow her to explain in her own good time where she'd been all night. But she could've telephoned and informed him she was away for the night, eh?

Not if it was meant to be a secret!

The side garden gate clicked. Jack stretched a smile he was far from feeling and waited with a ready explanation until the man appeared brandishing garden shears.

"I'm not doing any harm," backing away.

"I recognized your Cadillac from the weekend." The man stopped at the foot of the deck. "No good ringing the bell, she's away."

"That's for sure. I was concerned. I tried contacting her all last night."

"Oh, no problem. The police took her away in a cruiser."

There wasn't a reply Jack could think of uttering. He stared openmouthed at the man with a larger, overlapping stomach than he'd ever exhibited; but then, he was in his sixties, so was entitled.

"They waited for her to come home last night," the neighbor continued. "Came inside, then marched her away." He shrugged. "Don't know why though, seems a nice lady. A lot better than the previous resident." He eyed Jack enquiringly, hoping to be thrown some light on the subject.

But Jack was completely in the dark.

JACK TELEPHONED the Bonnie Doon Police Station on his cell phone immediately he was in his car heading north. "I'm making enquiries about a friend of mine. Why did you pick up Jean Morningbird yesterday?"

"Who's that who wants to know?"

"A friend who's heard the news from her neighbor. Why'd you take her?"

There was a pause, then: "A friend, eh?"

Jack assumed he had verified the situation through police computer files. "That's what I said."

"Does Jean Morningbird's friend have a name?"

"Sure has, but he isn't saying another word until you explain why you picked up Jean Morningbird last night."

"Maybe you'd like to come into the office and bring us up to speed on your association with Ms Morningbird?"

"And then again, maybe I wouldn't," and deliberately erased the call from the cell memory bank.

Did they use 'Call Display' phones at Police Stations with the caller's name and number? Was a cell phone traceable? His removal of the call probably would not deter them tracing him. He was treading dangerous ground here; never done anything reprehensible enough to have the police on his back. He certainly wasn't going to follow up the invitation to allow them to question him on his association with Jean.

How embarrassing, not only explaining to Jean he was a cowardly drongo who couldn't pursue a lady unaided without his condo mate's list of girlfriends, but also display his inadequacies to a skeptical police force.

He'd sooner fend off Jeffrey Olivera's snide remarks.

Then again, sooner not.

DICK CHALMERS FELT randy. He stalked his prey around the desk in the Claims Office in the hope she would soften her resolve and allow him to woo. Apparently, the more resistance, the more he pursued. Jessica always ensured she had a desk or another body between herself and the director, unfortunately for Veronica Boehme, who became the sacrificial lamb.

"Oh, look at what Veronica's done, Dick." Jessica pointed over Veronica's shoulder. "Can you see the fine writing on this ledger?" Dick obligingly bent over Veronica and admired her writing, along with her other attributes.

Jessica fled the scene determined not to feel sorry for throwing a victim to the wolf: she had enough on her plate.

JACK TURNED into his parking space at Shellack Oil Exploration, sat in his car with the engine turned off. What diabolical situation deserved Jean's apprehension by police? It could be anything.

Like what, for instance?

"Well, maybe she ran over a dog at the kennels."

What a relief, that was it! There'd been an incident where she worked.

During a quiet break he'd telephone the SPCA and ascertain from Jean herself exactly what occurred to warrant police activity. He alighted from his car his mind leaping ahead. She'll require a ride home from work seeing the police took her off in their cruiser.

Yeah! The perfect excuse for telephoning her.

By the time it was convenient to telephone Jean from the office, he decided not to divulge his secret identity: least said, soonest mended.

"Jean who?"

"Jean Morningbird"

"No one here of that name."

"Is that the SPCA?"

"Yes, and there's still no one here of that name." She hung up on him preventing further enquiries.

Curious! He automatically picked up his pen. Might as well continue working he was getting nowhere with Jean, but he'd phone her at home after work. There was a mystery here, and he loved solving mysteries, usually of a geological nature; but this was close to the heart, caused adrenaline to flow, and at the end of the challenge the reward of Jean herself.

Nice! And she was a good kisser. And he sort of liked being called 'lad'.

JESSICA ALIGHTED FROM the one fifty one bus on 92nd Avenue, walked a few yards, went around the corner and she could see her own front footpath. What a relief. A pretty house and frontage without a police cruiser gracing its length. She was home, free and alone, answerable to no man, especially that misbegotten weasel of an ex-husband who made a game of passing her onto a masher.

On the garden path a hail reached her from the next door neighbor on the other side of his hedge.

"Good evening." Jessica ambled towards him across the grass.

"Hi! Your friend called last night. I told him you'd been taken by the police."

104

Cripes! "Er, which friend?"

"The one with the Cadillac. He was sure concerned," his curiosity obvious. "What did they take you in for? I found out your phone number from Directory Enquiry and tried several times to get in touch with you."

"The previous occupant planted something illegal in the back garden. I had to convince them it wasn't my doing." Now Brian would know she wasn't Jean Morningbird. A sensation of relief followed. Thank the Lord, she didn't have to lie anymore. She smiled at him. "I'm looking forward to sleeping at home tonight and not in a police cell."

"Ah yeah, don't blame you. Never experienced it myself, but it sounds sort... She was a real mess, Jean Morningbird. Used to have parties 'till the early hours. I told your friend, she wasn't much. You're a nicer neighbor than her." He indicated the freshly painted house and neat flower borders. "Your house looks great. A credit to the neighborhood."

"Thanks for being so helpful," she turned to go. "I'll telephone my friend and let him know I'm all right."

She went indoors by the front door and left it open, checked everything was in order from the previous evening's hurried departure and opened wide the French windows to freshen up the place which had been enclosed for too long.

She delayed telephoning Brian, feared his anger at her pretense. There'd been too many hassles the last twenty four hours, she needed a respite.

She had a ground beef pie and vegetables on a tray in front of the television set foregoing the sausage and mash in the fridge. Her mother and father always reverted to English meals whenever they walked around a supermarket and spied steak and kidney pies, meat and potato pies, shepherd pies, ground beef pies, and Jessica was no exception. She had dropped into Save On Foods on the way home from work.

"Pity there isn't a Marks & Spencer in Jasper Avenue. I did used to enjoy their Pork, and Stand Pies."

She smiled, remembered the previous evening meal. Nice for a change but it was good to be home. Here, she could enjoy watching Wimbledon Tennis replays.

"Wow, it's sunny there... when it isn't raining."

And during the television advertisements she switched to the National CBC to bring herself up to date on the Lobster Pot debacle. Were licensed lobster fishermen still blocking the fishing boats of natives determined to fish for their rights?

Events had moved along. Now Chief Lawrence Paul of First Nation Congress was negotiating reparations. He suggested five hundred million dollars be offered to Burnt Church not to fish over forty two Lobster Pots.

"And good luck to you, mate!"

The telephone rang. Jessica eyed the instrument. Should she answer, it would be Brian? Her limbs refused to move, she could not pick up the receiver and listen to acrimonious remarks about her dual personality; she was worse than Jean Morningbird, druggie, prostitute and probably pusher.

The ringing stopped. He must be heartsick at her duplicity. Suddenly saliva dried in her mouth. She couldn't swallow. She put aside the tray, rushed to the sink and spat out chewed pie. The telephone rang again.

She sank to her knees; tears of hopelessness ran from blinded eyes. It seemed everything she touched turned on her: marriage, Vancouver job, Dirty Dick boss. And she couldn't even cry properly. Tears should bounce off her cheeks not run down inside her nose.

She wished her mum and dad were here. Oh, why had she left them so far away? Her mum would answer the phone and put Brian in his place. Her dad would sock the police on the jaw...

Maybe it was best not to have them near at this time.

JACK EYED THE replaced telephone. She either wasn't there or was declining to answer. She was hiding something, that's for sure. Why wasn't she at the SPCA where she was supposed to be working? Why was she picked up by the police? Why were the police interested in his association with Jean Morningbird, native to this city? On reflection, he thought not. Not your usual part-native anyway.

He went into the bathroom, viewed himself in the mirror. A sad face stared back. No wonder he couldn't maintain a relationship, he was too miserable a guy. At the first hurdle he crumbled. He'd been found wanting. Where was his compassion? Where's the love he felt for Jean? He should love her even if she's committed murder.

"Geez, I'm not that stupid!"

He'd phone again in an hour, she'd be home by then. That's if the police hadn't picked her up again.

"Oh, shut up, you whinger!"

He went into the lounge and switched on television to watch Wimbledon, sympathized with the English champion who, once more, experienced defeat at the hands of an American.

Thoughts of Jean and himself in the canoe and on the lake intruded. When he held her in his arms she felt right, belonged there. He eyed his watch, checked with the wall clock. In fifty minutes he'd phone Jean.

Chapter Nine

Jessica telephoned Brian after she had wiped her eyes free of tears feeling more than a little stupid. She wasn't a schoolgirl for heaven's sake, she was an adult; probably why the tears resembled large raindrops. The tears of frustration over a wayward husband were nothing compared to the avalanche produced by not taking Brian's phone call.

"Hello?"

"Hello Brian. It's me."

"Oh, I'm pleased you called. I've been sort of apprehensive. Your neighbor said the police whipped you away in their cruiser."

"Yes, you were right, Brian. That cannabis in the back garden. They were really annoyed about it."

"Is that what it's about? Phew, what a relief, Jean."

He didn't realize she wasn't Jean. She smiled in relief.

"You said you pulled them all out."

"They re-grew, apparently."

"How did they discover you'd illegal plants growing?"

"I couldn't hazard a guess, and they didn't say. They just appeared at my front door."

"Someone must have ratted on you."

"I was thinking about you all last night Brian."

"Were you? You surprise me. You didn't call all day."

"I had to give minute details of what I did to the plants, they were so fussy. And they examined my garage and cellar, but as you know there's nothing there."

"I don't have any knowledge of your garage or cellar."

"I didn't mention you knew about the plants because they're onto the Landscape Gardener seeing he didn't report them."

"You don't say."

"I thought it was best to keep your name out of it."

"Thank you, I appreciate that."

What else could she say? Brian seemed to be waiting for her to make all the moves.

"I was thinking... I'd like to go to Bonnie Doon Swimming Baths sometime this week, Brian. Do you fancy going tomorrow?"

"Thanks for the invite, but tomorrow would be awkward."

"Oh, how about Thursday night?"

"That'd be difficult. By the way, how'd you get home from the SPCA today?"

She froze momentarily. She used the bus, of course.

"A colleague gave me a lift to Jasper Avenue from the Clinic and then I caught the number one fifty one bus."

"Which colleague was that, Jean?"

"The one on the station platform in Churchill Square, remember?"

"I didn't see her. What's her name?"

"Julianne," was the first name that sprung to mind. And that was something else to worry about: another flaming name! As if she didn't have enough to contend with trying to remember her tribal ancestry.

"Julianne, uh?"

"Why are you curious about my colleagues, Brian?" Did he suspect she wasn't all she was cracked up to be?

"The entry phone bell's ringing. Thanks for calling, Jean."

Jessica eyed the dead telephone. Tears sprang up unbidden which made it difficult to replace the receiver. She sniffed, wiped her hand across a dripping nose. She'd lost him and it hadn't required much effort. She'd blown it but good. She'd have reacted the same way if he'd given her a similar run-around.

JACK STAYED his hand on the instrument to retain contact with Jean. He was adept at deception, what next? Computer fraud? Better still, manipulate geological data and create an imaginary gold bonanza. He'd retire a mogul, a multimillionaire.

"Don't be stupid! It's plenty impersonating Brian, the skydiver. I'd sure as hell not manage to impersonate a dubious entrepreneur."

He didn't enjoy being made a fool of. Did she think he didn't know nuts from bolts? Someone at SPCA was out of their tree, or she didn't work there. Which was it?   He stroked his bald spot and sighed. He enjoyed swimming. Pity he'd felt bloody-minded and cut off his nose to spite his face.

Was Jean proficient in swimming like her canoeing?   He smiled, remembered her determined rescue at the lake. She'd immediately swung into action concerned for his safety. And the moment on the beach locked in one another's arms, and his trying to avoid a knockout punch.

"Jean's no shrinking violet, that's for sure."

He crossed the lounge into Brian's bedroom and eyed the interior. How would Brian deal with Jean's secretiveness? How would his gung-ho condo mate act?

The room resembled Brian in many ways; skis propped against the wardrobe door in decorative fashion, and pictures of him covered the room alongside posters of air shows in which he'd participated.   Jack straightened the counterpane by the pillow, noticed pajamas stuck out untidily, and shoved them out of sight, sat on the edge of the bed undoing his good housekeeping, and viewed his feet.

"He'd solve the problem. What did Jean say she enjoyed doing?"

He shot over to the desk, removed and re-read Jean's first letter to Brian. A smile appeared at the corners of his mouth which gradually spread to his eyes making them crinkle.

"What a lovely person she is. So bright and bubbly."

When she's not hiding something.

"Oh, shut up, doubting Thomas."

Brian would know what to do. Brian would…

"The skis, yes!"

He covered the floor in a bound, opened the wardrobe door. Small parachutes used in skiing jump offs from high peaks were packed against one wall. He'd never attempted jumps, but he'd para-glided with Brian. It'd been exhilarating!

He hurried to the lounge telephone, sat down, checked the telephone legend then called the City Airport manager.

"Jack Haversky, here. My condo mate Brian Swartzkoff, Airborne Brothers, said I could help myself to equipment during his absence."

"That's his problem."

"Okay with you if I make use of the facilities?"

"Sure. If you have the keys you can gain access. If you haven't, then you can't. Good-bye. Thanks for calling."

"You're welcome. Have a nice day."

Jack hung up the receiver with a glow of triumph permeating his whole body. He quickly took out his pen and used the phone pad to make an itinerary.

First: Familiarize myself with Brian's hangar

Second: Invite Jean on a surprise date

Third: Find out where she really works

Fourth: Ascertain her background

He stared at the script. Anger mounted, he tore off and screwed up the page.

"I'm pretending to be Brian, not damned Hercule Poirot!" He tossed the missive viciously into the waste basket.

JESSICA WASHED up her dishes, cleaned the stove top and then threw the elements into the sink full of hot soapy water.

"Needs a cleaning anyway."

She busied herself with the interior of the oven on her hands and knees and even scrubbed the back and sides with oven cleaner.

"Stupid really, it hasn't been used that much."

IS THIS ALL THERE IS?

So she scrubbed harder to demolish the hurt; sat back on her haunches after rinsing down soapsuds, and confronted by a gleaming oven, started to cry.

"Oh, you crybaby! You blubbering crybaby!"

She whipped off rubber gloves and rose unsteadily.

"I must look a right mess with water cascading down my nose and chin. He'd really think I looked like a drowned dog if he saw me now."

She hurried into the bathroom, washed face, neck and arms then dried herself with a cuddly, but rough towel before eyeing her reflection, glowing with rude health.

"That's better, Jessica. Put a brave smile on it. Be positive, not negative! If you don't think you're worth something, no one else will. That's a fact!"

JESSICA CALLED IN at the YWCA, following work, to offer her services. She discovered from pamphlets at the Reception Desk in the entrance, 'Keep Fit' was scheduled for Sir Winston Churchill Square during 'Youth Activities Week Festival'.

She had fond memories of a certain man in the square. They'd laughed a little; consumed a lot; she'd lied atrociously; a suspicious dog sniffed her.

Marcia Murchant, rowing captain and on the organizing Festival Committee, emerged from the elevator, crossed towards Jessica with an outstretched hand.

"Good to see you, Jessica. How're you keeping?"

"All right, thank you Marcia. I've settled into my new house but it's lonely without you lot. I tend to rattle around like a pea in a drum, at times." She smiled fondly at receptionists busy taking in newcomers to stay for a few days. "Everyone made me feel so welcome." She'd been disconsolate on arrival at the 'Y' but they had extended the hand of friendship, included her in many activities including swimming and exercise sessions. She hadn't realized how much she missed them until now.

"I certainly felt a loss when I was making up teams." Marcia opened up a clipboard, a biro hovered expectantly.

Jessica got the message. "What do you want me to do at the festival?"

"I'm sorry it's short notice. Originally I thought of using you on reception."

112

"Reception would be fine with me."

"Yes, unfortunately you're needed elsewhere." Marcia took hold of her arm, led her towards the lounge with its spacious seating arrangement and tables to accommodate snack parties for residents and visitors. "One of my rowers sprained her wrist, so I'm caught short. Now, I'm okay for some slots, but Saturday...?"

"I'm all right for Saturday, I think, at least... I'm sure." Brian obviously wasn't asking her out, she might as well do something worthwhile to occupy her days. At least, it stopped her thinking of another man found wanting.

"I'm so pleased, Jessica. You've no idea how difficult it is to replace someone."

"Oh, I think I... What do you want me to do? Circulate and hand out pamphlets?"

"No, I'd like you to demonstrate the rowing machine, the roadrunner, weightlifter for firming butts etcetera, and any equipment on show." Marcia determined not to show weakness asking for a lot, ticked Saturday activities on her sheet.

"By crikey, I'll need a sponge to wipe off excess sweat."

"Ladies don't sweat, only horses remember? Ladies glow."

"So! I'll glow then, profusely."

"We'll supply the towels of course, and leotards with our initials. We want all the advertising possible in the time at our disposal."

"Oh gosh, everyone will see my all."

"Don't be shy, Jessica. You looked okay in leotards when you worked out."

"Glad you thought so. But that was here, not on show in front of gawking eyes."

"Come in for a workout and tighten up your muscles." She patted Jessica's stomach and hips with both hands. "We haven't seen you for three weeks. You're obviously in need of exercise."

"I've been busy, sort of, even worked out canoeing off Edmonton Beach."

"How was it?"

"Okay until we went for an unexpected swim when the canoe overturned. So you could say I'm keeping fit."

"Good on you. When are you coming in?"

She was persistent, Jessica had to give her that, and walked back to her Cavalier parked at the curb, climbed in and tried not to grin at feeling so wanted. She'd been hard pressed to say when she was available to attend Keep Fit classes. A priority for Marcia aware Jessica had rowed for Vancouver: she'd be an asset for their reserve.

She moved out from the curb bucking the traffic. She'd been occupied in more ways than one since she pretended to be Jean; dancing and dining, canoeing and picnicking. Don't forget the unexpected swim and roll around and passionate kiss on the beach.

"Forget him, Jessica. Just forget him."

Unfortunate the swimming session at the baths hadn't transpired. He was curt refusing Wednesday, then Thursday.

"I can't get away from Brian, darn it!"

She turned into Jasper Avenue at the lights. Strange, how everything beautiful tumbled to an inglorious end. She wasn't wanted by Brian, obviously; was yesterday's menu. Instead, on Saturday, she'd be sweating out her guts on physical education equipment in front of overdressed spectators. Talk about a spectator sport! She hoped they'd be suitably entertained.

"I wonder if they sell meat pies at Festival stalls?"

But then, the Health Department mightn't like open stalls selling meat pies. Pork especially would go off quite easily in the heat of the...

"Hey, wait a minute! They have fridges in those stalls."

DORINDA WAS IMPRESSED when Jessica explained at work next day she was assisting at the Youth Festival on Saturday.

"I'll bring David and have a look round." She patted Jessica on the back. "We'll be entertained, I know, watching you on the rowing machine. Maybe it'll get us motivated to join the 'Y' Keep Fit. David says a healthy body makes for a healthy mind."

"He's right, your David," the first time a David saying made sense. Jessica saw out of the corner of her eye the director approaching via Veronica's desk. Would he stop and chat with the poor girl, or lope over in their direction.

"I hope he doesn't find out, or I'm finished," indicated the office lecher touching Veronica. "I can't imagine anything worse than him seeing me in a leotard."

"No sweat if he does, if your Brian's there. He'll stop Dick's unwanted attention, that's for sure."

Jessica looked at her friend in dismay, reminded she hadn't mentioned Brian had cooled off; didn't want to mention it in case Brian took it into his head to restart the association. Then it suddenly struck her! What if Brian happened to come along to the festival? He'd discover she wasn't Jean Morningbird, but Jessica Walters! Oh, hecky thump!

"I'm not asking Brian along. I don't want him to see me in leotards!" She didn't wear a stuffed bra in leotards; bore the rounded look of all athletes.

"Oh, I'm disappointed, I'd like to have met him." She picked up a claim form due for processing. "Watch it," out of the side of her mouth and went to her desk. Both surreptitiously eyed the director head in their direction.

Jessica sat down, picked up a completed claim form and checked for errors. A shadow fell on her hands on the desk, her bottom pinched with familiarity.

"That you, Dick?" Without turning to check, she removed a bottle of wipeout from the drawer. "Of course it is, who else would..." Unscrewed the top; removed the heavily laden brush.

"Of course, Jessica, who else would?" Dick breathed hot breaths on her neck and fondled the overlapping cheek bottom. The tone of voice indicated the recipient was open to suggestion.

"Whoops-a-daisy!" Her arm jerked, white liquid shot onto his face. "Oh, dear!"

She turned, the brush of wipeout stroked against his lapel. He was frozen in shock momentarily before his fingers loosened their attachment to her cheek-bottom.

"Oh, I'm sorry about that." She emptied the contents on his head. "Wow! It's happening again, all over your hair, Dick!" She slipped out of her seat, strove to maintain a respectable distance from goo running down his face onto his collar. "You shouldn't have startled me, Dick," edged away. "Really you shouldn't."

Dick Chalmers stood upright, blinked rapidly and shook his head. Was it in disbelief or sheer necessity? Jessica and Dorinda didn't have a clue, but dodged flying wipeout.

"Look everyone!" Jessica pointed a finger at the sorry figure of the director. "Dick made me jump and I accidentally got wipeout all over him."

Everyone sniggered; aware she wanted witnesses in case he pressed for dismissal.

Dick felt his way blindly to the next desk, picked up a handful of tissues and wiped his face, staggered past desks on the way to the partition opening, with not a hand lifted to assist.

There was an appreciable silence whilst everyone listened for his walk onto the landing, then the closing of the washroom door brought instant relief.

"You've some nerve." Dorinda could hardly speak for laughter and bent over her desk. "Wait 'till David hears, he'll be in hysterics!"

"Hey, Jessica, where'd he touch you up?" Veronica and the others hurried up with thinners and tissues. "He gets me underarm from behind."

"He goes after my knees," thin Freda opened a bottle.

"He likes my hair." Brenda rubbed away spots on Dorinda's desk. "Likes to twirl it round his fingers."

"He blows on the back of my neck." Fran shuddered. "Gives me the creeps."

"He was fondling my bum, the dirty bugger." Jessica held out her arms for them to examine. "I know it overhangs the seat but he shouldn't make free with my parts."

"Reckon he's got any Thinners in the washroom, eh?" Thin Freda rubbed gently on arm spots.

"Who cares," Fran answered.

"It was in his hair as well as his face and neck." Veronica poured thinners onto a folded tissue and rubbed at spots of whitener on Jessica's chair. "He'll be a mess."

"He should be so lucky having friends with thinners." Jessica was turned around by the girls examining her attire. "Wonder what story he'll spin his wife?"

"Not the true one," chorused everyone.

For the remainder of the day Dick was noted for his absence; speculation abounded he visited an emergency department for treatment, but nobody really cared enough to pursue the matter.

Jessica got through the rest of the day half pleased and half apprehensive. Since the action wasn't planned, surely she couldn't be charged with 'Malicious Intent'?

JACK WORKED WITH a feeling of contentment at his desk. Doing something constructive, acting like flamboyant Brian was the answer, not timid Jack who...

Hey, don't be a downer. Think of Brian's strategies.

Each time anyone passed his open door in the corridor he looked up and smiled. It was mostly accounts clerks, engineers and draftsmen who benefited from his inner glow. Unfortunately, the only person to put a damper on him was Jeffrey Olivera.

"What's the matter with you, looking like you've scored?" Jeffrey's grin was pure evil. "Had a bit of rough last night, eh?"

"It's a problem for you I have a lady friend, Jeffrey?"

"That was no lady putting a mile wide smile on your face, Jack." Jeffrey sidled into the office, glanced at the geological graph Jack was working on as if it held a clue. "That was a hooker!"

"Piss off! You've a sewer for a mind." He stood and ejected him from the office with a persuasive push on both shoulders.

Jeffrey staggered into the corridor and the arms of the finance director, Mike Walsh.

"Wahoo!" Mike righted Jeffrey and stepped into Jack's office. "What's happening, Jack? You've some disagreement regards costs on the Yellowknife operation? If Olivera's running Accounts' objections past you, I'll deal with it. No need for violence."

117

"Nothing like that, Mike." Jack eyed Jeffrey dusting himself down to excuse himself from not jumping in to answer. "I took exception to something he said totally unconnected with work. It's all over with. No problem."

"Well, let's be adult and maintain a distance between private and official affairs. Remember our priorities while at the office, eh?" He looked at the conglomeration on the desk. "How's it going with the estimated yield? Worked out if it's a viable operation?"

"That's for sure. Excellent for putting down further cores."

"That's what we want to hear, Jack"

Jack opened up his cross-section map. "I'm looking forward to working in the field again. I guess I'm an outdoors man at heart."

Isn't that the truth? What with Jean and her secrets on the home front, and bigheaded Jeffrey at the office... I'm away!

THE WORK-DAY ended, eventually. Jack left the office with alacrity, he had things to do; he'd wasted enough time and wasn't getting any younger. He passed Jeffrey Olivera in the corridor and delivered a sour look. Jeffrey answered with a smile and a small salute which surprised Jack considerably. He'd expected retaliatory measures after ejecting the guy from his office.

So that's what put down the smart aleck. A bit of rough!

In his parking space at the back of Shellack Oil Exploration, Jack discovered a flat back tire on his Cadillac. How had that happened, he was careful about retaining air in his tires? He traversed rough tracks in the back blocks and good tire maintenance was a necessity.

He removed the jack from the trunk, jacked up the car and commenced pumping the tire. When it was full he listened for escaping air: there was none.

It didn't take a professor of psychology to determine what had occurred. Smart-aleck Jeffery had retaliated, not to his face the smarmy bastard, but behind his back. He'd watch him in future! And he'd also maintain a keen eye on his back!

He headed for City Airport, a short distance from work, and passed through the entrance gates to the hangars. A guard on duty flagged him down.

"Going to Airborne Brothers." Jack drew up alongside. "Brian Swartzkoff."

"They're away on a touring air show."

"I know. Brian shares my condo and I have his keys," dangled the evidence in front of the man's nose. "I've his permission to use the equipment."

The guard waved him on with a smile.

"I'm coming with a lady friend this weekend." Jack leaned from the window. "You'll be on duty, eh?"

"Unfortunately, but it's double pay on Sundays, so who's complaining?"

"See you. Have a nice day." Jack moved off.

He maintained a sharp lookout for maintenance staff and airport personnel when he drove past hangars with small craft visible through open doors. He'd been to the airport occasionally but not to reconnoiter whom he'd meet on the way.

Airborne Brothers' hangar was second to last in the line and he had traversed the run from the road without encountering anyone. Large commercial airlines were banned from City Airport, overseas and distance internal flights routed to International Airport; private planes were permitted to use airport facilities, and small businesses like Airborne Brothers, hence the quietness and lack of activity.

Fortunately for Jack, there was nobody around to ask awkward questions. He opened the hangar side door with his key, entered the cavernous dome and put on the light switch. Instantly, gloom was replaced by a bank of overhead lights that ran the length of the hangar.

Good, lights needed to ascertain the layout; engines, tires, gears, jacks, uniforms, coveralls: everything! He walked around the hangar mentally compartmentalizing and hoped it wouldn't be necessary to recall so much.

The paraglider engines were in an off section, and there were six of them, left behind from the Air Show. Maybe their itinerary didn't include paragliding activities, or they could be spares. Jack chose two and started them up one after the other, checked there was sufficient gas and they were ready for takeoff.

The parachute room contained huge tables which took up almost the entire length, the examination of canopies and ropes a priority. He chose two spined wings from the paraglider stand which held the clearance form: 'Ready for Use'.

In the office he opened drawers and unlocked filing cabinets, noted briefly the contents, which firms used Airborne services, where stationery was stored. He closed up, checked everything was secure in the hangar, put out the lights and left the way he had entered.

Chapter Ten

Jessica looked at the telephone in an injured fashion each time she arrived home from work. Traitor, why don't you ring? Each day it became more difficult to enter the house with the realization she was alone, not surrounded by workmates. A house wasn't a home unless it was shared. She remembered earlier days of her marriage, when coming home from work meant companionship with a husb...

She stopped thinking at that point not wishing to be reminded of pain filled days of discovery over Ronnie's perfidy, when she had been literally gobsmacked.

Each day that passed she didn't hear from Brian indicated more positively she was in the past tense, a has-been. Her marriage had failed and now a man friend had failed, just because... Why had it failed?

"Your marriage capsized on the rocks of harsh reality, and a man's friendship's floundered on the beach like a tossed up fish. There's something wrong with you. You turned Ronnie in the direction of a bit of crackling, and turned a lovely man off you, because you're stupid!"

She plugged in her newly purchased electric frying pan, rubbed Canola Oil on its surface, threw in two strips of bacon and waited for it to sizzle. Normally she enjoyed watching bacon fry, but not today.

Why did it have to change? He could have overlooked her deception if he'd loved her. He'd said as much when they'd rolled around on the beach and she'd tried to gouge out his eyes. She'd reminded him of a mongrel.

"Very nice!"

They'd overcome that obstacle. They went to the native stall and bought beads and a Canada Goose. She left the kitchen and in the foyer eyed the bird; every feather stood out under a layer of varnish.

"Lucky bird, you can't hurt, you can't even fly. Your wings have been clipped like mine. We're both flightless -"

The telephone rang.

"Yes?" It could be Brian.

"Hi, Jessica!"

"Hello, Marcia. Forgot something?" She had phoned into the 'Y' before leaving work and gone shopping; been thoroughly versed on what time to start on the morrow: eight o'clock sharp.

"Sorry to inform you, Jessica, but we've struck a rock. The guys helping set up the tents. Well, one of them has gone down with the gripe, and another got struck with a puck at hockey this afternoon. He'll be out of it completely according to his X-ray."

"Any more good news?"

"Could you arrange to be at Winston Churchill Square at seven am?" Her voice had a cringe at the start but quickly changed. "That's an angel! See you at seven, Jessica. Must rush! Bye for now! Have a nice day!" She hung up without waiting for a reply: hadn't dared.

"So what? I'm not going anywhere else," replaced the receiver and fluffed up her hair in the reflection above the bird. An image of Brian stood by her. "Oh boy! Now, I'm seeing things."

She reluctantly turned from her vision. No Prince Charming was coming to whisk her away on a white horse, and time was no problem. She'd go to bed and rise at her usual work time.

She returned to the kitchen, turned the bacon, and took a packet of macaroni cheese from the cupboard and a packet of mixed frozen vegetables from the freezer compartment on top of the fridge. What would she have for dessert?

The telephone rang again. Jessica turned, wondered whether she should answer or not. She walked into the living room and eyed the telephone. It would be Marcia with more good news, no doubt. She picked up the phone.

"Yes?"

"Jean, it's Brian,"

"Oh Brian," her heart leapt into her throat, knees became weak.

"I've been busy and unable to contact you. Have you missed me? I've suffered pangs of deprivation not seeing you."

"Oh yes," she perched on the edge of the armchair. "I was wondering where you were and what you were doing, and why I hadn't heard."

"I guess you've been busy walking your animals, grooming and giving them injections at the shelter, eh?"

Her stomach hit bottom. Good thing she was sitting already with weak knees or she'd be prostrate on the floor.

"Ha-Ha-Ha! You know me, I love walking, whether it's with a dog on a lead or just by myself. But tell me Brian, what have you been up to? High flying? Testing planes? Canoeing or fishing?" There was a long moment's pause. Had she been disconnected?

"I was organizing a surprise for you. Could you come out to the airport with me tomorrow morning? I've arranged something special."

"Oh, I can't tomorrow, Brian. It's Saturday, you see."

"Yes, I'm aware it's Saturday. I'm off from slaving during the working week and so are you. What are you doing? Can't you rearrange it?"

"I wish I could, but I've promised to help out someone. How about Sunday? Sunday is free... I think."

"Sunday is free? You're sure? I wouldn't want to impose on your commitments."

Oh boy, sarcasm she needed like a kick in the head.

"Yes, Sunday, would be best for me if you've no objection to me having a life of my own before I met you."

"I'll phone you again then."

He hung up before Jessica could say she was sorry, of course she would meet him on the Saturday. What did she care if the YWCA was short of demonstrators, her love life came first. A stomach bug and a puck injury took priority. Why couldn't her broken heart be attributed to a life threatening problem that required immediate attention?

A slow walk back to the kitchen to turn bacon which had passed the point of no return; savagely open the packet of macaroni which took revenge, and missiles flew in all directions across the kitchen floor. She sobbed, got down on her knees and picked up macaroni one piece at a time to replace in the box.

Why was everything so difficult? Why couldn't he be nice to her? Why was he so sarcastically suspicious?

"Because he suspects you're not all you make out to be, you stupid moran! You gave him plenty of reasons for mistrusting you."

She eyed macaroni in the box becoming wet with tears. Will salt tears spoil the taste? She rose to her feet, hung onto the kitchen unit for support.

"Naw, I'll just add less salt in the water."

The telephone shrilled.

Jessica dropped the packet on the countertop where it disgorged its contents; noticed the bacon curling with burn and hurriedly switched off the plug, raced into the living room and flung herself at the telephone.

"Yes?"

"Is that Mrs Walters?" A female voice.

"Why? Who wants to know?"

"How are you today, Mrs Walters?"

"What do you want?"

"I'm Jenny from the Leprosy Mission -"

"I'm not interested, Jenny. I've just lost a boyfriend, and burnt my bacon!" She slammed down the phone and stomped into the kitchen. "That'll teach them wanting me to contribute my hard-earned money."

She saw scattered macaroni on the kitchen top. At least it wasn't gathering dust on the floor, it would still be edible. She placed the macaroni in a sieve under running water before proceeding to cook it in a saucepan. And there was only one fitting end for the burnt bacon: the rubbish bag under the sink.

"Flaming Brian! Flaming bacon! Flaming cadging calls!"

JACK WALKED AWAY from the telephone. Why had he bitched at Jean? He had taken extreme measures to rectify his previous, surly behavior?

"Why, oh why?"

He wanted to fling himself into the lounge chair overlooking river valley, but the wisdom of age prevailed; he lowered himself into its depths and considered events.

124

Maybe he was too old for this game of courtship; he couldn't retain trust when faced by discrepancies. Why did she speak like a recently landed immigrant? No aborigine would have an English accent. No amount of service abroad would have a Canadian acquire the speech patterns Jean used when excited, off guard -

"That's it!"

When Jean was off guard she let down her defense; when on guard she stopped... speaking... gave herself time to think. He struck the side of the armchair decisively. Jean wasn't whom she pretended to be. She was afraid. Of what? Her nonexistent job at the animal shelter? He groaned. He was going round in circles.

To hell with it, he had enough to worry about with Jeffrey Olivera. Now, how could he spike that guy's guns? He rose to his feet, stretched, and ambled into the foyer, picked up the newspaper he'd left on his arrival home, too excited to read at the thought of asking Jean on a date tomorrow, highflying over green hills and...

Could she ski even? He'd only seen a photograph of her in ski clothes, holding skis. Maybe she'd been posing for the photographer. Maybe her ability to ski was as big a lie as being a kennel maid at the SPCA.

"Oh, geez!"

He sat in the armchair determined to eliminate all thoughts of Jean, looked at the amusements page. A lot to choose from. What would Jean like to visit?

"Oh, geez!"

JESSICA SAT in front of television and watched a documentary on salmon fishing. They were having a problem on the east coast. Fresh salmon weren't returning from the seas to breed in the rivers, only one in a hundred compared to previous tallies. Farm salmon fed with antibiotics had escaped over the years, mingled with fresh salmon out at sea, and either killed them with new strains of germs or eaten the smaller, fresh salmon.

A scientist indicated the spill that young farm salmon used on their way to the sea; couldn't understand why the salmon didn't return the same way. His demonstration had Jessica so openmouthed she forgot to eat.

First of all the scientist netted the young fresh salmon from the tributary where it had been born; placed it in a measuring box, injected a color trace into its skull, cut a piece out of the dorsal fin, and dropped the fish into the spillway. The fish tumbled down the slope head over tail, dropped down a small waterfall and landed in a wooden bucket which overturned to eject fish and water into rapidly flowing waters.

"You've got to be kidding! I wouldn't return, either!"

She was thankful she wasn't having fish for dinner. But her plate on the tray bore evidence of someone playing at eating. Despite the first disastrous attempt at christening the new electric frying pan, the second lot of bacon had proved a resounding success; vegetables and macaroni cheese had turned out well too, but she was too depressed to appreciate the meal.

"Between Brian's suspicions and Dirty Dick's shenanigans, it's no wonder I'm a casualty. And I'm still recovering from that Vancouver bastard's infidelity!"

Dick Chalmers had been absent for two days. When Friday came round it had surprised everyone in the Claims Department, just before they finished at four o'clock, to see him arrive and go directly to his office.

A buzz of interest had permeated the secretaries.

"Guess who's just turned up like a bad penny?" Veronica hurried up to Jessica.

Jessica looked up from signing a consent claim form for the recipient to be entitled to money whilst she had her baby, and for three months afterwards, or until Social Services traced and put the bite on her deadbeat husband.

"I don't need to, Veronica. I could sense him."

"Way to go! Do you have extrasensory perception, eh?"

"Nope! I got a whiff of his aftershave over the partition. Did you manage to see him? Was his face white?"

"Baby pink." Veronica giggled, picked up coat. "Reckon he was blushing?"

"It'd take more than embarrassment to make him blush." Dorinda joined in from the filing cabinets where she was locking up. "My David says it always comes round to everyone getting what he deserves."

Veronica paused buttoning up her coat. "I guess we're back with our leader when we start the new week?"

"I suppose so." Jessica removed her handbag from the drawer. "Sad isn't it? We enjoyed his absence!"

All three had parted on a laugh, aware the following Monday there would be a totally different atmosphere.

The ringing of the telephone brought Jessica back to the present. She pushed aside the tray, stopped and stared, finally lifted the receiver.

"Yes?" determined to be even nastier if it turned out to be another panhandler after her hard-earned cash.

"That you, Jessica, love?" A Yorkshire voice came down the line. "How are you, love, we haven't heard from you for ages? What have you been doing? Are you getting out and about meeting new people, and forgetting that Ronnie?"

What could she tell her mum? She'd behaved like Peter the Apostle, not denying but omitting their very existence to Brian. She shouldn't have committed such a reprehensible act; it was unworthy of a dutiful daughter. Her parents had disagreements, cajoled Jessica to take sides but that was nothing, a mere annoyance; indicated only how deep their feelings were for her and for one another.

As a seven year old she had suffered each pulling her onto their side of an argument. She learnt to be discerning, argued both for and against, which finally targeted their wrath on her; alienating her whilst they aligned themselves against their judgmental daughter. Afterwards, it was a case of hugs and kisses, until the next time.

Jessica smiled. Each had a role to play in life and hers as peacemaker made her an easy target. But now, she had to square her conscience with her parents.

"Oh Mum, you've no idea how good it sounds hearing your voice. I miss you Mum. You and dad, I do miss you."

"Ee, love, you sound downhearted. We're just over those blessed mountains."

"Those mountains aren't the only obstacles for me, Mum. I've other things gnawing away at my inside."

"You've not got cancer, have you?"

"No! It's the worry about my new job, and… and people and other things."

"Don't worry any longer love. Much as your dad hates the thought of mountain roads going up and down, twisting bends and precipices, we'll be coming as soon as possible: if he knows what's good for him."

AT THE YOUTH festival, hustle and bustle predominated in the un-orderly manoeuvre of spectators from one exhibit to another in Sir Winston Churchill Square. They meandered freely, ignored walkways of grass matting in the search for space, unused oxygen to breathe; some used benches spread around or dashed into tents to view and finger objects on sale; others entered tents connected to youthful endeavors, how to educate, train, excite, to hold the attention of little darlings.

Jessica, at the rear of the YWCA tent demonstrated the stationary cycle amongst a group of housewives with young children. Hardly the place that would interest children, but mums were tired of walking and it was entertaining watching sweat glisten on the demonstrator's forehead.

A child came close to the spinning front wheel and smiled. Jessica's heart gave an extra beat. Was she going to be friendly or was this a put-on? Not having any children of her own, she was in unchartered territory. The child put a finger onto the spinning tire that resembled a fairy spinning wheel and made a whizzing noise.

"Don't do that!" Jessica quickly brushed away the hand.

The child looked at a finger bearing evidence of rope burn. Her face screwed up, mouth opened wide, eyes narrowed. A scream rent the air.

"Ah, good grief!" Jessica stopped peddling, held out a sympathetic hand.

"Excuse me!" The mother stepped forward. "Leave my kid alone, vicious woman!" She struck Jessica's hand and snatched up her squealing child.

"But I didn't want her to get hurt!"

Jessica sat on the exercycle shattered at the turn of events. There developed a gradual movement away from the perfidious demonstrator by wary mums. Everyone could hear the child's wail as she exhibited her damaged finger.

"I tried preventing her touching the wheel." Jessica slipped from her perch and went over to the mum. "But she was too quick for me, honest."

"Keep away from us. You're trouble, eh?" The general consensus seemed to bear out that statement. "You've no right to be around kids."

Backs were turned on Jessica; mums and children headed for the awning covered entrance. Jessica hurried to Marcia at the table handing out literature on YWCA and YMCA activities.

"Ran into trouble one hour after opening?" Marcia watched the general exodus. "What happened, Jessica?"

"The mum blamed me for allowing her child to touch a spinning tire." Jessica rubbed the hand where she'd been smacked. "And she walloped me."

"Walloped you? With what?"

"Her hand, the cheeky beggar! It was her responsibility to look after her daughter, not mine. How did I know she'd stick her finger where it wasn't wanted," which reminded her of Dirty Dick: not a pleasant thought.

"Never mind, it's all in the past now. Mums and kids've gone." Marcia gave her a comforting pat on the shoulder, pointed her in the direction of the rowing machine. "How about going on the rower? The equipment needs a good workout, it seems to be stiff. I've tried it. I think transporting it here in the truck, did some damage."

"Right!" Jessica eyed the rowing machine with no bodies around it. Good, she'd be able to vent her anger on rowing. "See you later." She ambled over, sat on the long leather seat, inserted feet in the forward stirrups, and grabbed the handles to row.

Good grief, Marcia wasn't kidding! The machine was intended the demonstrator made it appear easy, to encourage others to take up the sport. She strained every muscle lying full length on the seat to pull back on the oars; sat up, turned to the right and with both hands pushed back an oar, turned to the left and pushed back the other oar. With both oars in her hands she could row, once more ending up prone on the seat.

Gradually, spectators arrived and as Marcia predicted, rowing became easier, no longer requiring pushing back the oars one at a time. Instead, she exerted every muscle flat on her back, pushed the oars forward then sat upright to row properly.

Like a flaming, slave ship navvy!

IS THIS ALL THERE IS?

Sweat dripped from armpits, covered ever-widening circles on the leotard, and glistened down her forehead, along her nose and into her eyes. However, her eyes were closed with the effort of concentration so it didn't bother her. Her nostrils weren't blocked though; she could smell aftershave, a hated aftershave.

Oh, dear Lord, he'd arrived and was leering over her. She squinted through eyelashes when in the prone position, but couldn't see properly, blinded by running sweat. Would he place a hand on her? She was surrounded by people, he wouldn't dare be familiar. Maybe he'd move away if she kept on rowing, it couldn't be a pretty sight, so much sweat and effort. But then, he enjoyed breast watching. Was he titillated eyeing her flat chest, observing it pump up and flatten with the strain of each pull on the oars?

Oh dear, why did she volunteer for this humiliation? She hadn't wanted to do it. Marcia had made her! Marcia made her feel wanted; she wasn't a cast-off. She was ashamed at pretending to be someone else; ashamed at denying the presence of her parents; ashamed at fooling her mother and friends at work; ashamed at taking in Brian, who was so lovable and kind. She made him nasty and disagreeable. She wasn't a nice person. She deserved to be punished on this flaming contraption with a despicable pervert staring at her.

"I'm putting oil on the joints, Jessica," Marcia's voice reached her through the pain of remorse and muscle agony. "Keep on rowing."

All right for some! She was pleased she couldn't continue self mortification, she'd struck bottom.

"See! That's working better." A pat on the shoulder and a word of encouragement from Marcia before Jessica felt her presence departing. Then wonders of wonders, the rowing became easier, then easy. She no longer had to lie full length on the padded seat exerting reluctant oars to work; she could remain sat up and row properly. She could even open her eyes! Stinging sweat made her close them.

"You're putting a lot of effort into rowing, Jessica. It's a great spectator sport from where I'm standing."

She recognized the voice; it went with the aftershave. Don't answer, keep on rowing. Anyway, what could she say? Pleased to see you? Like hell!

"Maybe you'd like to be cooled down?" A female voice Jessica couldn't recognize.

"It'd be welcome." Jessica opened her eyes in time to observe a cascading milkshake leave a shaker, headed for her; the next split second her face was drenched in milkshake. She realized it was strawberry when she licked parched lips.

"How'd you like having something flung in your face, eh?" the same spiteful voice continued. "Bitch!"

There was a murmur of disapproval around Dick Chalmers and his wife when Jessica blindly stood with splayed legs astride the machine. She eyed them blearily through milkshake; at least she could now see without smarting sweat in her eyes. The rotund, angry woman by his side? Dick's wife, obviously. What story had he told her about the whitener?

"You didn't have to do that, dear." Dick took hold of the milkshake carton. "It wasn't necessary."

"Call yourself a man allowing that flat-chested woman to take liberties?" She elbowed him and snatched back the carton.

"What liberties, you crazy woman, she was flat on her back?" A fat man with a skinny wife stepped forward, waved his fat finger in front of Dick's wife's face.

"You should be put away, eh?" another man contributed. "You're the bitch, not her."

"You're a nasty bitch," from skinny wife.

"She wasn't hurting you."

"You've some nerve, lady."

"She's no lady behaving that way. She's a cow!"

Jessica was assisted from the rowing machine by solicitous hands which tried to avoid direct contact with milkshake.

"You okay?"

"Yes, thanks," she accepted a tissue.

"Sure you're okay, eh?"

"You'll be needing a wash, I reckon."

Jessica observed the Chalmers' ignominious departure under escort from the tent by male demonstrators and Marcia, and the enthusiastic help of witnesses to the incident.

"Thank you so much, you're most kind." Jessica smiled at the remaining people and went towards the entrance. How, in all that's wonderful, could she explain this second incident to Marcia?

DORINDA AND DAVID were on a different walkway to the one the Chalmers used when exiting the tent. Dorinda drew her husband's attention to her boss and his wife.

"Would you like to say Hi! to my boss, David?"

"Sooner say, 'Good-bye,' to him."

Dorinda giggled, then observed Jessica wiping down her frontage at Marcia's station, and pulled her husband in that direction.

"Hey, Jessica!" Dorinda eyed her friend's wet leotard. "You're supposed to be demonstrating how easy and enjoyable it is."

"Dick's wife threw a milkshake over me. I was just explaining to Marcia about our randy boss."

Dorinda eyed the departing Chalmers. "If that's what he has to live with at home I don't wonder he acts out a fantasy at work."

"Bosses like that should be pulled out of the workplace." Marcia handed out literature to a youth with a Mohican haircut. "They're gone Jessica. Don't let it worry you; the guys have their number if they try to come back."

"Sure looks tough work, Jessica." David walked around her. "Hope they're paying you well."

"She doesn't get paid, silly." Dorinda whispered to David. "It's volunteering."

"For that hassle I'd expect payment." David held out a hand for Jessica to shake. "Seems silly asking how you are, when it's obvious you're exhausted."

"It's only spilt milk, David. Nice to see you." Over his shoulder she saw Brian standing stock-still on the walkway looking at her. Directly at her! Oh Lord, she was in a leotard with a flattened bosom, wet through with milkshake and with friends who knew her as Jessica Walters, not pusher, Jean Morningbird!

"I'll be back in a minute." With a hand covering her face, and an apologetic smile to Dorinda and David, she scurried under the awning and dodged around spectators to the back of the tent.

What an idiot! There was no back door to a tent, she was trapped! She hid behind a group watching push-ups by enthusiastic keep fit artists with muscles that glistened with sweat, not milkshake. She observed Brian stretch his neck to see from the back of the group, and ducked down. With bent knees she shuffled around people; got another spectator sport between them. Kung Fu. Here, there were boys and tall men who afforded plenty of coverage for her to escape detection.

Marcia appeared surprised at her approach, walking apelike, with knuckles almost touching the ground.

"A little cramp, I suppose." Another flaming lie to remember! "Or maybe a creak in the back after rowing."

"Don't worry, Jessica. Go on the trampoline when you've dried off. It'll loosen cramps and sort out any aches and pains."

"You're all heart, Marcia."

David and Dorinda caught sight of her hurrying along the walkway into the mobile toilets, and shrugged.

"Perhaps another occasion will present itself for a visit., eh David?"

"So long as it's not a brush-off like the last one."

JACK FELT LIKE a stalker in his search of the YWCA tent. So that's why Jean couldn't meet him that morning, she was demonstrating equipment. But why hadn't she mentioned it? Was she ashamed of the all too revealing leotard? She looked flat-chested, but then everyone did. That was no reason for holding out; he wasn't a bosom man, but a nice eyes and mouth man. After going around the tent twice he conceded defeat.

She was hiding! Well, to hell with her! He wasn't a monster from which a woman had to run and hide. A stalker, maybe, but not a monster. He'd have a drink at the Territorial Club before going home and try to eliminate the taste of unrequited love.

"Do you know when Jean Morningbird demonstrates again?" He asked Marcia busy delivering literature at the entrance.

"We don't have a Jean Morningbird with us. Maybe she's at another tent." She handed him a pamphlet. "Our itinerary."

"Thanks. I reckon I made a mistake."

"Come and have a workout free, to assess if it's suitable for you."

"Okay, that sounds, that sounds... Thanks."

He departed, with the low esteem of a moran. How come he misinterpreted Jean so often? She didn't work at the SPCA and now she wasn't demonstrating at the YWCA. Either he was stupid, picked up incorrect signals, or he was seeing Jean when she wasn't there. He knew he... loved her...

Was that it? He saw Jean because he wanted to, hoped to?

A fluttering in the pit of his stomach brought him to a halt on the walkway. A man following with a tray of fries, hamburgers and cokes from a stall, halted quickly; spilt contents and an angry tirade followed Jack's hasty departure from the scene.

JESSICA DIDN'T HURRY cleaning herself in the toilets. There was a handbasin with running water, mirror and a bountiful supply of paper towels, for which she was truly thankful, for sponging down her leotard.

"Thank the Lord she doesn't drink acid, otherwise I'd be full of holes."

What tale had Dick spun his wife? What possible excuse for getting wipeout on him? Not the truth obviously for her to be so angry at Jessica. She shrugged, eyed herself in the mirror. She'd pass for muster. Anyway she'd shortly be working up another sweat on the trampoline.

She was wary exiting the mobile toilets; eyes swiveled in every direction in her search for Brian along the different walkways. He probably left the tent once he realized she wasn't there. Where was he? She couldn't miss him he was so tall, and his bald patch shone on his handsome head. When it was evident there was no Brian, she experienced an indefinable sorrow knowing she'd lost him yet again: it became more hurtful each time.

In the tent Jessica scurried on bent knees towards the trampoline, just in case. She was pleased he wasn't present to observe her calisthenics, and sad because he missed her showing off. Every time she reached the peak of her bounce, well above the heads of spectators, she searched for him; also maintained a sharp lookout for Dick's wife who might be inclined to pounce on her once more: not with harmless milkshake this time, but hemlock.

If she hadn't been occupied watching out for Brian she wouldn't have missed a small boy's action. He placed an inquisitive hand in the opening where tarpaulin and steel supports met. A scream of agony on her next bounce had Jessica double over in midair and land on her stomach, eyeballing the small face puckered in pain, pulling back on his trapped hand.

"Oh, what have you done?" Jessica's face screwed up also when the mother smacked the exhibitionist's bottom.

"Get off quick! Let loose my kid!"

Chapter Eleven

Jessica spent a night tossing and turning in agony, aware she'd thrown away true love; love she could no longer deny. She hadn't been acquainted with Brian very long, but realized, this was the man with whom she wanted to spend the remainder of her days.

And they'd be extremely short days if they were anything like the diabolical occurrences in the YWCA tent. It wasn't enough for a child to almost lose its finger and be upbraided by an irate mother; assaulted by a mother when her child placed his hand where he shouldn't, there was also the angry wife of a lecher to contend with. Would Mrs Chalmers come to her home and resume where she had left off in the tent? And then, to crown all, silly Brian appeared.

Maybe he wasn't certain it was her. Maybe he thought he'd made a mistake, hadn't recognized her for Jean but a close facsimile. What in all that's wonderful could she say if he asked her straight out? She could hardly tell the truth: 'I didn't want you to find out I wasn't Jean Morningbird'.

Oh, what a cloth head she was making up such a lie. She should have realized when she pretended to be Jewish it would be difficult, but then she opted for being aborigine. She hit her forehead a blow lying on the pillow.

"There's something wrong up there, you hear?"

She arose early thinking of the possibility of Brian phoning. He'd mentioned a surprise outing in store for her. Maybe, just maybe he'd forgiven her brusqueness when she retaliated at his sarcasm.

"And pigs might fly!"

She tied loosely the short, striped black and white satin robe on her still damp body after a quick shower and went into the kitchen to prepare breakfast. Shortly, the three and a half minute egg was removed from bubbling water and placed in the eggcup on its own patterned saucer.

"Looks nice." She put toasted fingers on the matching side plate. "A good buy, Jessica. You did all right for yourself choosing this set."

The doorbell rang.

"Yippee! Brian's come." Jessica hurried along the corridor, flung open the door. "Good morning!" Her robe parted, showed an abundance of flesh with her grandiose gesture.

"It sure is." Dick Chalmers strode past her with a bunch of flowers. "Enervating to say the least. Similar to the feelings of arousal when you displayed your all on the rowing machine." He leaned against the foyer divider, the visiting beau come to woo.

"Get out, you... you randy warthog!" Jessica flung wider the door, gestured for him to leave, not realizing her robe showed leg up to the thigh line.

"Not a nice name, Jessica. You can do better, I'm sure. After all I'm bringing you flowers." Dick strode into the living room, observed how his supervisor lived; flowers in a vase on the coffee table long past their sell-by-date. He thrust the bunch into it not heeding water overspill.

"Didn't you hear me, Dick-head? I said, Get Out! And put a hold on that thing in your trousers!"

"You can do the honors, my dear." He gestured to the flowers. "A small tribute to make amends for my wife's stupid action with the milkshake." Lust rose. Jessica stood with arms akimbo, a deep V breast indentation forming. "Oh, Jessica..."

"Sod off with your wife's actions!" Jessica stormed towards him with a raised arm. "It's your action I'm worried about. Get on your bike, moran! You're neither needed nor wanted."

Dick didn't wait for the arm to fall, he turned and hurried into the kitchen with a hop, skip and a jump of joy.

"Oh, in time for breakfast, Jessica. You were expecting me?" He negotiated the island between himself and oncoming Jessica. "You bought this lovely patterned breakfast set for my benefit, I know," hand to chest, hamming it up to the hilt.

"Spare me the nauseating act of seduction, you pitiful man, you. I said to, Get Out!" She rounded the island. "And I'm not kidding, I want you out of here!"

"Oooe, Jessica," moved to the side. "Excite me more!"

"You can leave in one piece now," Jessica opened the island knife drawer, "or several pieces later." She withdrew a chef's carver, wielded it menacingly.

"Take your choice. I'm not particular whether I start on your neck or your John Willie," and leapt.

"Oooe, Jessica!" Dick sprang to the opposite side of the island, held the top and leaned towards her. "You're giving me a turn on."

"You dirty, rotten sod! I'll turn off your water!" She leapt with a swinging carver.

"Oooe!" Dick sprang to the opposite side. "Stop it, I like it!"

JACK DREW UP behind the Daimler. Who was visiting Jean at this time of the morning? Or, had someone stayed overnight? And why was the door open?

He left the Cadillac, hurried up the path and nearing the house heard sounds of altercation issuing from within.

It's a good thing he'd arrived in time to protect Jean!

Intent on rescue he failed to notice the neighbor across the way, apparently walking his dog, pause, and peer curiously over his hedge.

JESSICA SAT astride Dick on the kitchen floor, the carver at his throat.

"How do you feel now, stupid moran? Still in the mood for a bit of nucky? Still feel randy, you dirty bastard?"

"That's for sure." Dick grinned; sensitive hands played up and down her bare thighs. "What strong muscles you have." His voice deepened to the low growl of the wolf man. "All the better to grip me with, eh?" His hand slid inside her leg. "Come on Jessica, do a Monica on me."

"You dirty bastard, as if I'd -"

"Jessica, undo my zipper and give me a stroke."

"I'll stroke you, you dirty bugger! I'll Cut It Off!"

She was unable to complete the swing. Her hand was caught by Brian's, his face glowering, standing over them.

"Leave him to me, love," pulled her off her perch.

"Oh Brian," relieved beyond measure. She'd been all set for the kill and prevented at the last moment from going beyond the point of 'no return'.

"You rat-bag!" Jack hauled Dick upright by his waistband. "You filthy, rotten rat-bag!"

"Cut it out!" Dick pulled back from the madman. "Loosen up!"

"Go on! Give it to him, Brian!" Jessica cajoled from behind him.

"Get your effing carcass out of here!" Jack jerked him viciously out of the kitchen. "You despicable rat-bag!"

"Thank goodness he's going." Jessica followed them. "He was fouling up my kitchen with his presence."

"Get off me!" Dick was propelled across the living room and into the foyer. "Leave me alone!"

"Who is he?" Jack spared her a glance. "Do you know the guy?"

"He's my boss." Jessica wielded the carver in case Brian relaxed his hold and the slime ball escaped justice. "Let me at him, Brian. Just let me prick his bit of pride with this."

"Don't let her near me with that pig sticker!" Dick belatedly concluded Jessica offered bloodletting not love play.

"Your boss, eh? The one who prevents phone calls reaching you at the SPCA?"

Jessica was mute: her chickens had come home to roost.

"Here's a message from me, bonehead!" Jack placed both hands on Dick's shoulders and shook him, then clouted his face left and right with open hands. "Get the telegram, piss-pot, or do you want an e-mail?" And twisted his nose end.

"I think he's got the point now." Jessica prodded Dick's rump with the carver to further impress the idiot.

"Don't let her injure me!" He held his nose with one hand; the other outflanked a prodding carver.

"You're attentions aren't required, horny guy!" Jack's face in his. "You bother my lady again and I'll be doing the castrating, not you."

139

Naturally, he was speaking from the assumption he was addressing a veterinary surgeon, but Dick wasn't to know that and experienced a sudden fear: there were now two about to abort his manhood.

"I'm okay with that. Let me go now."

"And don't harbor ideas about retaliation at work, because I'm onto you, guy." For the moment Jack imagined he was speaking to Jeffrey Olivera. "If my lady says one word about you bothering her, or preventing any phone calls getting through, then I'm after you!" He thrust his face into Dick's straining backwards. "Comprehend?"

"Ye-es, I do."

Jack threw him out of the front door.

Dick hurtled down the steps and didn't stop galloping until he arrived at his car.

"Thank goodness, he's gone." Jessica touched Jack's elbow as he stood arms akimbo watching the scum-bag's departure.

Dick put his hands on the hood to steady himself and looked at them standing in the doorway. She's a cow! Sends out the wrong signals. No wonder her ex-husband said I was welcome to her.

Jessica noted the absence of the neighbor with his invisible dog. Funny, he was usually about. He couldn't have missed the arrival of her visitors. He was probably watching from behind his curtains.

"I hate violence but sometimes it's necessary." Brian dusted himself down feeling slightly ashamed. "That's the only message that kind of guy understands."

"I liked being referred to as My Lady, Brian." Her sentimental mood swung to one of horror. The next door neighbor on his front porch held the Sunday morning newspaper delivery and was eyeing, openmouthed, the happenings across the hedge.

He's thinking he was premature imagining she was different from Jean Morningbird. She was having a brawl on a Sunday morning when decent people were attending church! He'd assume they were lovers fighting over a whore? She shuddered, drew back and placed Jack's body between her and an accusative stare.

Dick Chalmers clambered into his car with a different perspective on neighbors. He gave the inquisitive guy a rude two finger salute.

The neighbor staggered back into his hall as if struck with a fist.

Jessica shuddered again. Oh dear Lord, will it never end this humiliation she'd brought on herself pretending to be something she wasn't? Then reality kicked in. What a silly Billy! She was known as Jessica Walters to Dirty Dick, not Jean Morningbird. Her impersonation had nothing to do with this unfortunate incident. Good thing the two men hadn't taken to discussing her name, or names.

Jack waited to see Dick drive off before he turned to Jessica backed into the foyer, chest heaving, worry lines between her brows.

"You are My Lady, Jean. Come on, I'm here," held out his arms and closed the door with a foot. "Let it all hang out; tell me everything."

"What, what do you want to know?" What on earth could she tell him? More lies, that's what. She was relieved that bastard had been expelled from her home. He'd got the message all right, this time. She wasn't a desperate, wronged woman seeking solace in the arms of a lecher. Jack's arms tightened around her, the meat carver hung loose, touched her knee. Would she really have used it?

"I want you should know I'm here if you need me." He kissed her head and felt Jean's arms tighten around his waist, hard. The carver, he guessed, was what hit him in the butt and hoped it wouldn't cut the material, or worse. Jessica needed love and strength, apart from his requiring the 'Use Of'. "I'll spill his guts if you say the word, love."

"Oh Brian, you don't know how good it sounds to hear you call me, 'love'." She hugged him hard.

"Is that vet the reason they don't acknowledge you at the SPCA, love?" He pulled her free to look into her face.

"Who did you speak to?" She made certain her eyes were round, surprised and innocent.

"I couldn't get passed the reception."

"Er... Maryanne is jealous of me." Another name to remember with Jean Morningbird! "No reason why, because I don't encourage him. She gives out negative replies to any enquiries about me." Would this suffice, had she

141

explained enough, his expression was still suspicious? "And they do like to keep lines open for emergencies."

"So that's why she hung up on me." His face cleared and he almost smiled. "That makes sense. You don't tie up emergency lines with unnecessary trivia."

He'd bought her explanation. Oh, the relief!

"I've just boiled an egg." Jessica headed for the kitchen, led him along by the hand. "Would you like one? Have you had breakfast yet?" She decided she'd wash the carver before it went back into the knife drawer, it had been on the bastard's throat and he could have spread germs on the steel. Jack was looking at her delayed breakfast hungrily. She smiled, took placemats from the linen drawer and set them on the table with cutlery.

"Your egg and toast looks better than the bowl of cornflakes I had an hour ago. And that exercise sure worked up a hunger," and wondered if he'd said the wrong thing. Hunger for what, she'd be thinking?

"I'll pop an egg in for you. The water's still on the boil, or would be if that randy Romeo hadn't put in an appearance."

Jack put his arms around her waist, followed her step by step when she took an egg from the fridge.

"I'm a two egg man, actually, love." He kissed the top of her head. "Your egg will be cold, cook another."

"Right you are, love." Jessica was thrilled to her toes. He loves me, he loves me! She took out two more eggs.

"I'm pleased you have brown ones. I've always enjoyed the taste of brown eggs since I was a kid," and cuddled her hard.

"I think it's supposed to be our imagination, love. All eggs are the same, whether they're brown, white or speckled. I'm lucky, a chap brings these eggs into work."

"Of course, the vets will be in on fresh farm produce."

Wow, be careful, stupid git! Change the subject quick! "Would you like toast, I've Winnipeg Rye or plain white?"

"You choose," turned her face up to his, so open and trusting, "but I prefer Rye."

He helped move her arm to open the freezer top door and take out a loaf of Rye bread. She removed from the wrapping three slices frozen white with frost.

"Good thing we're toasting it." He kissed her hair. "Do you always keep your bread in the freezer?"

"Where else, love? It only takes a jiffy to defrost."

"I use a breadbox."

"But there are two in your apartment. Your bread won't go stale like mine."

She snuggled into his arms after replacing the bread in the freezer; it felt she was home, belonged, beloved.

Jack turned her face up to his, their lips met and clung together. They parted, eyed one another, imprinting on their retinas the fine lines around the eyes, the color of the iris and the shape of eyebrows, hairline and lips.

"You kiss with your mouth shut," perused her lips. "Every time?"

"And my teeth clenched. I don't like swapping spit. Never have. Ever since I was a young girl at a party. We were playing post office and a boy wouldn't let go my lips. It turned me off wet kisses ever after."

"A dry kiss it is then, from here on." He chortled and squeezed her. "It's a good precaution with the prevalence of AIDS; you can control the mixing of intercourse juices with a condom but the salivary tract is a different matter."

"Oh boy, you make it sound cold and clinical."

"I was just stating a fact."

"Talking about sex, do you know if your sperm has fins?"

"I believe spermatozoon have tails," smiled impishly. "But you know, I can swim."

"I know you can dogpaddle," smiled back impishly. "That isn't swimming."

"Do you want to get pregnant?"

"I do. Can your sperm swim upstream?"

"The last time I looked they appeared in excellent condition. However, we can practice and if unsuccessful -"

"It's a hard job for sperm, having to race against a million others and latch onto and fertilize an egg. If the egg's difficult to penetrate, it'll fail." Had that been her problem?

"Especially if it's hard-boiled."

"That, my man, hadn't crossed my mind." They both checked the water was ready for the eggs.

"Make it easy for the little guys," he cuddled her closer, her cheek-bottoms fitted neatly into his hands. Stand on your head then they'll be swimming downstream, my lady."

"They probably wouldn't be able to concentrate, for laughing, my man." She reluctantly moved out of the circle of comfort and placed three eggs in bubbling water.

Jack observed her carefully from his relaxed stance, his weight on the island. It wasn't the first time a woman had cooked breakfast for him, but the only occasion he had enjoyed this type of conversation. He loved watching her movements, so graceful, deft and capable.

"I thought I saw you at the Youth Festival in Sir Winston Churchill Square, yesterday, Jean."

The strident crash when the lid clattered onto the pan shook both of them.

"Ah, what did I look like?" She spun round to look, eyes wide and innocent. "Ha-Ha-Ha! Youthful, uh?" Turned back and propped the lid properly on the pan.

"You wore a delightful leotard." He looked abashed. "But I couldn't see properly. And this look-a-like-you disappeared. But she was a dead wringer for you, Jean."

"That's nice. I have a double." She placed slices in the wide toaster then checked there was sufficient butter in the butter dish.

"So good, they made two of you." He laughed with her. "I even asked them when Jean Morningbird was coming back to demonstrate."

"Ha-Ha-Ha!" Jessica dropped the butter dish lid. "What did they say?"

"Made me feel more of a love-sick calf. Said you didn't belong with them and to try another tent." He struck his forehead gently. "Geez, I felt stupid."

144

"Anyone can make a mistake, my man." Jessica carried the new egg side plates to the table. "What tent were you in?"

"The YWCA tent." He looked into cupboards until he found the eggcups, took one and placed it alongside Jean's on the bench and tossed the cold egg into the garbage bag under the sink. "It was geared for demonstrating equipment at the 'Y'." He stood over the pan and moved the eggs around with a spatula. "I was handed a pamphlet and offered a free session of Keep Fit."

"I've been thinking of you recently, Brian. Quite a lot, in fact, and I think you should know..." Jessica wet dry lips, saw him stiffen and stop stirring the eggs. "It's probably because I'm getting attached to you."

Now, you idiot now! Tell her your name isn't Brian!

"Your name's printed on my forehead; always, Brian - Brian - Brian!"

She heard the groan of despair. He wasn't looking at her but at the eggs. She'd said the wrong thing, pushed him into a corner. She felt choking disappointment. It was happening like at the beach: he'd gone off her.

Tell my lady, your name is Jack, idiot!

She looked through French windows at sunlight streaming through the branches of Mountain Ash and glinting on bunches of berries; they'd be brilliant red in winter apparently, there weight even now bent branches to form arcs over the herb garden.

"I wonder if there's any more cannabis growing?"

"I sincerely hope not." Jack sprung to attention. Something else to think about but Jack the silly, Jack the stupid, Jack the scared rabbit. Anything but Brian, the skydiver!

"I haven't had a look since the police came."

"We'll check it out. We don't want you serving more jail time."

"I'll go along with that. Once was enough. I learnt my lesson, thank you very much." He wasn't even looking in her direction, just concentrating on breakfast.

He turned off the electricity under the eggs; they'd been bubbling for three and a half minutes. The toaster popped up three slices of toast.

"Ah, golden brown, just perfect." He beckoned her over with a fond smile. "Come on. Which egg, my lady? We'll search the back yard for illegal plants, afterwards."

He was all right apparently. Her heart resumed its normal position in her chest and she practically danced across the space to choose an egg.

DURING THE TOUR OF THE yard they held hands, their search for cannabis unrewarding, but they weren't disappointed.

"I'll come do some digging when your vegetables are finished. That is, if you don't consider me pushy." Her tightened clasp of his hand answered him. He admired feathery carrot tops. "Did your landscape gardener put in vegetables?"

"Yes, I'm not much of a gardener. My dad..." Good grief, she'd been going to say her father grew the vegetables at home, her mother concentrated on flowers.

"Where is your father, Jean?" He touched one of the carrot tops nonchalantly to avoid a direct look in case she thought him inquisitive. "On the reservation?"

"He's dead." She abruptly let loose his hand, walked quickly to the garage. Poor dad, she'd killed him off!

"Geez, I'm sorry I asked you, Jean. I realize it must hurt to lose a parent. I'm sorry. I promised I wouldn't ask about your... your, and I did. I'm sorry, Jean."

"You weren't to know." She bent to straighten a Dutch Iris stem growing alongside the garage, to avoid his gaze. "It's all right, Brian."

A feeling of love smote him. She was lovely and gentle, had deep feelings to be tapped into. He should handle her with a velvet glove, not a catcher's mit.

Jessica felt his presence before his shadow cast across her hands and the flower border. What is he going to ask now? She couldn't handle any more questions; she'd answers coming out of her ears as well as her mouth, and that was difficult with a big foot in it.

"I've organized a surprise for you, Jean." He lifted her upright, gently, her eyes still lowered to the flowers.

"The surprise you phoned me about for Saturday?"

"Uh-huh. I'm taking you to City Airport."

"Oh!" She looked up. "Sunday's all right then?"

"Ye-es." He had the grace to look embarrassed.

"Is it to your workplace?"

Blue eyes shone. "Sure is." He cupped her face in his hands, kissed her forehead.

"Are we going flying?" At his nod. "In one of yours?"

"Unless you've sprouted wings, my lady." He cuddled her then turned them both towards the house. "Come on, I can't wait to show you my treat."

They glided indoors on a feathery cloud radiating love and happiness.

Chapter Twelve

They traveled in a state of euphoria all the way from Bonnie Doon, across river valley, up 109 Street and into 111 Avenue. A moment of trepidation entered Jack when Shellack Oil Exploration hove into view, but the feeling soon evaporated once past the place.

In Kingsway, the City Airport buildings were outlined against the skyline. Jack slowed, turned into the commercial road and wondered if their passage to the hangar would be without incident. He looked sideways at Jean seated so quietly, taking in everything. She looked at him and smiled. His stomach did a flip-flop and he smiled back until they arrived at the gates and the duty guard.

"Hi, still earning double-time, eh?" Jack waved a greeting. The guard grinned and waved them through.

"You know him well I suppose, passing every day." Jessica made the polite observation but not really wanting conversation to interfere with that feeling of well-being.

Jack smiled assent saying nothing; whatever he said would bury him deeper in untruths and prevarications. He headed for the hangars, assumed a familiarity with the layout traversing frontages and explained which company owned what and their sphere of operation, until they arrived at Airborne Brothers hangar.

"This is it, the end of the tour." He turned the Cadillac to run alongside the hangar, to the side door.

"Big, aren't they? I'm feeling quite overawed."

"Need big hangars for big planes."

"But you said commercial flights didn't come here any more, they've gone to the International Airport."

"Yes, but hangars require plenty of space for equipment. Anyway, commercial planes were housed here before they were transferred to International."

"Oh, that makes sense."

She waited whilst Jack locked the car, then together they ascended the side steps and he opened the door.

"Hold on a tad." He stepped inside, switched on the overhead lights and extended a hand for Jessica. "This is where we house the planes," indicated the emptiness with a loud clap of his hands.

"Hecky thump! Doesn't it echo?" Jessica laughed out loud. The hangar echoed back her laughter. "Ha-Ha, Ha-ha!" and again the echo repeated.

"It doesn't echo when the planes are parked, or undergoing repairs on ramps. It's certainly eerie, when empty." Jack took her arm to head for the equipment shed.

"You said we were going flying, didn't you, Brian?"

"We certainly are, my lady."

"Tell me, how do we fly without an aeroplane or -"

"Here's your transportation." He switched on the lights illuminating two glider engines, framed and mounted on wheels, standing by a long table.

"So, how do we fly?" She approached the engines and touched metal. "Even if I flapped my wings energetically, I doubt I could lift one of these beasts."

"I know you enjoy skiing and canoeing."

Jean Morningbird again! What else did she excel at?

"Let's see how you," carefully pulled along the table one of the spined wings. "Paraglide."

"Paraglide? Ha-Ha!" Jessica ran a tentative hand over the object. "I've never paraglided. I haven't even glided in a plane. I've skied behind a boat though." She'd seen skiers take off wearing water skis and a parachute, the crazy ones, the younger ones whose bones knit faster when broken.

"You'll be okay; I won't let anything happen to you."

"Oh well, I'm game. My insurance is paid up." She tapped the wing carefully as if it were an unfriendly dog. Ha-Flaming-Ha!

"Now, we spread out the wings on the table and..." Working under his instruction, it didn't take long to attach the wings to titanium struts on the framed seat.

"What made you think I'd enjoy paragliding, Brian?"

"Your letter." He tested the tautness of the guide rope. "You'll have to show me your favorite ice hole, by the way."

Jessica ducked her head and pretended she had dropped a screw. She must have misheard him; he couldn't possibly have said 'arse-hole'. She followed the Yorkshire axiom: 'When in doubt, say nowt'.

"Your grandfather must have enjoyed having you along."

Along for what? She smiled and tightened the screw.

"How did he get the fish to bite? Did he use native cunning?" He went over her handiwork, recalling her carpentry on the mailbox. "What was his secret?"

Oh dear Lord, will it never end? Now he's on about fish! Ah well, it's better than what she'd imagined.

"Ha-Ha! That's for me to know and you to find out." Her cheeky grin in his face called for a peck on the cheek.

"You'll excel at anything you attempt, I guess."

"Thank you, sire," and curtsied. My word, she was putting out the right vibes if he thought that of her. "Thou hast a tidy turn of phrase. Twill turn my head, methinks."

"Talk naughty a tad more, you'll have me forgetting about flying on air-currants," checked a screw where canopy strut and bar met. "We'll be flying down here, my lady," and waggled the spanner in her face.

"Ooer, promises, promises, my man."

The paraglider wheels made movement easy towards the hangar doors. Jack pushed and Jessica sat aboard walking her feet, feeling like a Queen with wings, even though they weren't yet fully extended.

Jack assisted her into the harness. "This front bar you hold onto at all times. You tilt your body for starboard."

"That's right, isn't it?"

"Yes, and tilt to port, for left. And for elevation use the flap control."

"How do you stop when you want to come down?" She searched for a hand brake.

"You don't have brakes in flight," chuckled her under the chin. "You manoeuvre your weight on these side struts like I showed you; the wings will come round and you'll glide down to a stop in a circling movement." He tapped the massive helmet sitting in her lap. "Wear that, and don't remove it."

"I presume the helmet's for protection against bird strikes."

"Oh, for sure," headed for the hangar door, laughing.

"Hey! Planes won't be a hazard, will they?"

"I doubt our height will interfere in a plane's flight path." How did the doors open, he'd forgot to check? It was a huge rollup door which operated with a hydraulic switch. Was it located to the left or right?

"It's just as well because I don't fancy arguing with a DC10 on who has the right-of-way when I'm up aloft." Jessica called to him.

"I'll help you when I've finished," he called back. Jean was fiddling with her helmet strap and wouldn't see him investigating. He went to the left of the door, discovered to his relief, the switch. Hello, there's another switch, what's that for? He looked at Jean again, now helmeted and stretched to full extent checking how securely the wing was attached to both port and starboard struts.

Jack quickly ascertained the second switch was a manual override in case of cutout and pressed the automatic switch. The graunching and groaning indicated the door was opening upwards. How did it close afterwards? He ducked under the rising iron door, looked at the walls and mentally kicked himself. Naturally, it would be an open invitation to burglary if hangar doors operated from outside.

"I thought for a minute you were going to be dragged up on that big door," Jessica said, when he returned.

"It needs to be massive. We don't hanker after thieves coming in and making off with equipment."

"I'm getting excited, Brian. I'm quite looking forward to a new experience and flying high with you."

"Way to go, love. I admire your enthusiasm." He pushed her paraglider onto the smooth liftoff area on the far side of the apron. "I'll go bring out mine now," and dashed back into the hangar.

151

Jessica noticed light filtering through her overhead wings spread like a butterfly. Nice umbrella if it rains. Hey, what happens when it rains? Will water affect the wings, they appeared to be made of fabric, what sort she couldn't hazard a guess. But she hoped they were waterproof. Her musing halted when she sighted Brian pushing out his paraglider.

"I could have helped instead of just sitting here like a lady-in-waiting."

"Never mind. You are my lady-in-waiting." He turned his paraglider to face upwind. "Save your energy."

"For what, looking out for birds?"

"I'll be back after I've closed up." He re-passed her. "Don't switch on the engine until I give the word."

"You betcha!" She hadn't come down in the last shower, matey!

Jack ducked under the door, threw the switch for it to close and hurried across the empty expanse to the side door. He looked around carefully before he switched off lights and locked the door. Impatience had him gallop around to the front of the hangar.

Jessica standing on her seat, pulled on the connecting struts of the wings to re-test the workings, saw him approaching.

"I think I've got it worked out, Brian."

"Okay. Want any assistance getting strapped in again?"

"No, I'm a quick learner."

Jack strapped himself into his paraglider with many backward glances towards his traveling companion; put on his helmet, and a feeling of apprehension stole over him. Was he doing the right thing, the sensible thing, a safe thing for him to do with a novice? Hell, he was only just out of training himself. And it was well known, a beginner passed on his own mistakes to another beginner: a trainer, never. He shouldn't have asked Jean to paraglide, he was putting her at risk.

"I'm ready and waiting, sithee!"

"Is that, 'Ye olde English'?" He twisted to observe her sitting proudly on her steed.

"Nay, lad, that's Yorkshire. Sithee, means 'Look and Listen'. Sithee?"

"I'm switching on my engine." She's cute and adorable. "Follow me! Do what I do! Sithee?"

"And if I strike trouble, what then?"

"Sit there! Aerodynamics kick in and float you down."

"Wow, thanks."

She turned on the engine which sounded like a quiet version of a motor mower. Was she really trusting herself to the skies with a motor mower engine? She swallowed hard, noticed Jack's paraglider moving along the apron, blades revolving slowly behind him in their protective grid. He turned, beckoned her to follow.

"Giddee-up!" Jessica urged her steed forward with bum encouragement which had no effect. She tried moving it along with her feet, and it didn't budge. Now it worked previously crossing the hangar to outside!

"Giddee-up!" Nothing moved. She switched off the engine and walked the paraglider. "This is never the way to become airborne." She eyed the dashboard, strained to remember instructions, but her mind blanked. Then she saw a lever. 'Brakes'.

Brian had laughed when she'd asked about brakes. Obviously, they worked when the engine was switched on! She moved the brakes to the off position and switched on the engine. Instantly the paraglider moved forwards. She glanced back. Yup! Blades slowly revolved at her tail and gathered momentum. She lifted her feet off the tarmac as speed increased; put her hands on the side struts, body leant, to manoeuvre.

"Easy-peasy!"

Jack's wheels left the concrete and he was airborne, rising on an updraft with the remembered exhilaration permeating his body, of previous paragliding. He looked backwards for Jean. Where was she, she should have risen just after him?

Jessica looked up at Jack's paraglider. Why hadn't she left the ground? What was she supposed to do to take off? She eyed the dashboard again; saw a knob marked 'Flaps'. She'd forgotten it. She pulled out the knob and the paraglider shuddered. There followed an eerily swishing sound, then silence, wheels no longer vibrating on tarmac. Is this death? And, why couldn't she hear the engine? She looked back, realized she was in front of, not behind engine noise.

"God, I'm stupid!" Jack struck his hand on the dashboard in frustration. "I only explained how to manoeuvre in flight, not on how to land and takeoff."

Jessica leaned back in her seat. She knew how to operate a paraglider.

"Easy-peasy!"

THE TWO PARAGLIDERS sailed along two hundred feet above the ground. Jack fifty yards in front indicated upwards to Jessica and opened up his flaps; immediately rose and pulled away from her.

Jessica looked below at the ground then up at the open sky, blue with scudding white clouds way above. Did she really want to soar like an eagle in the stratosphere? No, she was darned if she did. She liked it here with one foot on the ground. When Jack's hand again beckoned her up to his level of two hundred and fifty feet and rising, Jessica waved back a negative: 'No thanks, matey!'

She carried on at her chosen height, maintained an eye on Jack above and the passing scenery below. A park was approaching; at least, there were plenty of trees and greens. Maybe it was a golf course.

The coughing of the engine bothered her a little at first, until she realized it was coughing out phlegm to clear its fuel intake. But when the cough came again, and finally the engine cutout altogether, she realized she had better regard it seriously.

· "On a range of one to ten, this is a number nine emergency." She patted the dashboard encouragingly. "Come along, engine. I can't run into the garage for cleaning rods, rags and petrol."

A quick look back at the blades made her swallow hard: they were revolving, but oh, so slowly.

She hung onto the bar, wind, hitherto unnoticed above the sound of the motor, whistled past her ears. Her eyes were drawn hypnotically to the altimeter needle hovering at two hundred and ever so gently losing height. She could deal with this. Stay calm. When the engine cuts out apparently, aerodynamics kick in and float you down, like Brian said.

154

"Easy-peasy!"

Jack saw Jean's paraglider losing height. He banked, made a pass over her. Yes, she was descending, the engine wasn't turning the blades. His lips tightened. He was one hell-of-a-fool, had no right assuming he could teach a novice.

He looked around for a landing spot and saw Coronation Park ahead. He maneuvered down and alongside Jessica. She looked over and shrugged her shoulders, pointed back at the engine. He nodded his head, he was aware of the situation, and pointed directly ahead. Follow me!

Jessica saw the green fields. Wise choice, a lot softer than landing on hard rocks.

Jack glided in front of Jessica to lead the way. It would be okay in front of the bandstand at the Scientific Museum of Technology; plenty of flat land, providing they missed the trees. He looked back and waved at Jean. She waved to him reassuringly. He operated the flaps for a steeper descent, concentrated on where to put down.

Jessica saw the greens spread out. Plenty of room to land, Brian chose well indicating this spot. She held onto starboard struts, moved her bodyweight in the same direction. The wings responded and she spiraled to the right in a rapid descent. Very shortly it seemed the ground was racing towards her. She straightened up, let loose the struts and hung on tightly to the bar. The wings extended to full measure, the paraglider hovered over the huge expanse of green and landed with a shuddering bump and a little wheel-drag.

Jessica unbuckled herself and hopped out of the seat smartly before the wings carried her airborne again; even without engine thrust, she didn't quite trust the thing. She looked for Jack and saw him a hundred feet above and to the west of her disappearing out of sight above trees. Was that where she was supposed to be? Wasn't this landing place good enough? She thought it ideal.

A man's irate shout intruded. Jessica looked in the direction of a large building. An arm waving man was running down the steps.

"Get off the green, ye great big, stupid woman, ye!"

Jessica spied the large lettering above the clubhouse. 'COMMONWEALTH LAWN BOWLING CLUB'. Apparently a club member was letting her realize she was on a beautifully tended green, well, one of them, the other three were untouched.

"I'm sorry!" She shouted back.

Her apology had no effect. Giant strides propelled the man along the four yard wide strip separating the greens, and she could easily imagine him swinging a claymore in heather crusted glens.

"Get off yon green!"

"My engine cut out and I had to come down somewhere," she shouted again, body turning to keep up with his pace.

"Ye should'na have come doon here, ye ken!" left her in no doubt he was of Scots descent. "Ye've all the park to use. Ye've no the right to use our greens for yon vehicle!" He halted, faced her from the walkway. "What the hell d'ye think y're playing at, ye gormless woman? Yer behaving with the stupidity of an alien from outer space!"

"I'm not an alien! I'm almost a Canadian citizen, I'll have you know." Well, in a couple of years, that was.

"Then y'er a blethering stupid almost Canadian citizen, ye ken that?" He removed his shoes. "I never use anything heavier than a roller on my greens, ye ken?"

He was going to hit her with a shoe? Jessica started backing towards the clubhouse, searched the sky. Isn't that just typical of a man? Never there when he's wanted!

"Stay put, woman!" With one foot on the green he saw her movement. "Ye're not wearing the correct shoes!"

Jessica looked at her fashionable clubfooted Cuban-heeled shoes, thankful she wasn't wearing stiletto heels. Now, they would have made indentations on the green, and that's why he was fast approaching in stockinged feet.

"I'm sorry, should I take off my shoes as well?" With that she immediately bent to rectify her mistake.

"Better late than never." His tone mollified until the approaching phut-phut of the paraglider drew the man's attention. "If yon Nancy boy dares to land here, he'll be sorry, ye ken?"

"Aye, I ken," she waved off Jack. "Shoo! Get away!"

Jack peered down on the arm waving green keeper who resembled the Australian Bower Bird in a mating dance on stones in front of its tree, and got the message. He hovered over the clubhouse and settled on the front lawn.

"Thank goodness for that, he won't be causing damage on your green."

"We'll no mention damage to yon flowerbeds."

"He didn't land on your flowerbeds, but on the lawn."

"His whirly blades blew off topsoil! Did ye no see, woman?"

She was in a 'no win' situation, so shut up; placed her shoes on the paraglider seat and watched him kneel down to examine ground scored by wheels cutting deep. With the best intention in the world she bent to join in the investigative procedure.

"Is there any damage?"

"Are ye blind? Can ye no see, woman?" His eyes were light blue and round in a face red with anger. "Ye've spoilt a year's work with ye're blessed contraption."

"Grass soon grows. What's the matter with you?"

She wished she hadn't made that insensitive remark when he rose to his feet with a roar that frightened her so much she jumped a foot in the air. Coming down, she observed the reason for his anger.

Jack was running towards them in heavy boots.

"Get off the green, yer great big, clodhopper!" The greenkeeper's roar and wave off, stopped Jack in his tracks.

"Take off your boots, Brian, you'll damage the green!" Jessica added her voice and actions to that of the greenkeeper's.

"Sorry!" Jack immediately bent to remove his boots.

"Now there'll be more of ye're blethering handiwork to put right, ye ken?"

"I ken, all right. Maybe if we pick up the paraglider together we could carry it over to that grass strip."

"Aye, we could'n'all, when yon gets here to help and not hinder." He looked beyond Jack who approached in stockinged feet, and saw his boots sitting on the green. "Would you credit the ninny?"

"Are you okay, Jean?" Jack touched Jessica's shoulder. "I was sure scared when I saw your blades not turning." He acknowledged the irate green keeper. "Sorry about the unfortunate landing, Sir, it was entirely unexpected. We'll have it airworthy once I examine the engine."

"Not here, ye won't, ye great big Jessy. Ye're not messing up my green with oil. Get this vehicle off or I'll remove it, piece by piece."

"All I can offer is my apologies, Sir. I'm sorry!"

"Brian. Over there to fix it, do you think?" Jessica indicated the walkway.

"I hope that's okay with you, Sir?" Jack bent over to peer into the man's face. "Can you help us lift the paraglider and carry it over there?"

"Aye, lift your end then, I'm not straining mesen for you, ye ken," and took hold of the engine cowling.

"I don't have a problem with that, thank you all the same." Jack put his hands on the port frame and struts. "Jean, I'll get this. You get the starboard frame and struts."

"Okay," and lifted. "My goodness isn't it light?"

"When it landed with a thump, my green did'na think it was light."

"Sorry about that," Jessica's smile was intended to be infectious. "I didn't know the aeronautical term for, 'Steady does it'." The man raised his eyes to heaven.

Jack cast her an embarrassed frown. "No, it was my fault, Sir. I'm sorry!"

When the paraglider was stationed on friendlier turf, they rested for a moment, then Jack opened the engine cowling and the green keeper returned to the gouged-out area.

"I'll collect your boots." Jessica tapped Jack on the shoulder. "It'll give him less to complain about."

"Thanks. I'll start work on this. I'll probably have to blow out a tube."

The damage to the green seemed enormous viewed against the pristine lawn neatly rolled and mowed to perfection. Jessica swallowed hard when she passed the man on his knees, examining uprooted turf with a keen eye. She picked up Jack's boots, noted deeper indentations where he had landed after his leap from the front lawn. Cor! She returned to the spoilt landing spot.

"I'm so sorry!" She knelt, pushed down tufts of grass torn up by its roots. "You require smooth lawns for bowling, I know. My father was a bowler in England."

"Ye ken right, gal." He flattened divots and ruts with the sides of his hands. "It teks years to bring a lawn up to standard. We've just finished verti-cutting this one."

"What does that do, I've never heard of verti-cutting?"

"It's a lot of blades. It de-thatches and thins the grass, breaks up clumps of matted grass under the roots."

"Can I offer to pay for repairs?" She realized it was an impossible task for a novice gardener and stood up.

"Can you manage ten thousand dollars?" His expression softened when he noticed her dropped mouth. "Canadian, that is, not US."

"You must be joking!"

"That's what it cost ta bring in yon guy from Melbourne, Australia."

"But that would be for four greens, not one." She eyed him. "You lose your accent when you're not angry."

"Ye're not almost Canadian born, lass." He stood up and for the first time smiled, his craggy features cracking under skin toughened by years of Alberta summers. "I'd venture ye're Yorkshire born."

"Wow! How'd you guess that?"

"Ye canna lose it, gal." He slapped his leg and laughed. "I've been here since the fifties and I still think and speak like a Scot."

And she was pretending to be a Canadian Indian, at least a Métis. Oh boy, who was she kidding? Herself, apparently. No wonder Brian looked at her askance at times!

Jack blew grit from the pipe and tried the engine which burst into sound. "Listen to this Jessica," he called. "It's singing like a bird dining on Taber Sweet Corn."

Jessica nodded and giggled as she and the green keeper walked towards him. What a lovely, sweet nature Brian had, totally different from this chap at her side.

"Yon gets lyrical on occasion, I'd say lass." He wiped his dirty hands on a rag and smiled at her.

She nodded in agreement. "Sounds just lovely, Brian," and stepped up onto the grass strip, dropped their footwear by a bench and listened to the engine close-up. "Wish it'd kept singing whilst I was up aloft."

"Ah, that's my fault." Jack tightened a nut.

"And the green damage is hers." The green keeper sat to put on his shoes.

"I've offered to pay for the small green repair, Brian," sitting next to the man.

"Small, is it, now? Give yon lassie a bit of rope and she'll hang me."

"How much really?" her grin wide.

"Naturally." Jack wiped his hands on a tissue. "We expect to compensate for the green damage, Sir."

"Wait until you hear how much?" Jessica warned. Brian had walked right into it.

The green keeper eyed her, the paraglider and then Jack. "A beer in the clubhouse," turned to Jessica. "That all right, lass?"

"It's a better offer than the original one." Jessica gave him a friendly shove on his arm. "We'll accept it."

"That's great." Jack smiled, held out his hand. "Very nice of you to be so understanding. I'll soon have this airborne, don't worry."

After they shook hands the man knelt down by the paraglider. "There's always someone behaves irresponsibly on the greens." He ran a hand over a wheel, noted how deep it sat on the rough grass. "One time we had golfers in spiked shoes." He stood up. "We've bowling shoes for hire, but these nanas just walked on and put spike holes in the green."

"Not for long, I shouldn't think." Jessica stood up. "I bet you had them running from the green smartly."

"And I made them put back the divots, ye ken."

Jack, about to turn off the engine, paused. "You want I should leave the paraglider here while we have a drink?"

"Yes, it'll be all right."

"It's mighty good of you overlooking my stupidity." He smiled in relief and revved the engine before shutting it off.

"Yon's no like you lass." The ex-Scot spoke quietly to Jessica. "He's true Canadian. Polite."

"You cheeky beggar!" Jessica made certain Jack hadn't overheard. "Like my mother says: 'It takes all sorts, you know'."

"Your mum's got it right there, lass."

Jack put on his boots and the three of them walked along the strip to the clubhouse. "Do you have a problem with winterkill?" He took hold of Jessica's hand, aware he'd nearly lost her.

"We do now and again. Frost gets under the tarpaulin covers. It's a bugger to work out; teks two years to bring back a real good lawn."

"What are the sedimentary layers of the greens?"

"Top layer's sand, so's water doesn't puddle-up."

Jessica let them talk. She was quaking inwardly. Would this canny Scot give away her secret to Brian? Would Brian discover she was a fraud as well as a rotten pupil?

They passed Brian's parked paraglider on the lawn. Jessica noted footprints where he'd bounded onto the green appeared deeper from this angle. Whoops! But the green keeper, if he saw it, and she didn't doubt he had, said nothing. Maybe he was played out after the initial outburst. She hoped so, she didn't like a mad Scotsman sounding off.

JESSICA HAD NO cause to be concerned about the green keeper disclosing the fact that she was not only English, but also a Yorkshire woman. Once inside the clubhouse he busied himself behind the bar, opened three cans of English Ale straight from the giant refrigerator.

"Seven dollars fifty." Jack had noted the price list displayed on the wall. "That's a cheap round," placed the correct money on the bar. "Cheaper than what we're charged at the Territorial Club."

"Yeah, club prices. We're -" The kitchen telephone rang interrupting the Scot in mid-flight. He indicated seating by the windows before leaving to answer the summons. "Go sit in yon chairs."

Jessica breathed an inward sigh of relief, the man would be too occupied to give away her secret. They took their drinks and seated themselves for overlooking the four greens through the picture windows which ran around two sides of the clubhouse; an overhead verandah extended beyond the patio which also contained tables and chairs.

"Nice outlook, Jean, and what an amiable guy."

"Once you get to know him, he's all right." No need to elaborate, the green keeper might still denounce her. She poured ale into her glass.

"I've curled since college days. I'm told lawn bowling resembles curling, but I don't know... To me it seems like it's for oldies. What's your opinion?" She didn't answer. Jack stole looks at her quietness while he poured his ale. "How are you feeling, Jean? Over the shock yet?"

"I suppose now we've to turn round and take those beasties back to City Airport, uh?" She wished it could be sooner rather than later, before the green keeper finished his phone call.

"Unless I hire a van to transport them back to the hangar." He couldn't blame her for being hesitant about paragliding again.

"I don't want to wait for transport. I'll manage back to the airport. But I don't think I'm sold on the safety value of paragliding."

"That's my fault, I didn't tutor you efficiently at the outset."

"I won't disagree with you. You even told me there weren't any brakes." She could have mentioned her dad would have clobbered him if he'd been there, endangering her life in such a manner.

"Yes, my mistake. I forgot in the excitement of introducing you to a new sport."

"You behaved irrationally for a flyer."

Jack was furious with himself, knowing she spoke the truth. He'd risked her life trying to be someone he wasn't; committed the cardinal sin, placed someone at risk pretending to be knowledgeable when he wasn't qualified. He saw over the open kitchen counter the green keeper still on the telephone. There didn't appear any reason for staying, he felt uncomfortable and knew she was. He took a large gulp, placed the glass on the table and stood up.

"Let's be away," hand out to assist her rise.

Jessica deliberately ignored the proffered hand, instead picked up her glass and can and carried them to the bar. Jack followed suit feeling very much in the dog box.

"Thanks for everything." Jessica leaned over the counter. "I'm sorry for the damage. I assure you it won't happen again," her smile infectious. The Scotsman smiled in return and waved.

"Thank you, very much. Have a nice day!" Jack waved a good-bye and followed Jessica out of the clubhouse. "I'll follow you back, shall I?" He paused at his paraglider. "Or, would you sooner I went first?"

"Please yourself."

"I'm sorry my treat turned out a total disaster, Jean," touched her arm. "It was meant to be a pleasant surprise."

"Ha! Treat!" She walked off two yards, stopped and turned. "Ha! Surprise?" She walked another two yards, stopped and turned back to him. "Pleasant? I think not. I'm asking myself a question, Brian. What do you do for an encore?" She turned and continued to walk along the grassed walkway.

"Hold on a tad, Jean." He knew he deserved her derision; nevertheless he hurried after and felt like a lapdog noting her stride lengthening as anger mounted. "Wait a minute! Let me explain!" Caught up and grabbed her arm to swing her round to face him.

"Leave me alone! I don't want to be mauled by you or anyone else!" His hand dropped off an arm, her eyes, wide, brown blazing orbs of loathing.

"Please don't be like that, Jean?"

"Please, don't be like what?" She mimicked him nastily. Very nastily.

"Like you hate me," his face resembled that of a hurt child.

"I... I..." Suddenly anger receded. She'd no right to be annoyed with him, it was all her fault. If she hadn't pretended to be drug pusher Jean he wouldn't have assumed she'd be capable of aeronautical endeavors. She rushed to retrieve the helmet from the seat of her paraglider. "Let's get out of here before I say something I'll be sorry for."

"Okay," assisted her into the seat and fastened her straps. "We'll concentrate on how we're getting back to City Airport."

"The same way we came, I assume," dragged up a smile. "I trust the engine won't cutout this time."

"No way! I made sure it was perfectly clear of grit. I should have tested it before we set out."

"You certainly should."

"You'll be okay." He touched her fondly on the shoulder prior to leaving. "Take care, Jean. I don't want anything to happen to you."

"Me neither." She looked at the dashboard, felt sick to the stomach at her behavior: Mrs Happy had been replaced by Ms Bitchy.

"The wind's coming from the west, so head in that direction for better lift-off," he pointed at the flag over the clubhouse, and smiled at her encouragingly before running to his paraglider.

Jessica went through the routine of feet walking briskly on the grassed area, engine on, brakes off, flaps down and the glider lifted off the ground. She was airborne again, engine phut-phutting nicely. The paraglider rose higher. She hung onto the struts, leaned her weight to head westwards and soared like a bird to fresh heights.

What a pity this feeling of exhilaration sours when the engine fails.

Jack saw with relief Jean had taken off okay. He shouldn't have brought her out; their friendship was doomed. He was Brian's shadow not his substance.

He followed Jessica's take-off direction, banked to the west on the approach to the clubhouse. The green keeper came onto the patio and waved at him. Jack waved back.

Decent guy. The situation could've turned out worse. He could have been nasty. They'd sure been fortunate.

Chapter Thirteen

At City Airport Jessica landed, but not at Airborne Brothers hangar. She became disoriented looking down on the scene, chose the hangar at the Kingsway end and realized her mistake too late. She switched off the engine and cursed her lack of direction before she noticed a security officer approaching from the airport terminal.

"Excuse me. You can't land here."

"I just did."

"Who is in charge of you?"

Charming! Subtlety wasn't his middle name. "I'm with him." She indicated Jack who began to circle sighting her misjudgment. "Blame Airborne Brothers."

"You shouldn't have landed here. Commonsense dictates all gliders retain a distance from commercial runways."

"I didn't think there were any commercial aeroplanes landing here anymore."

"We have private aircraft, madam, and weather machines. Practice some commonsense!"

"I'm a learner!" She pointed at Jack's paraglider on its approach. "Blame him! He shouldn't have let me fly."

"Airborne Brothers hangar is down there," pointed along the landing aprons.

"I'll be going then. But I'll walk it, thank you."

The officer sniffed, gestured Jack to land immediately, and walked to intercept twenty yards ahead.

Jessica stuck her legs through the stirrups to walk the glider. Good thing she hadn't attempted to fly again: Murphy's Law. Something else would go wrong.

So far today, she had been assaulted by Dirty Dick; almost killed by brainless Brian; nearly decapitated by an irate Scottish green keeper; and to cap it all an airport official wanted a piece of her.

"I shouldn't have got out of bed this morning. And I thought yesterday wasn't a bundle of joy. Ha-Flaming-Ha!"

Jack and the official were talking. Jessica padded past ensuring the paragliders had sufficient clearance, she didn't want to become involved with another confrontation, and the official was too angry.

"What's the idea coming down on this section of the airport? Don't you realize the danger you're creating with incoming aircraft? You're not a teenager. You're old enough to realize the consequences of this irresponsible action. What's your name?"

Jessica missed hearing Jack's reply. Funny! Why didn't the official recognize Brian, the Skydiver? And why had Brian hesitated opening the hangar door before they left, as if he didn't know what he was doing? She'd thought nothing of it at the time, well, not much, but now, in the light of the latest development she was beginning to suspect: something was definitely fishy in the State of Denmark.

INSIDE THE HANGAR Jessica came out of the washroom. "Trust men not to have a decent mirror in the loo." She must look a sight after wind exposure and a ton weight flattened her hair, that, on top of flattened brains imagining she could impersonate someone a lot younger than herself.

Oh, that rotter Ronnie Walters had a lot to answer for re-arranging her brain cells so she didn't know whether she was coming or going. She'd made a right mess of things since the breakup of a marriage. And he still hadn't finished with her apparently, sicking Dirty Dick onto her.

Jack emerged from the equipment shed. "Guys have a lot to answer for." He took a tissue from his pocket and gently wiped her face. "A bit of grease." Her breast was lopsided, but he wasn't going to adjust it and receive a haymaker.

Jessica followed his eyes. "Oh, to hell with this pretense!" She stuck her hand up her jumper, inside the bra and pulled out her Madonna look-a-likes. "See how you like it now, uh?" Stuck out her chest with the shape of the average woman.

"It'd be considered cheating if I stuck a pair of socks in my crutch."

"Oh, so I'm a cheat, am I?" The truth hurt so much it was painful. Brown orbs flashed and she threw the two shapes at him.

He ducked his head and laughed, immediately knew what was coming and dodged the swinging arm which he caught in a firm grip.

Jessica could have screamed in frustration, she was powerless to overcome his strength. It wasn't fair! Life wasn't fair! So box clever, gal! Capitulate! Walk away with dignity: well, what was left of it.

"Take me home," ceasing her struggles. "This friendship has run its course."

"Okay with me," released her abruptly. "I'm sure ready for cutting loose."

They started a quick walk in the direction of the side door. He looked back to check everything was in order to leave for the day and spotted the bra shapes on the floor. Pick them up or draw her attention to them? "Er... er..."

Jessica looked; saw him trying not to smile indicating her shame lying on the floor, points facing upwards.

"They were for your benefit! You pick them up!" She carried her head high, hurried to the exit with what dignity she could muster.

Jack retrieved the bra shapes, he'd no desire to answer awkward questions by Airborne Brothers' team. He switched off the lights and locked the door, turned to have a make-up conversation with her, but she was striding towards his car and once there, impatiently foot tapped until the car door was unlocked.

She'd show him, laughing at her aiming for beauty. Who did he think he was? He'd hid his bald spot under a toupee! She hadn't laughed at his bit of vanity. Well, not really, the laughter had exploded from within her. And anyway, he had laughed too. He shouldn't have laughed at her Madonnas.

"Buckle up, please." He too could be curt and ratty.

Her reply was to snap on the belt. The journey downtown was fraught with silent self recriminations. She was close to breaking point when a bus stop hove into view.

"Stop here, please," holding up a hand. "I'll catch a bus home the rest of the way."

"Okay by me."

Jack came to a halt, felt the color drain from his face with the shock of the final cut. He waited, not looking when she clambered out of the car, but heard and felt the slam of the door. He pulled the car into mainstream traffic; saw in the rearview mirror Jessica at the bus stop. If she had looked his way, he would have returned, persuaded her not to end the relationship, but she was looking in the opposite direction for an oncoming bus: obviously, he was a dead item.

IS THIS ALL THERE IS?

Jessica boarded a bus within a matter of minutes, a number eight fortunately going to Bonnie Doon. She just had to be moving, get away from that area smartly, and leave her one true love. Oh, God!

Traveling homeward she soul-searched and came to the conclusion it was her fault; she was a cheat, liar, petty minded and bitchy: deserved every flaming thing fate had dished out to her!

JACK ARRIVED HOME in less than ten minutes still in a state of shock at the suddenness of the breakup. He flung himself into his favorite armchair ignoring the pain to his lower back and eyed the river valley, always a restful view.

It had been restful looking into Jean's open face; chestnut brown eyes he wanted to jump in and wallow like a contented pig; large smile that indicated a welcome. He wished he could be a piece of toast and be bitten by those teeth, teeth clenched when kissing. His tongue would never explore her mouth.

He closed his eyes, leaned back for more comfort and felt the bulge in his jacket pocket, and removed bra shapes which he gently cupped.

"Oh Jean, where are you? You didn't have to pretend with me. I loved you as you were, not these additional objects."

He put the bra shapes on the windowsill, points facing upwards. Looked a tad provocative. He pushed them over to lie on their points. That looked worse! He altered their stance to points facing upwards once more.

"They're a part of you, Jean. I don't want to discard them like so much garbage."

He eased himself from the chair, walked to his computer and switched on to try and forget Jean's very existence. The study of geological charts for the upcoming trip could not hold his complete attention, his eyes often wandered to the window sill.

Would her scent linger, and for how long?

JESSICA ALIGHTED from the bus at Bonnie Doon Shopping Mall. She wanted people, light and sound about her; anything to blot out the pain of a love gone wrong.

Mall music was pleasant and accompanied her walk down the center aisle and into a dress shop. She looked at trousers provocatively pinned to the wall; blouses on models with busts she envied, which instantly reminded her of Madonna look-alikes and last seeing them lying on the floor of the hangar.

Her face started to pink-up in shame.

The shop assistant approached with a welcoming smile. "Hi! How may I be of help?"

"I managed without any help from anybody, thank you," and walked out of the shop in a dream state.

The assistant wondered where she had gone wrong.

JESSICA ATE HER dinner in front of the television set and discovered afterwards she couldn't recall the latest news when she washed the dishes: no fresh data in residence.

"I've overloaded my circuits. What with pretending to be Jean Morningbird, trying to look younger, paragliding, losing a lovely man and my breasts, I'm not only a physical wreck, but also a mental one."

What could she do, to whom could she turn for solace, a bit of comfort? As if on cue the telephone rang.

"It's Brian!" She ran and picked up the receiver. "Hello?"

"Hi, this is Jean Morningbird." The voice was female, low and husky, but perfectly ordinary.

The shock wasn't. Jessica's toes curled in her house shoes: her nemesis.

"I left something of mine in that place. I left in sort of a hurry. Okay if I come round and collect it?"

"If you mean the cannabis, the Bobbies have it."

"Oh, shame, eh? Marihuana's a good source of income."

"How'd you get my phone number?"

"Your next door neighbor gave it when I rang him yesterday and asked him to pick up my plants. He wouldn't, the miserable guy."

"The Bobbies are looking for you. You be careful."

IS THIS ALL THERE IS?

"You sound nice. Are you English?"

"Clever guess. Was it my accent?"

"Naw, you sound nice, eh?"

"That reminds me. There's a letter from Brian Swartzkoff arrived for you."

"Great, I'll come over and collect it."

"No you won't. I spent a night in a police cell because of you and your cannabis. I don't intend having a closer association or the Bobbies will throw away the key. And that cell didn't have a TV, you know."

"Tell me about it, eh? Cells aren't all that great. But they're okay for a hot meal and a warm bed by yourself when it gets tough on the streets."

"Oh, Jean..." She caught back the sob in her throat. "I'm in Social Services. Come to Jasper Avenue tomorrow morning at seven forty and I'll process an Emergency Claim for you. There's no need to sleep rough when you've money in your pocket."

"You've figured that out, eh?"

"You know where we are, don't you, off 106 Street? Seven forty tomorrow morning. Watch out for my Cavalier. I'll wait for you in front of the building. There won't be anyone else there until eight, so we'll have a clear field."

"No cops then, eh?"

"I promise, Jean, there'll definitely be no police activity."

"Okay, I'll be there. See you." The phone went dead.

"Poor, poor Jean, and I thought I had worries."

She went to her writing desk, withdrew Brian's letter and felt tearful when she read it.

"It wasn't to be, Brian. Maybe you'll be better suited with Jean Morningbird." Tears sprung up; she sniffed, and wiped her nose on an investigative finger.

"Not with her, Brian. You won't like her, whatever she looks like. It was me you loved, not her." She allowed tears to overspill and cascade down her face. The release of pent up emotions helped clear her head. She licked her lips free of tears.

"Boy, are they salty!"

AT SEVEN-FORTY Jessica drew up in front of Social Services. However, she didn't have to switch off the engine, a girl detached herself from one of the stone pillars and approached the Cavalier.

"Now that's a Métis, Jessica. You're not even a close facsimile."

She was lovely; a light olive complexion, face and figure eye-catching, age about twenty-three; the pink outfit, a loose mini-coat over a miniskirt and blouse; the heels were of the break your ankle variety. The message was clear: Buy me!

Jessica leaned over and opened the door. "Get in quickly!"

"Hi!" Jean smiled warmly and leapt into the seat. "Thanks."

Jessica didn't wait for her to fasten her seat belt, she accelerated to the top of the down ramp parking before she slowed down.

"From Brian, eh?" Jean retrieved the envelope from the top of the dashboard. "Thanks for keeping it for me."

"That's all right. Any trouble whilst waiting, Jean?"

Jessica didn't want to think of Brian again. She was a fool to give him away, but he hadn't been hers in the first place so there was no great loss: only a fractured heart.

"No cops, but a John propositioned me." She laughed at Jessica's look of concern. "No problem, I told him I was waiting for my date."

"Then I picked you up. Ta, ever so."

"What's your name? That guy next door refused to give it to me. Said your phone number was enough."

"Jessica Walters. Don't strain yourself remembering, I don't intend putting my life in jeopardy, knowing you. I wasn't turned on by a night in a cell."

"I look forward to it, sometimes," and shrugged her shoulders.

Jessica bit her lip hard, determined not to allow sympathy to overcome good sense and let this girl into her life.

Jean half read Brian's letter. "Sounds a nice guy."

Jessica could have told her how nice a guy he was, that is, if the Brian of the letter was the same as the Brian she knew. She doubted it, there were too many imponderables. His being overweight for a skydiver; lack of knowledge of the hangar door; the brakes incident, and the official who didn't recognize him. Well, that puzzle was now Jean's, she was welcome to it.

"Good, no one's around." Jessica pulled into her parking space and switched off the engine. "We'll go upstairs and process you before the arrival of the rest of the staff."

"Why don't you want anyone to see me? Is it dishonest what we're doing?"

"No. It's just that I'm taking shortcuts. Your case is urgent." Liar! She wanted her off her conscience; had usurped her place in Brian's affections; was indebted to her.

They alighted from the car, hurried to the metal staircase door then heard the hum of car tires coming down the ramp.

"Whoops, someone's arrived early." Jessica ushered Jean through the door, then paused. "Hey, Jean, come back a minute, will you?" She pulled her back into the garage. "See that Daimler parking over there?"

"Uh-huh, makes for an easy screw in back of a large car."

"Thought you'd appreciate the comfort factor."

"A mini's okay but my legs go into cramp if I'm not careful."

Jessica didn't really want to visualize what position she adopted with her legs, so encouraged the girl to squat low.

"Now, that's Dick Chalmers." They watched him emerge from his car. "He's my boss. A randy bloke; all mouth and trousers, sort of chap. He'd appreciate your favors." Dick flicked dust off his windscreen. "He's got plenty of money, and it's meat here, not on the street," eyed Jean, meaningfully. "Savvy?"

"I figure he's been putting it up against you, eh?"

"Astute girl, aren't you, Jean?"

"I'm streetwise, Jessica."

"I wasn't buying what was on offer." Jessica patted her on the shoulder and smiled at the girl she was beginning to like. "But for you, in your situation...

Go get him girl, hanky-panky is his middle name, and he has got a bitch of a wife. But, after we've processed you. Come on." She led the way to the door.

IT DIDN'T TAKE long for Jean Morning Bird to be placed on the Emergency Claim register and a check issued for instant cash.

"What address do I put down for you on our files?"

"Yours will do."

"It won't, you know, the Bobbies got the wrong idea."

"Okay then, put down 9620 - 103A Avenue"

Jessica typed it. "That's never your address."

"No, but it'll do. It's the cop shop downtown."

"I realize that now. I was incarcerated there overnight." She erased it and reinserted her own address. So what!

Jean read the screen and smiled. "That's nice, of you, Jessica. I said you sounded nice, and you sure are."

Jessica took Jean along to Dick Chalmer's office and knocked on the door.

"Come in." His hopes rose when he sighted Jessica come to do homage at the feet of the master, especially after the unfortunate occurrence at her house yesterday morning. Maybe she'd fallen out with her new man friend; maybe wanted to dangle her finer points tantalizingly. "We've plenty to discuss..." He saw the pink apparition behind Jessica. Apparently, Christmas had arrived early.

"This is Ms Jean Morning Bird, Dick. She was having a problem with her Emergency Claim. I've processed it, but maybe you could give her additional attention; put her wise on a thing or two."

"Yes, certainly." His eyes traveled up and down the lovely young thing ready for the taking. "Leave the young lady with me, I'll work out something to her advantage." He stood up, held out a welcoming hand towards Jean. "I'll give her my best attention."

"She couldn't ask for anything better." Jessica winked at Jean before she left, to give her encouragement, but Jean was already into her act, sitting on the edge of the desk showing off her several charms to the eager John.

Jessica returned to the Claims Department to find the rest of the staff had arrived. She beckoned Dorinda and Veronica over to her position and enlightened them on the latest clash with Dirty Dick.

"Brian arrived in time to throw out the creep?" Veronica missed the hook to hang up her coat and it fell to the floor. "You don't say!" She bent to retrieve her coat, felt around the floor not removing amazed eyes off Jessica. "He defended his lady's honor like a knight in shining armor."

"He did, he arrived like an avenging warrior. Strode in and took over. Gave that creep what he deserved: a thick ear!"

"Sure good timing, Jessica." Dorinda took lip salve from her purse. "You could have been raped, that's for sure."

"He'd have been minus a few vital parts if Brian hadn't interceded." Jessica sat on the edge of her desk. "I'm not fussy when it comes to dissecting rabid animals." She could be brave, now it was all behind her.

"So, you've no need to worry about his intentions anymore, eh?" Veronica both looked and sounded wistful. "He got the message, that's for sure. I wish -"

"I shouldn't think any of us will have to worry about his dishonorable intentions for the time being, Veronica, he's got other things on his mind," and tried not to laugh outright.

"Wish I didn't have to worry. I'd like him off my back, as well."

"Especially since..." Jessica giggled, beckoned them close and whispered.

Both women clapped a hand to their mouths and eyed Jessica in total disbelief.

"You brought in a hooker?" Dorinda's lip salve missed its mark. "Oh, what a solution. My David always says, a bigger hook catches a bigger fish."

"A street hooker?" Veronica's eyebrows were in her hairline. "She might have brought in the clap, Jessica."

"You betcha!" Jessica immediately sobered. She thought back to when she had picked up Jean in the car. Had she touched anything apart from the door handle and dashboard? She determined to disinfect the car when she arrived home. But then, Jean had wondered about at the back of her when she was typing. She looked around casually, tried to visualize what had been touched.

"Where did you pick up a hooker, Jessica?" Dorinda put away her lip salve. "My David will want to know." She caught the exchange of looks between the other two. "He's interested in everything I do and say at work. Says it's enlightening."

"I didn't bring her in for that purpose, Dorinda," Jessica said. "I put her on an Emergency Benefit and pointed her in the direction of the pervert." She turned to Veronica. "A prostitute would take precautions, wouldn't she?"

The two ladies eyed her askance, saying nothing.

"It's in her best interests to wear something to prevent..." They still remained mute. "So, when we're in the car park and see his Daimler vibrating, we'll know what's causing his big end to shimmer and shake."

"Oh, Jessica, you're so funny." Dorinda fell against her and gave her a hug.

"It's what keeps me going," hugged her back. "Or, as my father says: 'Sheer bloody mindedness'. But I prefer to think of it as, a sense of humor."

Veronica looked sad. "I guess I'll ask my boyfriend to pick me up at home time, it sure worked for Dorinda."

"Dirty Dick won't have the energy for playing patsy with you, Veronica," Jessica took a couple of tissues from her desk box. "I told you. He'll be too occupied. Besides, there's too much competition. Jean's beautiful!"

"Thanks, I needed that!" Veronica walked away then turned back with a sad smile. "Guess I'll learn to live with it, eh?"

"Don't we all." Jessica wiped over the surface of the desk where Jean probably fingered. "You know, she's got to have beauty for her job, we get by on brain-power." A thought struck and she straightened. "Wow, I've just realized! I could be prosecuted as a procurer." And this, after being accused of drug trafficking! It seemed life was more than unfair, at times.

Giggles at her dilemma accompanied two coworkers to their duties. And whilst they worked the three maintained a watchful brief on Dick's office. He finally emerged an hour later to escort his latest acquisition to the elevators.

Jean winked at Jessica from the partitioned opening.

Jessica winked back.

IS THIS ALL THERE IS?

DURING LUNCH BREAK in the cafeteria Jessica brought her chums up to date on her paragliding. They insisted upon hearing every nuance of her experience.

"Gee, you're an adventurer, that's for sure." Veronica said when Jessica paused for breath. "I wish my boyfriend was a skydiver."

"I'd love to meet up with him, and so would David." Dorinda gave a slight giggle. "In bed last night, he said how great it'd be to make up a foursome."

"In bed? I don't think so, Dorinda." After they had all giggled, Jessica continued: "Brian left this morning for Nova Scotia, to join up with the air show tour."

"That's so sad, Jessica." Veronica touched her arm. "I am sorry you've lost your knight in shining armor."

"I'll get over it."

"Just when you were so happy with him." Dorinda shook her head and took a bite of her sandwich. "It's like what my David says: here today, gone tomorrow."

Jessica returned to her desk with uplifted spirits, there'd be no more lies again after this day. Well, just one. Brian had to be knocked off in an accident. Appalled, she scurried to justify the thought. You killed off your dad for him, why not Brian?

She looked around surreptitiously to see if she had spoken the words out loud, but nobody in her vicinity appeared interested in her murderous thoughts.

He was dead in the water anyway; wouldn't stand a chance against the charms of young Jean Morning Bird, providing she had the energy to take him on along with her boss.

Would Brian succumb to young flesh? Emulate the actions of randy, rotter Ronnie and dastardly, Dirty Dick?

Chapter Fourteen

Jack was eager for departure to the North West Territories; wanted to distance himself from Jean immediately, if not sooner. To this end on Monday morning he reexamined a scruffy, six inch diameter tube he'd brought back from a previous visit to the site; the geological core contained sections of sedimentary organic matter from different layers going back five hundred and eighty million years into the Paleozoic era.

He struck open a chip from the core on his desk.

"Not whistling a happy tune?" Jeffrey Olivera popped his head into the office. "Someone missed out on their oats, apparently?"

"What make is your car?" Jack tossed the core from one hand to the other meaningfully whilst he eyed the bastard through narrowed eyes. "A blue Mustang?"

"Yes, why?"

"If my Cadillac suffers any more damage I'll know on which car to retaliate."

Jeffrey got the message and withdrew his head. Jack resumed his examination of the chip. It would be good to leave Edmonton with all its frustrations. Jean's hurtful sarcasm was bad enough, but her cutting short, so abruptly, their deepening relationship, hurt. Really hurt, deep down. And, he was fed up to the back teeth with Jeffrey's snide remarks.

Mike Walsh entered the office in a rush. "Do you have the presentation slides up and running, Jack?"

"Sure, been ready since I arrived." Jack stood up, closed the blinds and switched on the projector. He demonstrated on the overhead screen with his pointer, picking out salient features. "This dark layer of carbon rich mudstone and the lighter clean porous sandstone, denotes the extraction will be a viable operation -"

"That's your expertise," Mike interrupted. "Does it justify the expense?"

"You have my word on it, Mike. But as you know, there's always uncertainty in geological field work. This follow-up trip for preparing drill sites and cutting disposal -"

"It'll be welcome news for the board with escalating prices at the pump." Mike left in a hurry. Jack picked up the telephone and dialed the secretarial pool.

"Jack Haversky here, Gloria. Make accommodation for me at the Yellowknife hotel for... three weeks, just in case. I'll arrive about three pm. tomorrow."

SHOULD HE SPEAK TO Jean before he went? Jack broke off packing his grips, stood in the middle of the lounge and contemplated the telephone. He'd be absent over two weeks measuring and having discussions with engineers where it was best to assemble wellheads. Maybe he should inform her what he was doing, where he was going?

Then she'd know he was a fraud. He sat down with his head in his hands, elbows on his knees. What was her problem?

He'd only said she was a cheat, hadn't he, he wouldn't stuff a sock in his pants? Some men would, stupid young men, not men in their forties. So why would she, a woman in her mid-thirties, he guessed, having seen her at her worst, wet through and dripping scads of water from her straight hair, bereft of make-up... Why should she pretend to be younger? Why was she secretive about her heritage?

"Oh, to hell with Jean, she's too much of a problem." He saw the bra points, picked them up and garbaged them in the bag under the sink unit, snapped shut his grips and strode to the door. He dropped the grips, dashed back to the cupboard and rescued the sponges, smiled and pushed them into a side pocket of the grip.

"I'm taking a tad of Jean with me."

However, leaving Edmonton did not lessen Jack's agonizing over Jean. It was a long journey and allowed opportunity for working out exactly where he'd gone wrong: pretended to be someone he wasn't.

JESSICA TRIED to assimilate to different circumstances without Brian; avoided Dick Chalmers almost as much as he avoided her. She supposed his new playmate was keeping him occupied, he sometimes arrived for work looking completely knackered.

Jessica heard nothing from Jean Morningbird, however she spelt it, and hoped she never would again, she didn't want the local constabulary hanging around her home. Had Jean contacted Brian, she'd seemed genuinely interested? But maybe she was too busy. It had been noticed on more than one occasion by knowledgeable staff the Daimler shook rhythmically with no sight of an occupant.

Forgetting Brian was extremely difficult, everywhere she looked at home she saw him laughing or smiling, holding her in his arms. Four days passed before she succumbed, she must see Brian and lay bare the truth about herself. What did she care about competition from young Jean, Brian loved Jessica the person, not a pseudonym.

After work finished at four o'clock, Jessica drove to City Airport, down the road towards the guard at the gates.

"I'm going to Airborne Brothers Hangar."

"The hangar's closed, they're away touring."

"But Brian Swartzkoff is here. I was paragliding with him on Sunday, if you remember."

"Not with Brian, you weren't."

"I was!"

"I'm telling you, madam. Brian Swartzkoff's been away air touring for over two weeks."

Jessica was too numb to thank the guard. She turned the car around and returned along airport road, her face drained of color. At Kingsway she edged into traffic. He was a fraud, an impostor! A cheat and a liar!

"Oh hecky thump, like me!"

She braked hard at the realization. The car behind came to a halt on a squeal of brakes and a loud horn blast.

"Get out of my exhaust pipe, idiot!"

She wasn't tolerating any more nonsense from macho men. She slowed down to allow the impatient fool to pass, she'd give the idiot a tongue-lashing, you betcha!

The car drew alongside. A little lady in her seventies glanced across at Jessica and smiled sweetly: they were both women in a man's world.

Jessica returned a sick smile, and felt like the bottom of a birdcage.

"I can't do anything right."

She allowed the car to travel six lengths ahead on the other lane. Should she go to his home, that's where the letters were addressed?

"No! I've had enough!"

She slapped the steering wheel and removed her foot off the accelerator. A toot of horns obliged her to pay attention so she moved on in the stream of traffic.

"Stand up the real Brian Swartzkoff!"

She hoped Jean would catch up with the right man.

"Leave the impostor for me, Jean. Pretty, please Jean?"

FRIDAY ARRIVED, Jessica telephoned Marcia at the "Y" to arrange a timetable for Keep Fit classes, then once arrived home, surrounded by visions of Brian and herself, she telephoned her mother.

"I want you to come so badly, Mum. I'm furnishing the spare room."

"Ee, love. That'll be right nice to stay with you," her voice brought a tear to Jessica's eye. "We didn't mind staying at your 'Y', but it wasn't homely."

"I'll expect you for next weekend. All right Mum?"

"It certainly is all right, love. And your dad will say so too, or I'll want to know the reason why."

"Oh, Mum, it will be lovely to see you both."

JESSICA SPENT Saturday morning purchasing furniture from Sears at Bonnie Doon, the delivery would be on Monday evening after work. Plenty of time before her parents' arrival on Friday.

Time off for good behavior, she indulged at the Second Cup to enjoy a cinnamon buttered bun with an Irish Cream coffee and watched shoppers in the mall; mums with babies and linked couples, they all seemed to have purpose.

"Is this all there is from hereon? A watcher? This can't be all there is?"

She looked to see if anyone had overheard, but couples at adjoining tables were intent on their own affairs. She'd better take heed, talking out loud to herself was a sign she'd gone bonkers. She'd have to do something constructive. Use her brain.

The solution struck like a lightening bolt.

She smiled, finished her treat and hurried to the car park and her next project.

THE BOWLERS WERE on the greens when Jessica walked through the gates from the car park of the Commonwealth Lawn Bowling Club. She was made welcome in the clubhouse after explaining she wished to join up as a member.

"We're always on the lookout for new bowlers," the kitchen lady said. "You can watch for a tad. See how you like it and pick up a few hints." She indicated the coffee urn. "Would you like a coffee?"

"Thanks, that'll be lovely."

She was served coffee and took it to the seats where she and Brian had sat. She'd watch the bowling and wait for someone official to sign her up as a member.

"You can go outside and sit on a bench overlooking the greens," the kitchen lady called from behind the counter.

"I'll do that, a lot better than being isolated." She stood up. "Is it all right if I take my coffee?"

"Sure, we're easygoing. Just bring back the cup."

"Thanks, I will."

Jessica went down the clubhouse steps balancing her cup of coffee against spillage. She walked past the empty green with two newly grassed in areas surrounded by yellow protective screens: evidence of some stupid gits misuse thereof.

The other three greens however, were occupied by men and women. On two greens, bowlers wore whites. On the third one casual dress was the order of the day; obviously, new bowlers and visitors to the city. Once she'd learnt how to bowl she'd buy whites, they looked attractive against the green grass and the blue sky.

She was pleasantly surprised to see the various ages of bowlers. Unlike previous misconceptions garnered from watching her father bowl when she was fourteen, lawn bowlers were not old men with stomachs protruding over waistbands. There were younger people in their twenties, vociferous in speech; most seemed in their forties and fifties; a great many in their seventies and older. Wow, she'd be a younger member.

There appeared to be several matches in progress on the two greens with white-garbed bowlers. She chose a bench where a familiar figure was stooped over a rubber mat, about to bowl. The bowl went up to the far end of the green and joined other bowls around a white jack. The bowler straightened, saw her, smiled and came to the edge of the green.

"Ye'll be wanting to join up with us, I suppose?"

"Aye, you suppose right." It was nice to be herself, not have to worry about every word. "You turned me on with your charming welcome the other day."

"Good lass! You're name's Jean and you're almost Canadian."

"It's not Jean, it's Jessica Walters. What's yours?"

"A double Johnny Walker, but after the game, eh?"

"You cheeky monkey!"

ON MONDAY EVENING Jessica walked into the spare bedroom and checked again her newly acquired furnishings. Her parents would like it, she'd aimed at imitation antique, like the furniture they'd had in Bradford: solid, dependable. Not like some people who're less substantial then drifting sand that runs through your fingers.

She felt the counterpane, the quilting and stitches felt reliable, durable, long-lasting.

MR AND MRS MAYHEW arrived on Friday by car thoroughly depressed by the journey. Jessica stood at the curb to welcome them.

"There's nowt but mountains to look at," her father complained once he slipped out of the car.

"And nothing to listen to but your complaints," added her mother climbing out of the offside seat with Jessica's assistance. "Never stops complaining, Jessica."

Mr Mayhew put suitcases on the front path. "The bloody radio broke. Nothing to listen to but the hum of wheels on the road."

"The radio broke because you were forever twiddling with the knob." Mrs Mayhew shook her head at him.

"Well, I couldn't get a good reception winding through those mountains."

"That's right, you'd need to tune into different stations, en route." Jessica indicated the house to change the subject. "How'd you like the look of the house now, Dad?

"Looks a damn sight better than last time I saw it."

"Looks like a picture postcard, luvvy." Mrs Mayhew thankfully accepted Jessica's arm going up the path. "I'd love a cup of tea."

"Once we get you settled, Mum, I'll make one."

Inside the bedroom Mrs Mayhew murmured a thankful: "Homely, love." She set down her small case and handbag and stretched out on one of the single beds. "Lot better than the 'Y'."

"Of course it is Mum, this is a home." Jessica placed the suitcase at the end of her bed. "The Y is for transients."

"Eee, love, we've always shared a bed." Mr Mayhew came into the bedroom with a large suitcase which he placed on the other bed. "I don't know how we'll manage sharing a twin." His wife patted her bed, to encourage him to sit. "Ever since we married, we've slept in a double."

"That time at Butlins Holiday Camp in Skegness, we didn't." Mrs Mayhew patted her bed again. "We had bunks."

"That's different." He sat next to her. "That was a holiday, not a home."

"Never mind, Father, our Jessica's likely got other visitors in mind. She wouldn't want to saddle herself with a double bed, just because you want it, now would she?"

"Not really, Mum," Jessica opened up the large suitcase. "I remember my last double bed. I don't want a double in my house for a while, I can tell you. And there's no visitors planned, except you two."

"That's right love; you stay single for a bit." Mr Mayhew bounced on the bed to test the springs. "There's nowt like a good marriage, but when it isn't, it's lousy."

"Will you stop that bouncing Father?" Mrs Mayhew slapped his arm. "I had enough of ups and downs on the way here."

"You like my place, don't you?" Jessica sat on the bed to open the smaller suitcase.

"Aye, it's right nice, love." Mr Mayhew took his wife's hand and stroked it fondly. "You've done yourself right proud with the house, our Jessica, hasn't she Mother?"

Jessica felt a lump in her throat. At times they were so loving: when they weren't jumping down each other's throats.

"And now for that cup of tea I promised, Mum." Jessica stood up. "It'll go down a treat after that long journey, I imagine. How did it go by the way, apart from the mountains, that is?"

"You're right there, love, a cup of tea'll be fine," Mrs Mayhew's face soured. "Your dad dropped the flask when we were picnicking... Where was that place, Father?"

"I'll take a look at that." Mr Mayhew got up to examine the window mountings. "It's double glazing, isn't it?"

"It has to be apparently in Alberta, Dad. They go in for double insulation in a big way." She joined him at the window, watched him run an inquisitive finger around the pane of glass. "The temperature gets to minus forty at times, I'm told. I'll take you on a tour after, to see the furnace. How's your business venture going?"

"Where was that place you dropped the thermos, love?" Mrs Mayhew persisted.

Mr Mayhew bent over and eyeballed his wife. "Just before that roadside café where they dragged the teabag through lukewarm water." He straightened, eyed his daughter. "Honestly, the way Canadians make tea, they ought to be put up against a wall and shot."

"He goes over the top, your dad sometimes. Fair makes me sick! You ought to have seen the palaver in that café! Made my hair curl!"

"Well, the water was off the boil!" Mr Mayhew started unpacking.

"He had the waitress hopping up and down for boiling water."

"Boiling water?" He gathered up neatly folded socks and threw them into the top dresser drawer. "Ha! Not on your life! It was off the boil! I told her to stick the pot in the microwave for thirty seconds."

"I could have sunk through the floor with shame."

"Well, what a bloody way to make tea!" He put his hand under his underclothes and lifted them out of the suitcase very carefully. "Warm water, not boiling, bubbling water! Don't warm the teapot! Serve a single cup of hot water with the bloody teabag in the saucer." He threw his underpants in after the socks. "There's no hope in hell of tealeaves steeping in a saucer. It needs water to steep! Bubbling, boiling water!"

"All right, I've got the message!" Jessica hurried to the door and tried to hide her laughter. "Tea it is and strong. And no teabags I promise, it's loose tea."

"That's nice, love." Mrs Mayhew hitched up on the bed. "I don't go much on teabags, they're full of dust."

"I mean to say, would they serve their coffee like that?" Mr Mayhew was on a high. "A spoonful of coffee grounds in a saucer and a cup of hot water?" He fished out nylon tights from the case, stared at them. "Would they hell as like! Where do these go?"

"In a different drawer to your socks, of course!" Mrs Mayhew said. "And Father, shut up, you've said enough! And stop that swearing! This is a newly-furnished house and we don't want to sully the walls with your profanity!"

Jessica left them still straining not to giggle. It was good to have them here, gave her something to think about other than Brian Swartzkoff, whoever-he-was.

185

"Why can't they make decent tea?" Her father followed her into the kitchen to watch her efforts in that direction. "They're descended from us, aren't they? The Boston Tea Party was American? Canadians've no need to drink coffee."

"People are from all over nowadays, Dad," she kissed his cheek. "I went to a Citizenship ceremony with a friend in Vancouver before you came out, and there were only two British names out of thirty people claiming citizenship."

"I was born English. I'll die English."

"I'm going in for Citizenship as soon as possible. I think if a country is good enough to take me in, then I owe it allegiance."

"You can still be English and patriotic to both countries."

"I've arranged for us to go lawn bowling tomorrow, Dad," to change the subject. "I'm a new member, and you'll meet plenty of expatriates out there."

"Eee, Jessica, that sounds right nice, love. I haven't been bowling since Bradford." He turned round and called. "Hey, Mother, we're going lawn bowling with our Jessica tomorrow," his voice faded going along the corridor. "They'll serve good tea there love, they're ex Brits!"

Jessica smiled, knew what the tea was like at the clubhouse. She'd ask the kitchen lady to put in two extra bags to the pot. Or, suggest to her parents they copied her, stick to drinking coffee outside the home.

Yes, better than a scene in her new club.

JESSICA ENJOYED HER parents' visit, it indicated there was love and affection around if she only cared to search. Regardless of the spats, the fault-finding, they still loved one another. They weren't separate entities, they were a whole. She wanted to be in the same state of grace. She would, she determined, once her heart stopped aching at the thought of a tall figure with gorgeous blue eyes that twinkled when he smiled.

During a bowling session there was an incident that struck Jessica as extremely funny. Mr Mayhew was bowling on another rink to Jessica's. Mrs Mayhew sat on a bench to watch her daughter's team. Jessica and the opposing lead played their three bowls, and while the second and third bowlers played, Jessica joined her mother on the bench.

"Have you got over Ronnie's rotten desertion yet, love?" Mrs Mayhew patted Jessica's arm affectionately.

"Who?" She noted the opposition had more bowls surrounding the jack than her team. They must be better players. "Oh, Ronnie!"

"By gum, you soon forgot a husband of fifteen years."

THE NEIGHBOR ACROSS the road walked his invisible dog around the garden, peered over the hedge at the activity in front of the house.

Jessica carried a suitcase down her path to the parked car at the curb, gave him a wave which he returned. Mrs Mayhew carrying a thermos from the house saw the exchange and hurried to Jessica heading for her dad placing luggage in the car.

"Don't get too friendly with him, love," Mrs Mayhew whispered. "He's trouble."

"Mum, he's harmless," twisting her head so her father couldn't hear.

"So was the Yorkshire Ripper, 'till he and his lady friend got the bloodlust."

"Mu-um! You're on your own too much. Stop thinking and worrying." She went to her dad. "Going in the boot all right, Dad?"

"Aye," shoved in the suitcase. "I don't fancy that return trip one little bit, though. Next time, you come visit us, you hear, love?"

"Okay, I'll do that, Dad. And it might be sooner than you think. I've missed you both such a lot."

"Make sure you come soon then, love." He shut the boot and patted her arm. "You know there's always a welcome for you."

"I've got the tea, Father," Mrs Mayhew, opened the offside door. "We'll be all right if we drink sparingly." Mr Mayhew assisted his wife into the car, tried to take the thermos flask, but she held onto it grimly.

"Let go of it, I'll put it on the back seat."

"Not twice, you don't," smacked his hand. "You're not getting your hands on it, this time. And remember, I'm the one operating the radio on the way back, not you."

187

Jessica smiled, wished they had stayed longer, she wouldn't have time to think of Brian-what's-his name, then.

The neighbor emerged from his front gate with the invisible dog and started across the road towards them.

"Bye, Dad." Jessica leaned in and kissed her father at the wheel. "Remember, you're persuading mum to take up lawn bowling."

"I heard that," Mrs Mayhew said, and eyed the neighbor nearing. "If you think your dad and me can play together, you've got another think coming."

"No reason why she shouldn't," Mr Mayhew said. "There were plenty of women at your club, love."

"And you noticed, Mum," Jessica went around the car to her mother's window. "That husbands and wives don't play together on the same team."

"What's the reason behind that thinking, Jessica?" Mr Mayhew leaned forward for a clear view of his daughter.

"Obvious, Father." Mrs Mayhew answered for Jessica. "Husbands are always telling off their wives to do this, do that, do the other!"

"I know who tells me off, and it isn't a husband!" Mr Mayhew switched on the ignition.

"You join in and bowl with dad, Mum. That's what keeps a marriage happy. Togetherness."

Her father leaned across. "And you'll be an expert on th -" before his wife dug a quietening elbow in his ribs.

"Drive Father!" She turned to Jessica. "I'll think on it. Be careful of yourself, love," and pulled her daughter's face close and kissed it.

"I will Mum." Jessica peered across her mother. "Dad, take care on the roads."

"I've been driving longer than your age." Mr Mayhew put the car into gear. "Mind you, that was left-hand drive, not this stupid Continental way. Why did they have to follow the Americans?"

"She said, take care, so be careful!" Mrs Mayhew nudged her husband.

Mr Mayhew put his foot down. A bang on the front fender had him immediately release pressure.

"Bloody hell!" Through the windscreen he saw a man holding the invisible dog leash high, anxiously eyeing his front wheel.

"Drive on, Father." Mrs Mayhew had observed Jessica smile at the neighbor.

"His dog! I've hit his dog, Mother!"

"It's imaginary. Drive on!"

"It's bloody, what?" He glared at his wife.

"It's not there, it's in his head. He's pixielated!"

They departed on a squeal of tires. A furious Mr Mayhew grimly hung onto the steering wheel, eyes locked straight ahead.

Jessica waved and scampered along the footpath for a while, then the car turned into the main street and she was alone. Empty. Oh, so deflated inside. How to fill the void their going had caused?

The neighbor waited for her return, encouraged her to examine his injured dog.

And like an idiot, she did.

Is This All There Is?

Chapter Fifteen

Jessica continued her life, taking each day as it came; lawn bowled with new friends and exercised at the YWCA with old ones, sweated out glands not memories. Her parents visit and return home to BC with a new drop proof thermos flask, long gone as a time-filler; any intrusion of personal thoughts and she suffered pangs of remorse.

She should have informed Brian she wasn't Jean Morningbird earlier on in the relationship, he might have understood her reasons behind the pretense. Like cocoa! She couldn't understand why she had behaved so irrationally, so why expect him to?

She was naive to fool Brian. As naively stupid as the neighbor with his imaginary dog. But then, what of Brian's pretense? Who was he supposed to be? Who, in all that's wonderful, had she been dating for two weeks?

"I was falling in love with that man. He was so lovely, so loving."

Ha-Flaming-Ha!

THE RETURN JOURNEY from the North West Territories two weeks later was just as thought-provoking as the outward one; Jack still thought of Jean. Where had he gone wrong, how could he rectify it? He knew the answer. Come clean about himself. Admit to Jean his true identity, that he still loved her, wanted her.

Once arrived home he didn't wait to unpack but telephoned Jean and left a message on her answer-phone, then went to Shellack Oil Exploration to give his report. Fortunately, Mike decided the written report was worth more to him and the chairman than the chief geologist's verbal remarks; Jack could hand it in later.

Jack hastened out of the office with a quick wave, he had other fish to fry! In his car he telephoned his own phone, but there was no reply message from Jean.

"I have to see her!"

He eyed his watch. What time did the SPCA close?

"To hell with phoning them. I'll probably get that randy vet, or jealous Maryanne, or spiteful Julianne."

Jack put down his foot and soon arrived at the SPCA building, parked and went inside, up to the receptionist.

"I'd like to speak to Jean Morningbird, please?"

"I'm sorry, there's no one of that name here."

"Well, then, I'll speak to Maryanne."

"There's no Maryanne, either."

"Okay! Are you Julianne?"

"No," eyed him apprehensively.

"Where's the veterinary surgeon?"

"Have you a problem with a dog or cat?" Unseen, she depressed a bell under the counter. A man dressed in a white overall appeared from the dispensary.

"Need some help out here, Dora?"

"Are you the vet?" This was not the sex-maniac he'd manhandled out of Jean's.

"Yes, what is your problem?"

"You're the only vet here?" Bonehead had to ask.

The vet and receptionist nodded their heads.

"Sorry, guess I made a mistake, Sir, Madam." He made a hurried exit.

The two of them remained at the window long enough to ensure the madman really departed their parking space in his car.

Jack was in a foul mood on his return from the SPCA. She'd made a fool of him; strung him along with a tissue of lies. He'd become a substitute Romeo for skydiving Brian. She was obviously substituting for Métis Jean Morningbird.

"Oh, to hell with you, Jean-what-ever-your-name."

JESSICA FENDED OFF Dorinda's request to meet Brian, saying he'd been delayed on the air tour.

191

"Oh shame, Jessica. We'd kinda looked forward to meeting the guy." Dorinda hung her coat up on the coat hanger. "David says..."

Jessica didn't hear what David had to say on the subject, she'd learnt to mentally cut-off when his name was mentioned. She hadn't been able to bring herself to committing Brian to an early, messy grave. Much as she despised the pseudo man, he had been kind, considerate and -

"Later on Dorinda, when he's finished in Quebec we'll get together, I promise." And how she was going to manage that, heaven only knew.

"I'm holding you to that, Jessica."

Jessica worked at her desk unable to prevent thoughts of Brian entering her tortured brain. Apparently, some women attracted the wrong men. She was beginning to suspect the opposite sex was a no-no for her, whichever way she looked, she was a loser.

After work she exercised Brian out of her system on the rower and exercycle, arrived home feeling relaxed and switched on the answer phone. Immediately, her stomach went into orbit when she heard his voice after an absence of two long weeks. She could visualize her love, longed for his arms... Her resolve tightened, she would by-pass pseudo Brian's offer of friendship. He was a fraud and a liar and much as she loved him, wanted him, it was too agonizing.

There was only one way to exorcize Brian. Start another relationship quickly. She could emulate Jean Morningbird and the real Brian Swartzkoff. Jessica switched on her computer, scrolled through Edmonton Community Network and found the Introductory Service. She drew a deep breath, plunged in and placed an advertisement. This would change her life, but good.

> Lonely forty year old would like to meet sincere male WASP
> for a meaningful relationship. email:jessy@ECN.ab.ca

White Anglo-Saxon Protestant covered her requirements, exactly. She didn't care if she was stepping on anyone's toes. She wasn't associating with anyone of a different culture or religion, ever again: she'd been there.

She posted it and closed down the computer to make a pot of tea, her nerves needed to settle. She hoped Brian, what-ever-his-name, didn't come to the door. She'd die. She'd just die. She'd melt at the sight of that strong, tall, dependable -

"He isn't dependable! He's a liar and a cheat!"

That evening after she had walked around the spotlessly clean house and found nothing more to be done to make it sparkle, she conceded defeat and switched on the computer. She'd intended boning up on the latest bomb run by American and British planes in the Iraq 'No Fly Zone', but lettering came up: 'You have E-mail'.

"Wow! That's a quick result!"

She brought up the screen, discovered seven replies to her advertisement; four unprintable from sex-starved beings; two from hopeless homeless; the last a comedian stating he wasn't a wasp but a bee with a sting.

She'd struck out. She wiped the messages and hoped for better results later, it wasn't everyone who switched on their computer each day after work.

BRIAN ARRIVED HOME amidst a clatter of gear and an abundance of chatter about the tour. Jack, seated by the window overlooking river valley, responded with only a modicum of interest that intrigued Brian.

"What's the matter with you?" Brian paused on one of his visits to the front door to pick up more gear. "You look as if you've lost a dollar and found a penny?"

"You don't want to know."

"I do. What's the problem?" He ambled over and sat next to Jack. "You look real pissed-off. Come on, give."

"I did something completely out of character, Brian. I pretended I was you and answered one of your letters."

"No sweat, I suggested it." He arched a roguish eyebrow. "I didn't miss out on my travels. There was no lack of one night stands."

"You randy bastard!"

"Horny youngster sounds better," hitched forward in the armchair. "Which one was it? Was it Mary?"

"No. Jean Morningbird."

"Not to worry. I wasn't gone on a Métis."

"She was a lovely girl, woman. But you wouldn't have liked her; she wasn't suitable for you, Brian. About thirty five, and wore falsies."

"You discovered that? Way to go!" Brian slapped him on the shoulder before he noticed Jack's look. "Sorry!"

"I blew it pretending to be something I wasn't. And she isn't Jean Morningbird, Brian. English, yes! Part aborigine? No way!" And it hurt to remember brown eyes, a wide mile and loving arms, when they weren't about to fell him. "She's so nice, Brian, and I sure blew it."

"Hey, seems like you had it good, buddy," and stood up. "What went wrong?"

"Everything! In a way I'm relieved. I made a pathetic substitute for a fit skydiver with a full head of hair."

"You know the old saying, Jack," patted him on the shoulder. "When a horse throws you -"

"I'm not traveling that road again!"

"Not being me, but yourself, man!" Brian went into his bedroom, switched on his computer and after a while called out: "Come on, I've got it."

Jack shouted back: "I feel as if I've been put through a wringer and hung out to dry. I've not been myself at all."

"Come and look at them requesting soul mates."

"Soul mates?" Jack, intrigued despite himself, went into Brian's bedroom. "You must be joking," and looked over Brian's shoulder.

"How about this WASP Jessy?" Brian indicated.

"You must be out of your tree. She sounds desperate."

"Well, good buddy," Brian looked up at him. "We're all desperate for something. Dive in there, man! Get your feet wet!" Then an afterthought when Jack was leaving. "Under your own name, this time, eh?"

Nothing more was mentioned about the service during the remainder of Brian's unpacking. He related several amusing anecdotes of the air show then left for the airport.

Jack went to his own computer, whipped up enthusiasm and finally switched on. In the Introductory Service he inserted his own advertisement:

> Male: early forties, sci.bckgrnd, never married. Would like
> female companion of stable bckgrnd for outings. Enjoy

walks,   talks,   skiing,   boating   and   fishing.
email:havers@ECN.ab.ca

JESSICA RUSHED HOME from work the following day and brought up her email; maybe Mr Right had answered. There were fifteen replies. With a happy smile she commenced reading the first, then the second, then the third reply; by the fourth missive her lips were on a decided downward trajectory, no longer Mr Smiley.

"Stupid morons, you'd think they'd have something better to do than make asinine remarks to a stranger."

She went into the kitchen to make a pot of tea and allow time for her seething brain to settle down. How could men be such silly, stupid idiots? Had Ronnie behaved like that?

"I wouldn't know, would I? I was in blissful ignorance of that perfidious bastard's shenanigans."

She took her cup of tea to the computer, waded through the messages to the Lonely Woman who needed...

"Nothing there for you, Jessica. Clear them all away."

She enjoyed wiping the messages in one fell swoop, then went to the main screen and brought up the Introductory Service List. Maybe some male had placed a better advertisement than hers. There were many, but an exceptionally good one from a man called Havers with a scientific background.

"Right age group, and enjoys sports, walks and talks. All right, mister, you're it!"

Havers? Should she use that sign off name as a courtesy opener? She shrugged, there wasn't much option. She held back nothing about herself; she was recently divorced and forty, an immigrant of one year from England and just recently a Social Worker in Edmonton. She enjoyed sailing, loved boats of all kinds, member of a rowing club in Vancouver, liked skiing and most sports.

"Enough with lies. If the truth can't get me a man, I don't want one."

She checked every word, posted it in the Reply to Sender.

IS THIS ALL THERE IS?

JACK NOTED THE Jessy on the email and smiled, the desperate WASP lady, the best of many replies; he'd get his feet wet. He stated his name was Jack, and seeing she was English and newly arrived from temperate Vancouver, unused to Alberta weather, he thought she would be interested in what occurred last March.

> Alberta endured a harsh winter with Arctic Highs. Clear blue skies allowed ground heat to evaporate, early February, a continuation of winter coolness, everyone was desperate for warm weather. A clear indication of approaching summer is Groundhog Willie, a title for the animal across the whole of North America. Everyone was on the lookout for him to emerge from his burrow and cast a shadow which announced summer is close. People, young and old, took up a watching brief by the burrow to wait for the big event. Finally, the animal put out its nose, sniffed the air and cast a shadow. A cheer went up, winter was leaving, summer was almost here: it was official from Groundhog Willie.
>
> The newspapers carried several messages during the ensuing weeks of April.
>
> 'Groundhog Willie's in danger of losing his life. He emerged from his burrow, while the whole of North America watched, and said spring was here.
>
> He lied! It's been winter four times since then. He's gonna get hit!'

Brian returned home and peeked at the screen over Jack's shoulder.

"Who's this to?"

"The WASP lady, she answered my ad." He glanced up at the grinning face. "Sounds okay, Brian."

"Should turn her off, or on, I'm not sure which." He slapped Jack's shoulder before departing. "Give the lady a break, Jack. Lighten up."

"Everyone isn't a brash young guy, like you."

Brian paused in the doorway. "You've sure a peculiar way of seducing a female, old man."

Jack threw a pack of rubber bands at him.

JESSICA LAUGHED when she read about Groundhog Willie. Jack Havers seemed an extremely nice person, one with whom she could easily relate. Her mind emitted a warning. Don't be led down the primrose path again!

The ring at her front door produced a moment of panic. Was it Brian returning to lay siege to her heart?

"Well you won't know unless you answer, idiot!"

She opened the door to a good looking young man, and smiled. "Yes?"

"Are you Jean Morningbird?"

"She no longer lives here. Are you Brian Swartzkoff?"

"Yes," doing a double take. "Where is Jean?"

"I don't know where she lives, but I passed on your letter."

"I figure she doesn't want to know me, then, eh?"

"You never know. But, you should realize she may be a drug addict."

"Do tell," took a backward step off the mat.

"But she's beautiful. Very beautiful. And got a lovely nature."

"Tell me more," the grin appeared and accompanied a forward step.

"And she's probably a pusher."

"You mean. Go away, pusher?"

"No. Come hither pusher. Try my drugs, pusher."

"Tell on, please," took a hesitant sideways step.

"She's definitely a prostitute on the run from the police."

"That does it. I don't pay for it."

"Don't blame you, Brian." She grinned. "You might be buying AIDS."

"My sentiments exactly. That, I don't need." He gave a half salute. "Have a nice day!" And walked down the footpath.

The neighbor across the road walking an invisible dog looked enquiringly at him.

IS THIS ALL THERE IS?

"Nice day!" Brian called before getting into his car.

Jessica gave herself a mental shove as she followed the action in the street. Ask him Brian's name, the other Brian! But her lips remained closed, too scared to open up and ask.

The neighbor smiled, positioned his dog's head to say 'Hello', then held up and waggled a front paw in 'Goodbye'.

Brian retained a long investigative look at the man and his invisible dog through the rear vision mirror on his way to the main road.

The immediate neighbor pruning their dividing hedge caught Jessica's eye and waved to her. She waved back. She hadn't mentioned to him that Jean had telephoned her; the less he knew about her affairs the better. All the same, she bet he was pleased Brian had not been invited indoors.

She went into the kitchen, poured herself a cup of tea and pondered on the real Brian Swartzkoff, so unlike her Brian it was laughable. Why did the silly man try to emulate the characteristics of the suave and debonair young skydiver?

"Ha-Flaming-Ha! As laughable as me impersonating a young Métis."

She looked through the window at the garden.

"Another chapter in the book of life is closed. I've read Ronnie; rapid read Brian what's-his-name; a new chapter's about to begin."

She carried her tea into the bedroom and started typing.

Dear Jack Havers:

My name is Jessica. I thoroughly enjoyed your Groundhog Willie, funny.

I sailed around the Isle Of Wight once in a yacht. I was a substitute for someone with appendicitis. I'm an experienced rower and they assumed I wouldn't be totally ignorant on a yacht.

That was their first mistake.

I was knocked on the shoulder by a swinging yardarm, caught my foot in a trailing rope, hung suspended from the side of the yacht.

Their second mistake, pulling out of the race to rescue the novice hanging head down in the water.

Naturally, that was the only time I was asked to participate in a yacht race.

I never volunteered again.

JACK LAUGHED WHEN he read about the mishap at sea. His answer was on a more serious matter.

Dear Jessica,

In Toronto, where I was born, gulls are noted for their highly developed sense of intelligence. Small birds are chased by gulls into windows of high-rises; they fall to the ground, are swooped upon then eaten. Migrating birds in spring and fall have more casualties due to inexperience because their skulls aren't formed, so they become unconscious on impact.

It was estimated 10,000 birds died in Windsor until they changed the tower lights at the airport to strobe lighting; this frightened away both gulls and small birds.

Brian entered the apartment, walked up to Jack.

"Guess who I've seen?" He looked at the screen. "Is that WASP Jessy?"

"Yup! And I can't hazard a guess who you've seen."

"Your friend at Bonnie Doon. I went to see if Jean Morningbird was there. She wasn't," and winced at the plight of the birds.

"Did you say who you were?" Jack bit his lip in fear.

"Didn't have to. She asked if I was Brian Swartzkoff as soon as I asked for Jean Morningbird."

"So she knows I'm a fraud. Geez, that sure hurts."

"Guess she knows the truth about you. She's nice, Jack."

"I know."

"Sure put the bite on Jean Morningbird. She's a drug addict and pusher, and a hooker on the run from the police."

199

"My Jean was nothing like that!" eyes wide in shock.

"My Jean?" He tapped Jack's shoulder. "Go get 'em cowboy! Give my regards to Jessy!" He left the bedroom then turned back. "Oh, before I forget. What about that guy with the invisible dog, eh?"

"Did you find out her name?"

"Nope! Didn't ask."

"What about my name? Does she know it?"

"She didn't ask, and I figured you wanted out. Stick to Jessy, the WASP. If she can take what you're writing about, you've got it made."

JESSICA ARRIVED HOME after a workout at the YWCA. Before cooking dinner she started to run a bath; undressed whilst the computer warmed up, then brought up e-mail.

"Nice having a message to come home to. It's rather like having a friendly dog."

Pity she'd developed an allergy to long-haired dogs. Long-haired Dachshunds hadn't worried her in the show ring when she was young, showing her dad's smooth haired Standards. She could get a Chihuahua, they were almost hairless, they wouldn't make her sneeze. But they were scrawny, not cuddly. She'd settle for e-mail. And besides, a man was better than a dog, any day.

She smiled at Jack's letter until she read about the plight of the birds in Toronto. Why hadn't she heard of this? She'd only been on the other side of the country not on the other side of the world? Maybe his interest in scientific matters steered him towards calamities.

The sound of running water changed; obviously the waterline had been reached. Jessica dashed into the bathroom, turned off the taps, snatched up a fluffy white towel, returned to Jack's e-mail and sat on the towel in the nude. Maybe the next piece would be lighter.

> I realize you lack knowledge of Tornado activity coming from England. Maybe you'll find this interesting.
>
> One interviewee on television from Saskatchewan said he arrived home to find his garage roof off, then lightning struck

the house and burnt out all his appliances. He burnt his hand on the fuse box - one hour later!

When the 'Twister' film was showing in Alberta a couple in their car witnessed the real life event and were flung into a ditch. In Red Deer, an open-air showing of the film had patrons assume it was sound effects until their cars lifted a few inches before crashing to the ground.

Wow! Some film. She'd seen it advertised in Vancouver. She was experiencing a real life drama of betrayal and separation at the time from a twister, so the film had passed her by: interesting though.

The Monarch butterfly in the UK differs from the species in Canada; here it's a story of endurance and tenacity.

Their migration starts from Canada to Mexico in the Fall, and it takes months for the flight. On arrival in Mexico each butterfly lays approximately 400 eggs on milkweed. And, in the early spring they start out on their return migration. It's the second and third generation who finally arrive in Canada.

Jessica hugged herself. He was intelligent, sensitive and caring. She wrapped herself in the towel and typed.-

Dear Jack Havers:

I don't know if you've experienced the troubles in the UK, but I have.

Visiting London from Yorkshire, I alighted from the Victoria tube and other travelers got on. I saw someone had left behind on the platform an attaché case. I picked it up to find the owner. A man behind me said:

"Don't let go of that handle, it's probably been activated with a trembler release."

He pointed me in the direction of a concrete alcove, to wait, whilst he got the bomb squad, and went off. The other passengers left the platform and I was completely isolated. So I went to find someone, I didn't want to die alone! I

> walked up the stone stairs and informed a porter at the gates who spoke on his walkie-talkie.
>
> The bomb squad arrived and escorted me, still carrying the case, to a van outside the station back-entrance. They inserted my hand into a steel barrel and told me to release the case. I couldn't, my hand was paralyzed. They had to prize it off, then hustled me down behind an iron thingy. The case was exploded and business papers collected. I left with egg on my face, determined never, never to pick up a case again.

And she added her full name was Jessica Walters, (nee Mayhew) and she worked at Social Services, and recently taken up lawn bowling.

She felt her soul had been cleansed, she wasn't being devious; she could hold her head up high. She flung her arms wide.

"I'm a new person! I'm fresh born!"

She had a whiff of underarm perspiration.

"And I stink to high heaven!"

She hurried to the bathroom. Double luxury, a scented bubble bath and a feeling of well-being she'd discovered Jack Havers.

IT DIDN'T TAKE long for Jack to act as detective. There wasn't going to be a repetition of the SPCA fiasco. He still smarted when he recalled the reaction of the vet and receptionist.

He arrived at his office just after eight o'clock, looked up the telephone number of Social Services, then phoned and asked in which department Jessica Walters worked.

"Jessica Walters is in the Claims Department. Shall I connect you, Sir?"

"No thanks, I'll call later."

He hung up quickly, beads of nervous sweat on his brow. The Jessy with whom he was corresponding was for real.

"To hell with Jean, Jessica is who she claims to be."

He settled down to work with a gnawing feeling of regret at loathing Jean's duplicity so much. Why should he care? She obviously didn't, or she would have answered his telephone message. And she could have said something to Brian when he'd arrived on her doorstep. Curse that Jean, what's-her-name!

He couldn't wait to go home and write to Jessy.

Dear Jessica,

I was impatient to write to you, you told me so much about yourself I feel ashamed at holding out on you, and hopefully I'll prove to be as forthcoming as you.

I've taken up running recently, and it's doing wonders for my muscle tone which had begun to go slack with a sedentary life, sitting at a desk going over exploratory results. I'm Chief Geologist at Shellack Oil Exploration. While on a geological site I'm active, preparing for drilling and that keeps me fit.

THE FOLLOWING DAY Jessica was at her desk, a quiet moment. Dorinda was busy at the filing cabinet just a step away. Veronica, like the other girls, was busy working. Dick had not arrived. Strange, he was usually there before time.

Jessica looked up the telephone number of Shellack Oil Exploration. Chief Geologist was listed, but no name. She dialed the number.

"Hello, Jack Haversky?"

She immediately hung up. For a moment there she'd imagined it was Brian. She wafted a shaking hand over a heated face. Jack Haversky sounded Polish or Ukrainian. He'd used Havers as a sign off name which sounded English. Hold on there! She wasn't second-guessing anyone again.

"Anything the matter, Jessica?" Dorinda closed the filing cabinet. "Not getting a hot flush, are you?"

"Cheeky monkey, I'm too young for hot flush -"

There was a commotion by the elevators. They quickly peered over the screen.

Dick pulled and pushed two large suitcases out of the elevator, picked up a case in each hand and staggered down the corridor. At the opening he looked in.

His one eye did, the other one was closed, surrounded by a black and purple bruise.

Quickly, the office staff lowered their gaze, sniggering, they could do later when he wasn't around to rap them across the knuckles.

"His wife, or Jean Morning Bird?" Jessica whispered to Dorinda once Dick was ensconced in his own office.

"Those suitcases are from home. It must be his wife."

"Nemesis!" Jessica slapped a hand on the desk. "It's caught up with him. Let's hope he's caught the clap from Jean."

"Oooe, Jessica, that's not a nice thing to say."

"Well, you've never been on the receiving end of a broken marriage. It makes me bitchy. Not a nice person at all when I'm told I'm passed my sell-by-date."

"Oh Jessica, your husband didn't say that, did he?"

"As good as, dangling his bit of fluff under my nose."

The elevator bell rang. They peered over the screen, this was happening too soon after Dick. Out stepped a vision in pale yellow.

"Haute Couture personified." Jessica nudged her friend. "Didn't I tell you? What could be more like a bit of fluff than canary yellow?"

Jean's figure showed every curve beneath the tight fitting two piece suit. Her face beamed under the wide brimmed hat when she sighted their two pairs of eyes. She gave a little wiggle of gloved fingers beneath her elbow towards Jessica and winked conspiratorially when she passed the partition opening. Jessica reciprocated.

"Oh, Jessica, she's so beautiful," Dorinda whispered. "Dick doesn't deserve her. She's too good for him."

"Wow, I've just realized." Jessica clapped a hand to her mouth, turned her back on curious staff and whispered: "That's a replay of what happened to me! Wife out, girlfriend in." She made a play of straightening up her desk. "But I didn't deck Ronnie. I acted like a lady. I retired from the field of battle and left the field clear for his paramour."

204

"You can push a round peg into a square hole, my David says." Dorinda went back to her desk leaving behind a dumbfounded fellow worker.

Chapter Sixteen

Jessica arrived home that night elated Dick Chalmers had received his just desserts. How long would Jean stay with him? Ha-Ha! That's for him to worry over.

She started to cook supper, turned on the computer to bring up Jack's email. Wasn't this lovely? Much better than being greeted by a smelly, tail wagging dog who'd left doo-doos all around the place to be picked up by its owner.

Jack wanted to know when they could meet in person. Good as e-mail was it lacked something. Could she suggest a time and a place?

Jessica switched off the computer, ran to the bathroom and sat on the toilet for urgent relief. Why had he suggested meeting, they'd been corresponding so well?

Later, whilst watching a steak fry she pondered more. She didn't want to rush in and lose everything, she might be disappointed by the real person; he might be totally different to what his letters revealed. Could she take the chance? He must be uncertain because he hadn't divulged his full name. She'd discovered his proper name the hard way, and it had been a shock hearing him sound so like Brian, what's-his-name. She decided on prevarication, turned the heat off under the steak, switched on the computer and read comments on the Internet Chat Line.

"What a lot of twaddle, everyone's got a gripe!" She pulled in the e-mail and stared at his request. What to say?

Dear Jack:

I would love to meet you in person, but I'm hesitant. There's no problem writing on the computer, it's objective, but facing one another it might be disappointing.

But like you, I'm curious to see what you look like. So, I can meet you at Sir Winston Churchill Square at 4.30 tomorrow. I'll stand by the statue.

What should she wear so he'd recognize her? She couldn't possibly wear what she had worn when meeting Brian, what-ever-his-name, that would be both painful and naive.

I'll wear a brown coat and be carrying a Safeways Shopping bag.

Jessica ate an overcooked steak, hard peas and soggy Yorkshire Pudding, roast sweet potato with gravy sticking to the plate, from her tray, and watched television news.

Burnt Church had re-offered their claim for Reparations; were considering lowering the five hundred million dollars not to fish the disputed forty two lobster pots.

And the twenty five thousand acres in SE. Edmonton they claimed...

'Papaschase is not considered a band as they don't live on a Reserve or Settlement, therefore, are not entitled to the land their forefathers were forced off in 1888.'

"And I think I have difficulties! Poor devils!"

JESSICA COULD HARDLY wait for home time to come around the following day. A nervous sweat appeared under her arms when the hands of the clock moved slowly towards four. She went to the washroom to repair the damage with Lady Stick, which refused to be reasonable.

"Fat lot of good you are in a time of panic, My Lady!"

"Hi, Jessica!" Jean Morning Bird's head appeared around the door before she entered sporting a wide smile. "I thought you'd like to know. Dick's my guy from now on." She commenced to remove gloves from slender hands.

"Nice for you, love. Where are you living?" She eyed their reflections in the large mirror. Her brown outfit came out second-best against the mauve apparition. "Not in his Daimler, one hopes."

"No, in a penthouse suite." She giggled like a schoolgirl, arched her brows at her reflection and ran a wet finger over an eyebrow. "Guess I don't need Emergency money any more, eh?"

"You tell Dick to remove your name from the files. Don't mention me, there's a good girl."

"Okay," wiggled on gloves, one finger at a time, a pleasure to watch. "Been nice having you in my corner, Jessica," then when she was going out. "See you."

"Bye love!   Take care!"   And followed with an entirely unnecessary admonition.   "And don't take any crap from him!"   As if the streetwise girl needed her advice.

"I won't. Have a nice day!"

Jessica's nose followed her departure.

"Predictable! Channel Number 5 and I've got Lady Stick."

SOUND VIBRATED around Sir Winston Churchill Square. An exhibition of Cree dancing on the stage, and a standing audience foot tapped on grass; booths served edibles and trinkets; people meandered from one magical trick to another, and clowns played to scattered groups.

Jack emerged from the underground parking, stroked the top of his head, afraid of what was about to happen. He walked the pedestrian crossing knowing he would have to forget his Jean. Jessica sounded more like his sort of person, but it was going to be very hard to forget a wide smile, bright brown...

Jessica saw Jack's head above the crowd. Her eyes widened and brightened. It was her Brian! Or Jack Haversky? She'd no need for a Safeways shopping bag. Here was her man. He'd recognize her.

His searching eyes settled on her stood beneath Winnie's statue just like Jean previously. His face changed to an enormous smile of recognition. His Jean!

They hurried to meet. Jessica dropped the shopping bag, jumped into his arms and wrapped her arms around his neck. "It's you, love."

"It's you, my lady love."

Both held on hard and loving.

"Is this really you, Jack? My Brian is you, Jack?"

"Better believe it, Jessica." He swung her around off her toes. "I'm really me, overweight and loving you, and no longer Brian's shadow."

R. DRIVER

"Thank goodness I can be Yorkshire, not Métis, Jack. I hated the deception, love." She put her face into his neck. "At first it seemed so simple. I thought Jean was Jewish and you were too."

"You'd have made a far more credible Jew, love. As a Métis you were a tad unbelievable."

"And you went along with the pretense. How nice."

"Because I wanted to. I was stupid pretending I could fly well enough to train you. I nearly lost you, then, my lady Jessica. I'm sorry."

"Oh, you nearly did, my man. I was heartbroken thinking I'd lost you for good, that's why I was so bitchy. And I'm sorry for that. Thank goodness it's really you, Jack." She felt she'd arrived home after an exhausting journey.

A dog decided to join in the fun, to investigate dangling legs and the shopping bag. Jessica glanced down; she'd better come clean about dogs.

"I'm allergic to some dogs, Jack, sorry to say. The long-haired ones in particular."

Jack ushered away the dog with a gentle, lifted foot. "How about a greyhound then, or," couldn't prevent swinging her and grinning. "One like your neighbor's?"

"I'd sooner have children," her face buried in his neck, and cuddled hard enough to strangle him.

"Well, I have the equipment for the job." He lowered her but still held on tight. "I don't know if this is good timing, but I'm not holding back any more, Jessica."

She wondered what was coming, he looked so serious.

"Is your biological clock okay with a first baby... so..." fading away.

"Nay lad, that wasn't so bad to ask, was it? I thought something calamitous was about to descend on me?"

He cuddled her. "I hated asking you, but I'm concerned. I'd sooner adopt babies than produce an imbecile. Then there's the probability of me losing you."

"Whichever way we choose, my man." She patted his cheek. "I'm all right, whether I bear a baby, or we go shopping for one."

"I'd like one or two, Jessica."

209

"My mum and dad will love you, Jack. Especially if you make them grandparents, whether they're adopted babies or not."

"Oh, I'm pleased they're alive. Where do they live?"

"In Vancouver, where I lived for a while."

"If they're anything like their daughter they'll be okay with me." He cupped her face lovingly. "My Jessica."

"Thank God, you're you, Jack!" She felt naked looking into those blue eyes shining down on his beloved.

"My sentiments, exactly, Jessica. Sithee?"

"Hey, I know of Groundhog Willie and the flight of the Monarch butterfly, but not a lot of your background." She pulled back her head, eyed him quizzically.

"No problem, my love. My parents are in Toronto and I've a younger sister." He stroked hair off her forehead. "We've the rest of our lives to explore one another."

"Um, nice."

The End

Printed in the United States
6723